TYE

A Clifford's War Story

By: J. Denison Reed
and
Elliot J. Emerson

ISBNs:
978-1-7371640-8-1 - Paperback

This book is a work of fiction and non-fictional events based on expression. Some of the names, characters, places and incidents are products of the writer's imagination or have been used fictitiously. Any resemblance to persons, living or dead, actual events, locale or organisations is entirely coincidental.

"A bad father has never a good son."

-Latin Proverb

Chapter One: ________________________________

Late May 1994: Rural, Kentucky

Eleven-year-old Marcus Tye called out, "Dad?" when he reached the barn, but could not see his father.

Shrouded in the shade of the barn from the early morning light, the boy's father, Colby, turned briefly to face his young son before looking away.

After a moment, he exhaled the white smoke from his cigarette, "Go get your brother. We got chores to do."

Marcus ran off after seeing the ominous glow from the cigarette lighting up his father's eyes and face as he took another deep draw.

Even at his young age, Marcus knew not to question his father when given a direct order. To the outsider he and his brother, Darius, looked like well-behaved children. Their mother, a picture perfect and obedient wife. In truth, they were terrified of Colby. He ruled his house with an iron hand that sometimes connected with the flesh of his family. He would say cruel things one minute and then act loving the next. Neither boy liked being alone with the man and they much preferred the amazing father he pretended to be when they were in town and around other people.

Marcus continued, in full sprint, out of the barn and across the yard. The air was cool and crisp as he jumped up the three steps and stumbled onto the porch. Swinging open the screen door, he finally slowed to a jog as he went inside.

The dated farmhouse was old and worn but maintained. Reaching the kitchen, Marcus slowed to a walk and the wooden floorboards creaked under his feet.

"Dari, Dad needs us now!" he said to his older brother, who was sweeping the kitchen floor for their mother.

"For what?" Darius asked.

"Chores."

Darius turned around and glared at Marcus. "I'm already doing chores for Mom."

"He told me to get you."

Darius let out a deep sigh and leaned the broom against a chair. A small pile of dirt laid on the floor next to it.

"Okay fine, let's go," Darius said.

Marcus took off in another sprint, leaving his brother walking behind. As he got further ahead, Darius picked up the pace to catch up. Marcus was two years younger and still eager to please his father, but after becoming a teenager, Darius' disdain for his father started to build. He realized the way his father treated them, and especially their mother, was wrong, but felt he was too young and weak to do anything about it at thirteen.

Marcus slowed as he reached the barn. He looked around, "Dad? Dad?" Darius stopped running early and sauntered the rest of the way up to the barn with his hands in his pockets. "Where's Dad?"

"He was just here. He told me to fetch you," Marcus replied.

"Fetch?" Darius asked, questioning the choice of words. "I'm not a dog," he said, punching his brother in the arm.

"I can start treating you like one," Colby growled emerging from the old, rusted truck parked next to the barn. He slammed the creaky door with a swift motion.

"Quit picking on your brother, and get to work," he said, motioning toward the pitchfork and loose hay.

"Sorry," Darius quickly replied.

Colby walked toward Darius, gripped him by the shoulder, and squeezed.

"Sorry?"

Darius winced in pain.

"Sorry, what?" his father demanded.

"Sorry, Sir!" Darius yelped.

Satisfied, Colby released his grip and said, "Now apologize to your brother."

"Sorry Marc," he said, contritely.

With an overly firm pat on the back, Colby returned to the topic at hand, "Good! Now move that hay into the back of the truck."

Darius picked up a pitchfork and walked over toward the hay pile where Marcus was already working. He looked over at his father who glared, turned his back to them, and walked away to the other side of the truck.

Darius' eyes fell onto the tines of the fork and then back at his father. Shaking ideas from his head, he whipped the fork up and started loading the hay into the back of the truck as he was told.

The hay was transported to the Smithers farm down the road. Mr. Smithers, an elderly dairy farmer, needed the hay to feed the livestock he had left. In exchange for fresh milk and eggs, Colby agreed to provide him the hay. Unfortunately, Colby's baler was no longer in working order and Mr. Smithers wasn't comfortable with having such an expensive piece of equipment he owned on another person's property. This left the daunting task of getting loose hay down the road to be baled. Sometimes, the boys stayed to help the older gentleman with the latter part of the task. They were paid handsomely with fresh baked cookies from Mrs. Smithers who was like a grandmother to the boys.

Two hours and a few blisters later, the boys were called for lunch by their mother. Exhausted and hungry, they laid the pitchforks down and ran toward the house. The heat picked up in the afternoon and they were a little dehydrated. The boys made their way to the house and dragged their feet up the front steps of the porch.

Their father, sitting in the porch swing, enjoying a cool drink with another cigarette, looked over and reminded them, "Wash your hands and face before you sit to eat."

Limply, the boys nodded, and Marcus mustered out a quiet, "Yessir."

In the powder room, just inside the foyer, Darius turned the water on. Marcus hesitated because of a blister that had already popped open, and he winced from the discomfort.

Darius shook his head and whispered, angrily, "He could have given us gloves."

Marcus whispered, "It's okay. I'm fine."

"You're hurt. Look at your hands," Darius objected.

Marcus shook his head, "I'm fine. Really."

In the middle of scrubbing the dirt from their faces with the hand soap, their father knocked loudly once on the door, "You ladies finished in there?"

Darius replied, "Almost done, Sir. Just finishing up."

Colby stood at the door momentarily listening, but the boys were silent.

"Well, hurry up!" Colby said just before walking away.

Sandwiches and chips were waiting for the boys on the table in the kitchen, next to a large pitcher of homemade lemonade. Colby was already working on his second glass. Their mother, Margaret, reached across Colby for the pitcher to pour for her sons. Their father grasped her by the wrist and startled her. Slowly he looked over at her and asked through his teeth, "What are you supposed to say?"

Margaret whimpered softly, looking down and away as he held her wrist tighter, "I'm sorry," she whispered. Taking a second to find her voice and smile, she sweetly said, "Excuse me."

He released her wrist with a jerk and mumbled, "I just want manners and some Goddamn respect in my home."

Margaret considered herself adept at predicting Colby's moods, but something changed and she was always on edge.

With trembling limbs, Margaret did her best to quickly pour the lemonade into the two cups.

"Eat, boys," she said with a genuine smile, "You must be famished."

Marcus gingerly picked up his sandwich using only his fingertips. His mother noticed the extra care he was taking with his hands and asked what was wrong.

Marcus showed her his hands, "I have a blister."

Margaret spotted the open sore on his hand, "Oh my, why didn't you wear gloves?"

Darius cut in sharply, "We didn't get any gloves."

Colby's head jerked towards his eldest son. Darius could feel the heat in his cheeks rising as he avoided his father's glare. Margaret was too concerned with Marcus' hand that she failed to notice the tension building between her other son and Colby. She turned toward their father and asked as nicely as she could, "Why didn't you give them gloves, Cole?"

He looked at her in disbelief that she would question him in front of his children. He slowly stood up, locking eyes with his wife. Margaret couldn't hide the terror in her eyes as she believed she angered him much more than she thought.

"I'd like to speak with you in the hall, please." Colby said in a slow, measured tone.

He walked past her and into the hall. The boys looked over at their mother with a look of concern in their eyes.

"Mom-" Darius started to explain, but Margaret put a hand up to silently and politely shush him.

She mouthed, "It's okay," and followed Colby to the hallway.

The boys heard their mother let out a slight gasp followed by a loud thud when her body was slammed into the wall. The gut punch was barely audible, but Margaret's grunt was unmistakable.

"Never question me in front of the boys!" Colby hissed through gritted teeth.

Margaret blinked away tears. Her mind racing to uncover the offense she committed. She decided it was best to placate him and hoped he would explain what she had done so she could avoid doing it again.

"I'm sorry, Colby. I didn't mean any disrespect. I saw my son was hurt from-"

"Good!" Colby snapped. "They're too damn soft. I'm done watching you baby them. You just keep 'em fed and clean. I'm gonna do the raisin' of men now. And if those boys or you ever challenge me again, I will-""

"What, Colby?" She cut him off, "Kill us?"

His grasp flew to her throat and the back of her head made a soft thud against the wall. They were both surprised by her question. She wanted to close her eyes, but they were locked on his. His firm grip on her throat was holding her in place and if she tried to move, she knew he'd squeeze tighter. The silence was deafening. She didn't care when he threatened her, and she would happily take the beatings meant for her boys. She found her voice when she thought he was threatening them.

Starting to worry, Darius' eyes widened. He looked over at his brother who was blankly staring at his plate. They were too afraid to eat or move and neither could see their parents around the corner. Darius looked over at the kitchen knives wondering if he needed a weapon to defend his family. It was the second time today he thought about stabbing his father and it was only lunch time.

Colby was angered by Margaret's challenging tone. His face was barely an inch away from hers. He enjoyed the fear in her hazel eyes and when she did speak up, her bravado trembling, he would always feel a stirring. He loosened his grip around Margaret's slender neck and traced her pulse with his thumb. Her compliance calmed him.

He reached his hand around and tangled his fingers into her soft brown hair. She was still as beautiful as the day he saw her, fresh out of high school, sitting with friends in a park. Her laugh drew his attention from the conversation he was having with a buddy. He remembered seeing her with her clique. One of her friends, a guy, wanted her attention and eventually plopped down next to her, jokingly grazing her shoulder.

Colby didn't like this guy sitting so close to her. He immediately felt possessive of her and he didn't even know her name. He recalled thinking she was younger than him, which she was. The sunlight danced on the blonde highlights of her hair. He watched her, in fascination, stretch her arms skyward, showing her bare belly in the crop top she wore. He knew in that instant, he'd have her, and he'd make sure no other man ever came near her again.

"You will be performing your wifely duties tonight," he started as he tugged her head back, coming out of his reverie. His knee came up to wedge between the legs of her jeans.

"Make sure you're washed up real good before bed," he demanded quietly into her ear.

A tear slid down Margaret's cheek and he kissed it tenderly. He enjoyed tormenting his wife. His lips moved to cover her mouth. He could feel her tighten against him and it only excited him more. To show his dominance, he pressed his knee against her while bringing his other hand under her shirt to her right breast.

"You should feel lucky that I still want you after all these years."

"Colby," Margaret whispered in desperation, "The boys..."

Colby shoved away from her, "The boys!" he said in a mocking tone, "It's always about them."

"Well, we were just having lunch, and I know th-"

"It's fine. Let's go finish lunch. I know you don't like to miss a meal." He saw the direct hit on her self-esteem and decided to switch it up, "I mean, you don't like for them to miss a meal."

He gently pulled her to him and kissed her head, "I'm sorry my temper got the best of me."

Margaret inhaled his scent and allowed herself to relax into him. She knew if he felt her do that, he'd stay in a nicer mood. Compliance in everything is what Colby wanted. He cupped her buttock and whispered how he couldn't wait for the boy's bedtime.

Margaret excused herself to the powder room and Colby rejoined his sons in the kitchen. He glared at Darius who hadn't touched his plate since his parents left the room. Darius tried to hold his gaze, but fear made him avert his eyes onto the sandwich he was no longer hungry for.

After lunch, Margaret asked permission to bandage the hand that hurt Marcus the most. Colby's temper had cooled considerably, and he agreed as long as they didn't take too long. He wanted alone time with Darius anyway. Father and son walked back toward the barn.

"How old are you now, Darius?"

Darius, confused, looked up at his father not understanding why he'd ask such a simple question.

"Um-thirteen. Sir."

Colby looked straight ahead as he continued to speak to the boy, "Have you been in many fights? Other than your pathetic little skirmishes with your brother?"

"No. Not really."

There was silence for a brief moment when Colby purposely tripped his son. Darius fell to the dirt putting his blistered hands out to break his fall. He yelped, startled and in pain.

Colby stood silently while looking down at him.

Margaret placed a bowl of warm water and some bandages on the table after clearing the rest of the dishes. Marcus sat in a chair facing where she sat and held out his injured little hand. She noticed his sharp inhale when she touched the warm cloth on it. She hadn't sung a lullaby since Marcus was an infant, but she felt they both needed it now.

"Sweet mockingbird fly.
Higher and higher in the sky - where the angels fly."
Golden rain falls onto your wings as the sun rises high."
Oh, sweet mockingbird fly."
The shadows are near, don't you cry."
Clear your eyes and fly real high."
My sweet mockingbird fly."

Marcus smiled sweetly as he watched her soothe his skin. He rarely heard his mother's beautiful voice and he was so happy to have all of her attention. The red marks around her wrist were starting to bruise and he remembered his father grabbing it.

"You know, Dari and I are big enough now to pour our own lemonade."

Margaret didn't understand but decided to agree with him. Colby's vicious words still rang in her ears. She never minded doting on her boys. It brought her joy, in fact. It clearly bothered Colby and maybe it bothered her boys now, too.

She felt the stinging of tears welling up again in her eyes.

"I didn't mean to make you cry, Mom!" Marcus rushed to hug his mother.

Margaret winced from his embrace as he grazed the tender area of her belly that absorbed Colby's clenched fist earlier.

"Oh, my sweet baby boy, you didn't make me cry. Everything's gonna be fine."

She kissed his head and smoothed his hair away from his face, "I guess you're getting big enough to do some more things like that on your own now. Just promise me that if you need help or spill, you come get me, okay?" He agreed and rushed off to meet his father and brother.

Not saying a word, Darius picked himself off the ground and followed his still silent father the rest of the way to the truck.

Colby let out a whistle, "Wow. I didn't realize how much you boys got done this morning."

Darius was still fighting the lump in his throat, and if he cried like he wanted to, his father would be relentless, but his dad's praise jolted him out of his emotions. He sniffled and swallowed hard to reset his composure.

Colby considered the amount of hay he was looking at, the time it took to do it, and the boy's hands. He pulled his lighter from his pocket and lit the cigarette that had been dangling from his mouth. Darius remained quiet, unsure if his father wanted him to say anything. His hands felt like they were on fire, and he found that he could think of little else.

Colby looked back toward the house and spoke through his cigarette, "Tell you what, go get gloves for you and your brother from the barn." After a quick inhale, he pulled the cigarette from his lips, exhaled smoke, and continued, "You can give him his pair on your way back to wash that dirt off your hands."

Darius felt joy and relief. He couldn't help smiling, "Thanks, Dad," he managed to say as he sprinted towards the barn.

With fresh gauze and a band-aid on his hand Marcus started to make his way back toward the barn.

"Hey Dari, check it out!" He shouted, holding up his hand as his older brother jogged toward him

Darius stopped and wiped sweat from his brow. "Cool! Dad said we can wear gloves."

Marcus smiled, showing the space where his one canine tooth was taking its sweet time to erupt. He reached for his pair from his brother and noticed the dirt impacted bloody scrapes on his palm. His hands weren't like that at lunch.

"You should ask mom to clean up your hand," Marcus said with concern replacing relief.

Darius snatched his hand away and shoved both of them in his pockets, "I don't need to be babied like you."

"Okay." Marcus replied feeling hurt, "What happened?"

"I fell," was all Darius said as he continued to the porch, dismissing his brother before Marcus could notice that he was close to crying again.

The older boy ran into the powder room before his mother saw the tears streaming down his face. He lost the battle and cried. He closed the lid on the toilet and sat silently weeping while staring at his hands. He was tired. Tired from chores. Tired from watching his dad wreak havoc on their home. He was mostly tired of feeling like he couldn't help his younger brother or his beloved mother. The guilt he felt over what happened at lunch was eating at him. Taking a deep breath, Darius tenderly washed his hands. He was nearly done when a soft knock sounded on the door.

"You okay in there, Bud?" Margaret asked in her sweet and gentle voice.

Darius closed his eyes, feeling the sting of more tears and sighed. He said nothing. Opening the door, he showed her his hands.

Margaret looked at them and back, meeting her son's sad eyes. She didn't ask questions.

"C'mon." She put her arm around his shoulders and led him back to the kitchen to tend to his scrapes.

"That should be enough, boys. Let's get on the road," Colby announced to his sons an hour later. He slapped the hood of the truck, and the boys threw their pitchforks into the barn before climbing into the back of the truck with the hay.

Chapter Two:

The boys loved laying in the hay and watching the clouds. The breeze in the back of the truck cooled them as they lay in the bed, watching the sky. The Smithers' farm was only a few miles away, but Colby was happy for the bit of solitude in the truck's cab. The radio no longer worked, and his son's chatting would get under his skin even though he was determined to have them around him more to make men out of them. If Colby had to beat it into them, so be it. Margaret was going to need to be reined in from mothering and get back to focusing on being his wife. He had been patient long enough with her.

They turned onto an old dirt road and headed up toward a big red silo next to a matching red barn. The potholes of the barely maintained old road made the end of the drive a bit rougher on the boys and Colby's truck.

Jacob Smithers was an older gentleman farmer. He and his wife, Cheryl, never had any children and once had a bustling dairy farm. As time went on, hardships crept in. Cheryl was a breast cancer survivor, but the bills mounted, and Jacob had to let go of his farmhands years ago. His arthritic wrists made the chores difficult to accomplish and he was glad for the help. It was only a matter of time before he would have to sell his farm or close it for good. Colby was his closest neighbor but, although friendly, not his closest friend. He never much cared for Colby, and if he was honest with himself, Jacob feared him a bit.

Jacob walked out onto his covered porch tugging a cap onto his balding head. He was glad to see Marcus and Darius smiling in the back of Colby's truck as it came to a dusty stop. Jacob knew that most of the town was aware that life for the Tye family wasn't a good one and that the homelife Colby fostered was not ideal for the boys or their mother. He didn't like it, but he wasn't one to interfere in other people's affairs.

The brothers hopped down out of the truck, "Hi, Mr. Smithers!" Marcus said with a big smile.

Jacob smiled, "You boys are shooting up like weeds. I'd say you're both at least two inches taller than you were last time you were here."

Colby walked around the truck to greet the old farmer, "They eat everything in sight these days," he said with a nod and extended his hand, "Jacob."

Jacob grabbed and shook his hand, "Colby, how are you now?"

"Good and you?"

Mr. Smithers smiled, "Oh, just fine. Been working on the air conditioner. It conked out on us this morning and I haven't been able to figure out why yet."

Colby smiled back, "I can take a look at it. Not promising I'll be able to fix it, but I can look."

Jacob nodded while rubbing his sore wrist, "That'll be fine. Thank you. How's your lovely bride doing?"

"Mom's good," Marcus chimed in, noticing the older man's action, "Her wrist hurts there, too. Did Mrs. Smithers squeeze it too hard?"

The silence was palpable.

Clearing his throat, Colby changed the subject, "How 'bout we get the boys over to the barn and then I'll look at that unit of yours?"

Darius snickered at his misinterpretation of what his father offered to the old man. He couldn't help it. The look Colby shot him meant he was in trouble. He could feel his knees start to get weak.

He started to run for the truck, "Let's go, Marc!"

Marcus followed to get back into the hay for the short ride over to the barn.

Jacob would normally let the three drive up and then meet Colby back at the house, but today he felt his presence would be needed to keep the boys safe. Even if only for a few minutes.

"That sounds fine. Now, if you don't mind, can I ride with you?" he asked, following Colby to the truck, "I was going to walk up and check on things before you pulled up."

Colby clenched his teeth and forced a smile, "No problem."

Darius realized he left his pitchfork at home, "Marc! Where's your fork?"

"Home. Why?"

"Shit," Darius said under his breath, "So neither of us brought one?"

"Well, you tossed yours in the barn, so I did too."

"You don't have to do everything I do!" Darius yelled, feeling angry that he's going to be in more trouble.

"So, why'd you toss yours?" Marcus asked innocently.

"Shut up!" Darius had to think. Maybe his father won't hit him in front of Mr. Smithers. No, of course he wouldn't. He'd wait until they were alone again. Darius looked down at his hands and remembered the gloves fastened to the belt loop of his jeans. He looked at his brother and realized he was still wearing his. He smiled in spite of the pit in his stomach that was growing.

The truck stopped and the two men got out of the cab. Colby came around to the tailgate while Jacob went to open the barn. Darius was quick to launch himself off to the side and ran towards Mr. Smithers to ask if they could use a pitchfork of his.

"We didn't bring the forks, Dad," Marcus said, climbing out of the back.

"Are you serious?" Colby shouted at his young son.

He was quick to get his temper under control when he noticed Jacob's head turn their way.

He glowered at Marcus, "I guess you boys can do it all by hand then," he hissed.

"Everything alright?!" The old farmer yelled out.

"It appears my boys have a case of the forgetfuls today, Jacob, and will be taking a lot longer to do their job than we thought."

"Oh, now Colby, no need to get angry. It's a simple mistake," The old man started as he walked back over towards the truck, "Besides, Darius already told me and I have forks right here in the barn."

Before Colby could respond, Jacob invited Marcus to join Darius to each grab an old fork out of the barn.

Colby's jaw clenched, "With all due respect, Jacob, I'll be decidin' what's worth gettin' angry over."

"I'm sorry, Colby. I meant no disrespect. I just saw a problem with a quick solution to it."

Colby patted Jacob on the back and gave his shoulder a slightly stronger squeeze than was necessary, "I'm tryin' to teach them about responsibility. You don't know how they can be. Your wife couldn't give you kids."

Colby smiled and quickly changed the subject before his neighbor could react to what he hoped was a slight, "Do ya still want me to look at your A.C.?"

Hiding emotions, Jacob mustered up a smile and gave a motioning nod toward the house. It was easy to tell when Colby was in one of his moods.

The men left the boys to their task and made their way back to the house on foot. Jacob explained that the unit was in their bedroom which was on the main floor. Going up and down stairs wasn't as easy as it once was, and the older couple converted a portion of the lower level into a large bedroom suite. Upstairs was for storage, mostly, and one of the bedrooms was turned into an office for important papers in file cabinets. They did leave one bedroom as it was for any overnight guests.

Jacob stepped away momentarily to get iced tea for Colby and himself. He was met by his wife, Cheryl, in the kitchen.

"Are the cookies almost done?" He asked after kissing her cheek.

"The last batch is in the oven, and I already have some on plates for the boys." She turned, wiping her hands on the old apron she wore. She watched her husband look out the window facing the barn.

"I'm worried about them," He whispered. Walking away from the window, he held an index finger up toward his wife in a signal to hold whatever she was about to say. He checked that Colby was where he left him as he made his way to the refrigerator for the pitcher of iced tea.

"One of them mentioned a bruise around Margaret's wrist," he finally said, still keeping his voice down.

Cheryl's smile faded, "I know. She and I chatted on the phone. Something's broken in that man."

"I know. He seems to be getting worse," Jacob said, rubbing the stubble on his chin.

"I mentioned getting back to church."

"Somehow, I don't think that'll work," Jacob smirked.

Cheryl turned to face her husband of over thirty years, "He'd probably burst into flames."

Colby was adept at figuring out how some things, in general, worked. He had the air conditioner spitting out cool crisp air within the hour. He explained he patched it up for the time being but with one simple part replacement, it would be as good as new. He agreed to go into town with Jacob the following day to purchase the part. In the meantime, the boys finished unloading the truck. Cheryl Smithers took the freshly made cookies out to them with some iced tea. She enjoyed chatting with them and asked to check their hands after noticing their bandages had become loose and dirty from the work.

Colby and Jacob were sitting on the covered porch drinking more of Cheryl's lemon iced tea when she walked back to the house with empty plates and cups. Both boys followed close behind.

"Colby, I'm going to make sure the boys get washed up and re-dress their blistered hands, if that's alright."

She wasn't asking permission and continued into the house with the silent boys still following and not making eye contact with their father. Jacob watched Colby closely and was relieved when all he did was reach for another cigarette. He decided to keep the small talk going so his wife could care for the boys without any interfer-ence and approached the idea of the Tye's returning to the commu-nity church.

After a few minutes of listening to Jacob yammer on about the benefits going to a weekly service would be for the boys, Colby fi-nally stood up.

"Well, we need to be gettin' back home," he declared with an uneasy feeling of embarrassment as he walked into the house in search of his children. They were sitting at the kitchen table with newly bandaged hands chatting away while Cheryl gathered some cookies in plastic wrap for them to take home.

"I liked the chips and cookies and juice after!" Colby overheard Marcus say.

"After what?" he asked, startling the boys. Neither of them no-ticed that he had walked in.

"When we used to go to church," Marcus began to explain. "Re-member after the service, we could go up to that big room with all those snacks?"

Colby was getting irritable, "Why are we all talking about church, all of a sudden?"

"Oh!" Cheryl began, unafraid of Colby, "That's my fault. I asked the boys if they missed going to church." She turned to face him fully and gave him direct eye contact, "They do miss it by the way."

Colby imagined choking the life out of the woman he felt was interfering with his family. Truth is, Colby was deeply religious, but the church became more progressive than his personal beliefs. He also couldn't stand the conversations Margaret would get into. He had to keep her on a short leash and wouldn't let her get too far away from him.

The last service they went to, Colby let his anger get the better of him and he made the mistake of grabbing Margaret in front of some other parishioners. He remembered the raised eyebrows and whispers as he ushered his wife and kids to the car. Colby felt the embarrassment all over again and realized he was white knuckling the back of one of the kitchen chairs. His jaw clenched as he stared at the back of his hands trying to regain composure.

He imagined backhanding Mrs. Smithers across her face only to then bend her over the very chair he was gripping to teach her a lesson on her place in the world. Women who challenged men were the worst. He decided to use this fuel on Margaret later. He can't punish Cheryl for her insolence, but he can make his wife pay for the disrespect. The images he conjured up calmed him and took away the humiliation he was feeling.

A smile suddenly appeared on Colby's face, but it did not meet his eyes.

"Ya know, maybe we will go to church tomorrow. Maggie could use some time out of the house."

He turned on his heel and walked away. He continued out of the house and made his way back to the barn where his truck was. Cheryl gave Darius the pack of cookies and told the boys to hurry and catch up with their dad or he was going to leave them.

Cheryl Smithers joined her husband on the porch to wave to the Tye men as they made their way back down the driveway.

"Did I hear him say they may go to church tomorrow?" Jacob asked his wife.

She smiled, "I have a phone call to make."

Chapter Three:

Waking up to a much cooler morning, the boys prepared for church. The morning air was crisp with a slight hint of humidity lingering from the overnight thunderstorms. The sun rose just above the trees as the smell of the hot breakfast Margaret was preparing started climbing up the stairs. Farm fresh eggs and bacon wafted over the aroma of roasted coffee. Buttery sage potatoes sizzled in the pan, almost ready.

Darius and Marcus were aching a bit from the chores their father had them do the day before, but that didn't dampen their excitement of going to church. It would be a nice reprieve from all the other weekend chores their father placed on them. They were never allowed to have friends over, and Darius was looking forward to seeing some of his friends from school this morning. Even with the inviting smell of breakfast, Marcus couldn't stop thinking about the snacks.

Margaret moved about the kitchen as quickly as she could, as she was sore from the previous night. She was thankful that Colby gave her a warning this time. She kept a small bottle of olive oil hidden in their bedroom. She couldn't stop his attacks, but she could make the physical pain hurt a little less with minimal tearing when she had the opportunity.

She'd spent years training her muscles to go as relaxed as possible during his assaults too. It didn't lessen the bruising, but the soreness was better. Long ago, she willed herself to believe that as long as he used her body when he was angry or stressed, then he would not harm the boys. If she was compliant, she would be rewarded with a glimpse of the man she loved. Rather than run from the abuse, she adapted believing it was what was best for her boys.

After their morning meal, Colby read the paper with his coffee and cigarette in the living room. Margaret hoped he wouldn't find an excuse to back out of going to church. She missed seeing her friends on a consistent weekly basis. She especially loved watching her children play with others. Church was where the three of them could relax and be more of who they truly were. At home, they were only starved servants, hoping to be fed some kindness by their over-lord.

She couldn't remember exactly when he became this way. He had always been the jealous type and, admittedly, she liked that about him at first. He was always loving towards her and then, sometime after Marcus was born, he became different. Margaret believed that he wasn't adjusting well to the stress of a new baby, a toddler and a farm to take care of and asked her sister for advice. Her sister, Shari, was older and lived in Indiana with her husband and son.

"Ugh," Shari said, "I don't know. Men are weird. Why weren't either of us blessed with daughters?"

Margaret smiled over the memory. That was Shari. She didn't really give advice but would make a witty comment to make the problem seem small yet validated.

Colby walked into the kitchen as the boys finished up. He dismissed them to brush their teeth and to remind them they'd be leaving in ten minutes with or without them. He walked over to his wife cleaning the last of the dishes.

"You're wearing your hair down?" He asked.

Margaret could feel her face become hot. Without a word, she gathered her hair in one hand and moved it away from the back of her neck. She revealed the bruising his fingers caused the night before when he dug them into her skin to pin her to the bed from behind. The marks mirrored the ones he made on her from their confrontation at lunch the day prior. She was being matter-of-fact without saying a word.

Seeing his work on her body made Colby feel like a man and that made him want to do it again. He reached down to the hem of her dress and started to raise it up her leg when he heard the boy's footsteps on the wooden stairs coming back down. He muttered an expletive under his breath and walked outside to light a cigarette before they left.

The church was on the other side of town and sat along a wooded trail. The steeple could be seen over the acre of mature trees in the front. It was over a hundred years old and made entirely from wood. The donations gathered from the past few years were marked to start building a new place of worship closer to town, but it wouldn't be finished for another year. There was talk of conservationists restoring the old church and making it a museum due to its history, but a land developer was also making a bid for the expansive undeveloped acreage it sat on to put up a strip mall or a shopping center.

Colby parked farthest away from the church but closest to the main exit. Just right of the graveled lot and barely over the property line of the church, were the ruins of a well. The covering, wench and bucket were long gone and the masonry was becoming loose around the well shaft. Marcus spied the well as he waited behind the car for his mother to take his hand once she was out of the car.

"Can we have a penny to make a wish?" He asked with a huge smile on his freshly washed face.

Darius chimed in, "Yeah, can we Dad?"

Colby shut his eyes, "Every fucking time with the well," he said under his breath.

He opened his eyes to see Margret smiling at him, "Fine," he said as he fished two pennies out of the ashtray, he used to store his spare change, "Here you go. Just be careful."

The two boys ran off toward the well to make wishes, and Colby held his arm out for Margaret to take as they followed their sons. She looked up at her husband and silently made her own wish.

Marcus looked down inside the well and shouted, "HELLO!!!! ECHO!"

A loose brick broke away and fell into the well as Marcus leaned on it.

Colby quickly grabbed the back of his shirt and through clenched teeth, shouted, "God dammit!"

He pulled Marcus up and continued, "I said be careful. You fall in that well and no one will ever find you!"

Margaret rushed to her youngest son and smoothed his shirt. She noticed he looked close to tears, "Would you take Dari in and find us a place to sit?" Margaret asked Colby, looking up at him.

"I'd prefer to walk in as a family," he insisted.

Margaret could tell by his tone that there was no need for further discussion, "Did you make your wish?" she asked her young son.

Marcus could only shake his head no. The lump in his throat was too big for him to speak and he knew if he tried, he'd end up crying. She took his small hand and walked back over to the well. Margaret made sure the penny was in his other hand and told him to close his eyes and make his wish. While he stood there, she started to softly hum the same lullaby she sang to him the day before. He tossed his penny in and waited to hear it hit the bottom.

Colby was normally not a patient man, but he was glad for the delay going into the church. Waiting for the penny to make a sound took a long time and no one in the family was even sure if it ever did make one.

"How deep do you think it is?" Darius asked his father.

"Hundreds, maybe even over a thousand feet deep, I suppose." Colby said, thoughtfully.

Before the service began, the associate pastor, Ben Robins, walked the length of the pews to visit and greet each of the parishioners. His eyes focused on the Tye family as they settled into their pews.

"Oh my, what a handsome family we have here. Mr. and Mrs. Tye, it's God's blessing to have you in church today!"

"Good to see you, Ben. How are things?" Colby asked, standing to shake his hand.

"Each day gets better," he responded as he looked to the pew in front of Margaret and Colby. "Marcus and Darius! You two have gotten bigger! I can't tell which one is older anymore. How long has it been?" Ben asked.

"I dunno," Darius replied quickly. "Maybe a month or two?"

Ben smiled, "I'm pretty sure it's been a little longer. We have a youth group now. Would you two like to check it out?"

Darius turned towards his father, "Can we?" he asked.

Colby nodded, "Sure."

The older boy was eager to go to the other room, but Marcus was more shy, and after the incident at the well, he wanted to stay near his mother.

Ben was quick to pick up on the boy's hesitation and seized an opportunity he was worried he wouldn't receive. "Mrs. Tye, would you care to join us for a walk, and I'll show you the room your boys will be in?"

She glanced at Colby and then took Marcus' hand to lead him out of the pew, "That sounds lovely, thank you."

She looked back over toward Colby and said, "I should only be a moment."

It was a brief walk to the room as they retraced their steps from the nave into the vestibule, turned right, and down a short hallway. Once Darius and Marcus started talking to a group of kids over by a small bookshelf across the room, Ben decided it was time to unveil his true motive.

"I'm very glad your family came in today because I wanted to talk with the both of you. Perhaps after the service... or we could schedule something in my office."

Confused, Margaret questioned, "Talk with us? About what?"

"Well, it's a sensitive matter, actually," Ben started, lowering his voice and ushering Margaret back towards the door. "I'm sure you understand that the Church only wants the best for your family."

Still confused but intrigued by where the conversation was going, Margaret decided to simply nod in agreement. They now stood in the hall just outside the door to the room the children were in.

Ben reached down to gently bring up Margaret's right hand. The large bangle bracelet she wore slid down her arm. The beautiful piece of jewelry exposed the ugliness left behind by Colby's grasp. Still, Margaret was silent.

"It's a lovely bracelet." Ben said as he lowered her arm and met her eye. "The church would like to offer counseling for you and your husband. Would he be receptive?"

Margaret was stunned and quickly pulled her hand out of his. She could feel her face and neck getting hot and could only surmise she was as red as she felt. She wanted to speak but couldn't find the right words.

Ben placed his hands behind his back, "Maggie, I've known your family for a while now and we only want to help. We -"

"We?" She questioned with eyes wide. She crossed her arms in front of her chest. A defensive pose Ben knew all too well.

"I only meant the Church."

Several parishioners had quietly expressed their concerns for the Tye family in the past few months. Just the day before, he had a nice long phone conversation with Cheryl Smithers about all she had observed, and all that Margaret had confided in her. He didn't want Margaret knowing that her family was talked of so often, nor did he want this wonderful woman to feel betrayed by the friends who only wanted to help her and the children.

"He can't change, Ben." Margaret started, shaking her head vehemently, "He won't."

Pastor Robins laid his hand on her shoulder and replied, "If he cannot change, maybe we can help you and the boys differently."

***

"What the hell took so Goddamn long?" Colby whispered once Margaret returned to their pew just as the service was about to begin.

An older lady in a peach dress and obnoxious orange and peach plastic clip-on earrings turned from the pew in front of them to face Colby with a disapproving frown.

"Cole, please." Margaret pleaded as she smiled at the offended woman until she turned back around to face forward. Margaret reached for Colby's hand and then turned her smile to him. They locked eyes for a moment, and she wanted so desperately to see the man she fell in love with.

After a few seconds of silence, the sanctuary filled with the sounds of the organ and the choir. The Pastor and Associate Pastor walked down the aisle to start the service.

He leaned in to whisper to Margaret, "I was about to come look for you. Did you enjoy your little tour with Benny Boy?"

She smiled and shook her head, "He'd like to speak with both of us after the service."

Colby scoffed and shifted in the pew.

After the service, Ben and the Pastor, Alan, greeted each parishioner by the main doors before those who wished to stay a little longer and mingle, returned to a banquet room with the snacks Marcus dreamed of enjoying.

"Colby. Margaret. It brings me great joy seeing you and the boys in the house of God once again," Alan said with a huge smile.

Pastor Alan Bateman stood about four inches taller than Ben. His posture was that of a military background. Graying at the temples and wrinkles around his eyes that deepened when he smiled.

Colby released his grasp of Margaret's shoulder to shake Pastor Bateman's hand, "Well, the farm's been taking up a lot of our time on the weekends,' he started, "I suggested we take a break and see what we've been missing."

Margaret could barely contain the surprised expression on her face to Colby's lie. She met Ben's eyes and looked away but not quickly enough. Colby caught the look. He put his arm back around his wife, but this time he gripped her hip and dug his fingers in a little bit until he felt her relax into him.

"Besides, Marcus missed all the snacks afterwards." Colby quipped with a devilish grin.

"Ah, yes. Snacks have that effect," Alan said with a nod.

"Speaking of the snacks, please go enjoy some. Mrs. Grimes made the lemon pound cake and it's delightful," Ben interjected.

Colby smiled briefly, "I'm sure it is."

The couple met up with their boys in the small banquet hall. Margaret anxiously focused on the placement of her bracelet and smoothed her hair to be sure her neck was covered. Colby didn't want Margaret to leave his side and told the boys to stay close to her after they filled their plates so he could get his own coffee.

He picked up a familiar freshly baked cookie just as Cheryl Smithers walked up on the other side of the table to add more to the platter. Colby raised the cookie in approval toward her and noticed her tight-lipped smile perturbed him. She was never overly nice but each time he had been in her presence she was less and less so. It was at this very moment he realized their relationship was contemptuous.

Cheryl didn't know why Colby was staring at her, "Everything okay, Colby?" she asked.

Colby recovered from his revelation quickly with a smirk, "I was just realizing that you must have to fight yourself from eating them all."

His tone was innocent, but his expression did not convey, as his eyes focused on her belly in a subtle but cruelly obvious dig. Cheryl Smithers never backed down from a bully before and she sure as hell wasn't going to back down from this coward. She laughed and walked away to dismiss his childish quip.

Colby was left feeling unsettled. He'd never gotten that reaction before. She wasn't scared or angry. Hell, she wasn't even uncomfortable. Colby walked to the back corner to join his family at a benched table with his coffee and a cookie he no longer wanted.

"Ah, I see you chose Mrs. Smithers' chocolate chip cookies. Excellent choice," Alan said, moments after walking into the room, and up to their table.

Colby took the cookie, missing the bite he took earlier, and tossed it onto his son's plate, "It's not tasting the same today. You can have the rest, Darius."

"It was a lovely service today," Margaret said, looking up at Alan, keeping her right arm under the table.

Alan stood tall, squaring his broad shoulders as he thanked her with a polite nod and then asked if he could talk with the two of them on an important matter. Colby's eyes flew to his boys, "What'd you two do?"

Alan could see Margaret and her children tense collectively.

Before he could defend them, Darius softly said, "Nothing, Sir."

"The boys did nothing wrong, Colby," Alan said in a firm but gentle tone.

"In fact, it's just boring adult stuff," he said, making a silly face at Marcus.

Before Colby could get control of the situation, the boys asked to join their friends to play outside. Margaret quickly gave them permission, and Colby was flustered but quiet, as he tried to keep his composure in front of the other parishioners and not repeat his mistake.

He gritted his teeth before plastering a smile on his face, as he reached down to grab her hand, but slid her bracelet upward to give Margaret's bruised wrist a not so gentle squeeze and asked, "Do you want to talk here, or-"

"My office upstairs will do just fine," Alan said as he gestured for them to follow him.

Margaret and Colby were taking their seats in front of the Pastor's desk when Alan began to speak.

"This is where I offer all my counseling, as you know, from premarital, to substance abuse, to grief and," he took a moment to survey their faces and smiled, "I can counsel you through almost any struggle."

Colby finally picked up where this was going. He calmed his breathing, unclenched his jaw, and narrowed his eyes. "Our marriage is not troubled."

Alan smiled as he sat in his chair. "I never said your marriage was troubled. I said I could help you through struggles and every marriage has struggles. Counseling or having another perspective can help ease that struggle and make your union stronger and more loving."

Margaret smiled and bravely seized the opportunity to show Colby how much she loved him, "This sounds lovely. We should try it."

Colby was uncomfortable. He was also seething. How dare someone interfere with his marriage. He could barely hear his wife asking what harm a few counseling sessions could do. All he wanted to do was grab her and run out of the room. He took note of her hopeful smile as she was excitedly taking a brochure from Alan's hand. His mind began to focus on the conversation again.

"Sure. Let's talk about it some more at home and then we'll talk next Sunday, how's that?" he asked, standing back up and gesturing for his wife to join him in his departure.

Chapter Four:

The ride home from the church was a silent one. Margaret's mind was racing. She had no idea how Colby was going to react once they were home. He had become more and more unpredictable.

Colby pulled up to the front porch. "Okay, everyone out."

The boys jumped out from the back and before Margaret could reach for her door handle, Colby grabbed her arm. When she gasped, he lightened his grip.

"I love you," he said, giving her a smile.

"I know," Margaret flirted and then exited the car.

A cigarette later, Colby walked into the house while taking his tie off.

"Get dressed for chore'n, boys!" he shouted as he started up the stairs.

He rounded the corner and headed toward the master bedroom.

"Colby, close the door. I'm changing!" Margaret yelled, using the dress in her hands to cover herself.

He obeyed her command and smiled to himself. In her bra and panties, she started to slip the dress onto a hanger. Colby, in his unbuttoned shirt, walked up behind her and grabbed a fist full of her hair.

She gasped.

He pulled her up against him tightly with his other arm and nuzzled her neck. She could feel how hard he was up against her backside.

His mouth trailed to her ear when, in a harsh whisper, he said, "You owe me for that trip to the principal's office."

Margaret could feel panic set in. Colby surprised her and her body was not ready for him. He could feel her tense against him, and he no longer wanted to be gentle.

She could barely hear the boys arguing and calling for her when Colby grabbed at her underwear to rip them aside. She still held the hangar and her dress in her hands and bit down on the material burying her face into the pile when he roughly bent her over the ironing board left out from this morning.

"MOM! TELL DARIUS TO STOP!" Marcus yelled, stomping up the stairs.

Colby growled in anger and pulled his pants back up around his waist. "Jesus Christ!" he yelled.

He pulled the belt completely out of the loops and started to wrap it around his fists.

"Colby, don't!" Margaret snapped as she tried to grab his arm.

Colby shoved her into the ironing board, knocking it over. The crash sent the boys racing down the stairs and out of the house. Colby swung the door open and was faced with an empty hallway.

"Get to the barn and start your chores!" he yelled after them.

He heard the bathroom door behind him slam shut and turned to see Margaret was no longer by the fallen ironing board.

"I guess we're done?" he questioned through the door after checking to see if it was locked.

Her voice was shaking when she finally spoke, "I just really need to go to the bathroom, Cole, and the boys are restless so how 'bout we pick up where we left off tonight, huh?"

He mumbled something and she waited until she was sure he'd finished changing before she ventured back into their bedroom to get dressed.

Preparing for dinner in the kitchen, Margaret looked from the window and watched Colby talking with the boys under the shade of a tree before getting in the truck and driving away. She moved towards the phone.

***

"Hey, it was nice seeing you and the family in church today," Jacob said once Colby got the truck on the main road headed toward the town.

Colby scoffed, "May not see us again."

Jacob looked over, "Why? What's wrong?"

Colby snickered, "They think every married couple needs therapy."

"There's nothing wrong with therapy," Jacob stated.

"We're fine!" Colby snapped.

Jacob was quiet for a moment, "I'm sure you and Maggie are fine."

"We are!"

Jacob took a deep breath and changed the subject about understanding the part he was about to buy to fix his air conditioning. He fought to keep the conversation light and not anger the man who was doing him a favor, although he wished more than ever he'd insisted on driving. Colby needed his cigarettes and Cheryl would never forgive him if he let anyone smoke in their vehicles. Jacob got Colby talking about the new draft picks made by Cincinnati's football team the rest of the way to the store. On the way back, they talked about the new Ford and Chevy models coming out until they left the paved roads.

"You know," Jacob started, "My Cheryl and I had some dark times. But through some counseling of our own, we found our way back to each other and -"

"I'm just trying to be neighborly, Jacob, please don't piss me off bringing this bullshit back up," Colby warned.

Jacob threw his arms up, "Okay, Colby, fine! Just remember Maggie's a human being who loves you. "

"What the hell is that supposed to mean?!" Colby demanded, fishtailing a bit out of the last turn he took.

Jacob bit his lip and became concerned for his safety all of a sudden.

"Colby, I won't say another word. I'm sorry I said anything. Listen, -"

"No, you listen!" Colby snapped, "I don't need to get this shit from my customers. You want any more hay for your animals, get it elsewhere."

He slammed on the brakes at the mouth of The Smithers' driveway.

"I'm in a hurry to get home and will need to drop you here. Now get your shit and get the hell out of my truck." Colby said sternly and left the old man to walk the rest of the way home in a cloud of dust.

As he walked into the kitchen, he heard Margaret ending a conversation on the phone. "Okay. Thanks. Bye."

Colby felt suspicious, "That was an abrupt ending. Who was it?"

Margaret smiled, "Oh, it was just Shari. She called and you know how she can ramble."

Colby nodded, "And what were you thanking her for?"

Margaret was confused. "What do you mean?"

Amused, Colby walked towards her, "You said, 'Okay. Thanks. Bye,' when you ended it. So, what," he paused for dramatic effect, "were you thanking her for?"

"Oh!" Margaret laughed for a little too long, "while I had her on the phone, I asked her for a recipe. A chicken casserole thing she used to make."

Colby looked around at the kitchen table where he knew she liked to sit when she talked on the phone.

"Where is it?" He asked.

"Where's what?"

"The recipe?" He gestured toward the table, growing impatient.

"Well, we were talking so long, I already made a card for it and put it in my book." She pointed over toward the hutch that held her recipes.

Colby smiled at his wife, unsure of why she was lying to him. Before he could ask any further questions, she excused herself and hurried into the powder room. Colby walked over to the caller ID box on the counter just under where the phone base hung on the wall. He failed to see his sister-in-law's phone number within the past few hours since he'd been gone. He picked up the phone and pressed the redial button. After 4 rings the answering machine at the church picked up. Colby quietly hung up the receiver.

Margaret asked Darius to pour the lemonade for himself and his brother at dinner and took extra precautions to make sure Colby wouldn't get upset before they joined him at the table. Conversation over dinner was lively with the boys talking about how much fun they had with their friends earlier.

"Well, maybe we'll go again before school starts," Colby said.

Silence fell over the rest of the family.

Marcus was the first to ask, "Aren't we gonna go again next Sunday?"

"No."

"Why?" Margaret asked, not surprised by the fact that they wouldn't be going to church weekly, but surprised that Colby didn't weaponize it like he did with everything else.

"What do you mean, 'Why?'" He started, sounding smug, "I never gave any of you reason to believe this was going to continue. You idiots assumed."

Darius started to say something when his father interrupted, "And the next person to bitch about it will not sit for a fucking week. Do you understand me?!"

Both boys stared at their plates in silence.

Colby sat on the porch drinking a cold beer looking over toward the Smither's farm as the sun was beginning to set. He could see the top of their silo peaking over the hilltop. He replayed everything from the day in his mind. He was feeling cornered, ganged up on. He knew going to that damn church was a mistake, and then catching his wife in a lie angered him. He wanted to slap her lying mouth.

The boys were helping her clean up the kitchen and Margaret sent Darius out to see if his father needed anything.

"Bring me the six-pack from the fridge."

Darius was confused, "A beer or-"

"Did I say, 'Beer,' you little shit?"

"No." Darius meekly responded.

"'No,' what?"

"No, Sir."

"Go get me a six-pack now," Colby demanded. He flicked his cigarette toward his son, and it bounced off the storm door as the boy retreated into the house.

Three beers later, Colby found himself in the cab of his truck at the very spot he left Jacob Smithers standing. He coasted in neutral with no headlights the last ten or so yards and sat there for some time. He turned the key in the truck's ignition and drove over to the church. It looked eerie at night with all the trees surrounding it. Colby got out and dropped the tailgate on his truck with a fresh beer and a new cigarette. He pushed the can filled with diesel fuel for farming equipment over to clear himself a seat. He convinced himself that Margaret was having an affair, and he was starting to believe it was with Ben. Before long, Colby Tye convinced himself that Alan, The Smithers, and everyone else in town wanted to take away what was his. They were all against him and he felt like a fool. He became enraged.

He could hear Cheryl's laughter as though it were on a loop, and he envisioned the way Ben placed his hand on the small of Maggie's back when they walked away. Each new thought compounding the last.

He remembered the look those two shared this morning when they didn't think he noticed. After they came home, she flirted just after the drive, only to later bristle at his touch in their bedroom. She also lied about who she was talking to on the phone.

"Fucking whore!" he shouted into the night sky with only crickets to hear him. "Well, if she wants to be one, I'll treat her like one. Maybe give that lying mouth of hers something else to focus on." He had to reclaim what was his. He blamed her for everything he was about to do.

By the time Colby's truck reached his property line, he could hear the sirens. He looked in the direction of the church and smirked at the faint orange and yellow glow in the sky above the tree line. He quickly went inside as quietly as he could and ran up to the bedroom. He stripped out of his clothes, washed his hands and face and started to crawl into bed. Muffled sounds from the sirens were barely audible in their room. He paused, looking at Margaret's figure curled under the sheet. Rage started to fill his mind with images of things that never happened between his wife and the younger pastor. Colby couldn't tell the difference between reality and fantasy at that moment. He ripped the covering completely off her and rolled her onto her back, jerking her awake. Margaret was stunned when the back of his hand cracked across her face. She yelped and tried to shield her head with her hands, but Colby grabbed her wrists and held them above her head while he placed his forehead on top of hers and squeezed her legs tight together between his own.

"You've been fucking Benny Boy, haven't you, slut?!" he hissed, spitting as he talked.

Margaret could taste the blood from where her teeth made impact with the soft tissue inside her cheek. Her ears were ringing, and she was confused. Her crying was all the confirmation he needed. He struck her again with an open hand and began to choke her.

"Bitch." He snarled as he forced her onto her stomach. She tried to resist, and he struck her again. She could feel herself going in and out of consciousness as he stripped her naked from the waist down.

Colby reached for the pants he left on the floor and took his belt out of the loops. He cracked the leather belt across Margaret's backside leaving an instant red mark. She whimpered. It wasn't good enough for him. He wanted to make her feel the physical pain equivalent to the hit his ego took.

"You think you can make a fool out of me? Huh?" he asked as he felt the heat and skin welt on her buttocks from the belt with his fingers.

"What are you talking about?" Margaret finally managed.

"You've been giving it up to Ben, bitch, don't deny it. I know that's who you were talking to when I came home."

"I talked to him, yes, but-"

"Did you like it? Did he give it to you real good?" Colby was on top straddling her again and he gripped her buttocks with both hands.

"I never-" Margaret started to say when she felt him enter her in a place he'd never gone before. She could only feel searing pain and her body tried desperately to move away from him. She screamed and cried so loud he forgot about the sirens down the road.

"I guess I'll have to claim your ass since you give the pussy away."

Several minutes passed after Colby was finished with his assault. Margaret's battered body laid still in the exact position he left her when he rolled off and eventually passed out. She waited a little longer for his snores to turn into heavy breathing and then she went to clean herself and tend to her wounds. Her legs trembled down each step on her way downstairs. The grandfather clock she inherited from her parents chimed a quarter past two. She made her way over to a cupboard and poured herself a whiskey, straight. She grabbed an old afghan blanket off the couch and went onto the porch swing. When she looked up, she could see the glow of emergency vehicle lights by the Smithers Farm and only then realized the smell of smoke in the air. The night was very dark in this area of town that was void of streetlights and the moon was not yet full enough to see much. She prayed that everyone was safe and then noticed a fire and more flashing lights further away just west in the direction of the church as she took a sip. The whiskey stung her mouth and she started to cry softly. She now knew what she must do.

Margaret wanted to understand why her husband believed she was having an affair. And with Ben of all people. She wanted to sit outside in the cool air longer but the acrid smell from whatever was burning made it impossible. She started to walk back to the front door when she saw three empty beer cans next to the large ashtray filled with ash and cigarette butts and decided to clean it up. She assumed the other three cans were put back in the fridge before Colby went upstairs.

Chapter Five

The next morning the boys were telling their mother about the assemblies and class parties that were lined up for the final week of school over breakfast when Sheriff Hackett knocked on their door.

"G'mornin' Ma'am, I'm sorry to bother you so early, but I was hoping you'd have time for a couple questions?" The Sheriff asked, and then mentioned the two fires that occurred overnight at the Smithers Farm and at the church

"Was anyone hurt?" Margaret asked.

"Luckily, no one was at the church at the time, but it's a complete loss and the Smithers silo is gone along with a portion of their barn. It can all be rebuilt, thankfully."

Colby came down the stairs as Margaret was offering Sheriff Hackett some coffee.

"Are the kids getting escorts to school?" Colby quipped as he walked up to them.

The Sheriff gave a thin-lipped smile and explained that there were two suspicious fires the night before. He told Colby they were canvassing the neighbors and speaking with anyone near either scene to gather information that could help in the investigation. Margaret excused herself to call her friend to offer support.

"So, were you home all night?" Sheriff Hackett asked routinely.

Colby nodded, "Yes, Sir. We came home from church and then after the boys got going on some chores, I picked up Jacob to get a part for his air conditioner. I got home close to four-thirty, I suppose."

"And neither you or Maggie or the boys went out later or heard anything unusual during the night?"

"Huh-uh, no Sir. We didn't go anywhere, and I never heard a thing."

The sheriff asked Colby to join him outside on the porch when the boys ran past to finish getting ready for school.

"I hate to ask this, Colby, but why does your wife have a bruise on her face and a swollen lip?"

Colby laughed, "My wife's beautiful but she is clumsy. She forgot she left the ironing board out and fell over it. Damn iron was on top and fell on her."

"When did this happen?" Sheriff Hackett asked as he jotted something down in his notebook.

Colby's mind raced as he had hoped the Sheriff would laugh it off with him. "Um, well, if you must know…" His voice trailed off and he looked to see if Margaret or the kids were nearby.

"Oh, I really must know." Hackett said with very little amusement in his voice.

Colby smiled, "Well, shit was getting a bit passionate between us last night, if you know what I mean, and that's when it happened so, I guess around…" He was struggling to remember what time he came back home, 'Elevenish?"

"Are you asking or telling me?" The sheriff was losing his patience.

"I have to be honest with you, Sheriff Hackett, I had a few beers on the porch last night after dinner and then we got carried away. I wasn't looking at the clock at any point at all."

"And you didn't hear any vehicles racing down the gravel road by your house or anything?"

Colby shook his head.

Margaret joined them on the porch after a brief conversation with Cheryl, "I didn't hear anything at all. When I came out onto the porch, I couldn't see anything but the flashing lights of the firetrucks and the smell of the smoke."

"What do you mean?" Colby asked, unaware she left the bed.

"I came out here before two thirty this morning for some air. I saw the fire trucks and smelled smoke, so I went back in." she looked over towards the Smithers farm, "I didn't know what happened and honestly, I forgot about it until you knocked on our door this morning."

"I guess your run in with the ironing board made sleep difficult, huh?" Hackett asked.

Margaret looked at Colby perplexed, "You told him about that?"

Colby put his arm around his wife and kissed her gently on the top of her head.

"Of course I did. He noticed where the iron fell on your pretty little face," Colby said smoothly. "Speaking of," he turned his attention to the Sheriff, "My wife needs some rest, if you don't mind."

Satisfied, Sheriff Hackett left with his usual, "If I have any more questions, I know where to find you."

Margaret squirmed from Colby's embrace and headed back inside once the Sheriff headed down their driveway.

Colby watched as the sheriff continued off the property before joining her inside. He sauntered into the kitchen and watched his wife clean up after the boys. He noticed she hadn't started his eggs and bacon.

"Are you waiting for the boys to leave before making mine?" he asked.

Margaret stopped drying the plate in her hand and set it down, cursing at her inability to stop shaking.

"Actually," she turned to him, "I was thinking we could have a talk before your breakfast."

He glared at her for a moment, "Is there coffee, at least?"

She motioned to the carafe she already filled for him on the table with his mug next to it. His eyes followed, but he did not turn his head. Looking back at her, he tried to determine what she was up to.

The boys ran downstairs with their backpacks on to catch the bus. Margaret chased after them onto the porch with their lunches. She watched them race each other to the end of the drive where the bus waited patiently for them. The morning sun was blinding, and her eyes had barely adjusted after she walked back inside when Colby grabbed her arm and swung her into the kitchen.

"We can talk while you make my breakfast," he said, shoving her toward the stove. She stood still until he took his seat at the table.

"I'll be happy to, just as soon as we clear something up."

Her bravery usually amused him and on any other day it would turn him on, but not today. "You are lucky you're still breathing, lying bitch."

"Why did you accuse me of having an affair with Ben?" She tried hard to sound calm, but her voice betrayed her, and she visibly jumped when he threw his coffee.

"So, you want to know where you got sloppy, huh? I know your sister didn't call. I can use the caller ID, dumbass! And don't say you called her. I can use the redial button, too, and I got the church answering machine."

He saw the expression change on his wife's face.

"Are you kidding me? That's why you jumped to such an awful conclusion?" Margaret said, slumping into the chair across from her husband with a deep sigh.

The fact that she didn't race into denial or start crying threw Colby off. He sat in silence, allowing her to speak. He already came to his own conclusions and steadfastly believed them to be true. He also knew he'd never allow her to leave with another man so whatever she said wouldn't change his plans for their future.

"I did call the church yesterday after you left," Margaret said while occupying herself with a missed crumb on the table.

"She finally spits out some truth."

"But I didn't talk to Ben. I spoke with Alan. I had more questions about the counseling."

"Jesus fucking Christ!" Colby started, shaking his head. Margaret got up and fetched her husband another cup for his coffee and then continued her explanation while cleaning the mess his first one made. She then dutifully started to prepare his eggs and bacon.

"I knew you'd be upset that I lied, but I had every intention of talking about it further after dinner when the boys took their baths. You made it clear you didn't want to talk about the counseling yet." She finally said as she placed his breakfast in front of him.

She continued trying to explain her actions and he silently ate his meal. After he was finished, he placed his plate and fork in the sink for her to wash and kissed her head.

"Well, now you've learned a lesson on not lying to your husband," Colby said, smiling.

"I'm gonna go mow," and he turned on his heel and left her in the kitchen.

Margaret was exhausted. Her body had been aching for so many different reasons the past few days and all at the hands of her husband. She didn't sleep and pleading her case this morning felt like pleading for her life. She didn't know what to expect from Colby anymore and after what he did to her the night before, and showing no remorse for his actions, was the last straw. Margaret found herself on the front porch swing again. She noticed the smell of smoke still lingering and more cars going up and down the gravel road they lived on. Investigators and the curious townspeople, no doubt. A portion of the silo had collapsed from her view. When she spoke with Cheryl it was brief. The woman was clearly upset but had too much to do other than talk to a friend on the phone. Her eyes looked for the church's steeple and it didn't look the same anymore. She felt a lump in her throat.

She turned to see her husband walking back toward the house.

"Grab my keys, will ya?" he yelled up to her once he saw her on the porch.

Without thinking, she jumped to do his bidding, and cursed herself for it. She found his keys on the counter rather than the hook and hurried back out to toss them to him.

"Sorry it took so long, they weren't in the usual place." She was afraid of making his sudden good mood turn bad.

Colby smiled as he smoothly caught the keys, "No problem. Do you want to come with me?" he asked cheerfully.

"I don't think showing my face is a good idea right now, Cole."

"Oh, c'mon," he said, opening the passenger door. Laying on the seat was a diesel fuel can, an empty book of matches, a half empty carton of cigarettes and the plastic ring carrier from the night's previous six-pack.

She couldn't wait for him to leave, "I have too much laundry to catch up on. Besides, didn't you get the fuel for the mower last Friday?"

His upbeat demeanor swiftly changed. He slammed the door shut and walked around to the driver's side.

"Actually, you're right. Maybe you should just stick to the laundry today."

Chapter Six:

The morning of the last day of school started out like any other with the exception of Marcus and Darius' obvious excitement. The past few days were intense for Margaret. She never brought up the church or counseling again. She didn't see the use with church services, now held at the rec center, until the new one was finished in town. Besides, after last Sunday, it would be a cold day in hell before Colby allowed her or the kids to step foot in their church again.

Cheryl mentioned putting the property up for sale rather than rebuild. They were at the age where they could barely keep up with the demands of the farm. Both fires were obvious arson, and the Smithers weren't hopeful for an insurance pay out. It would be more economical to sell the property and find something more suitable and manageable for the older couple. Cheryl confided to Margaret the arsonist used rags soaked in diesel fuel to help spread the fire. A cigarette tied to a match was the ignitor. One of the bundled cigarettes and matches failed to ignite the fumes of its rag on the other side of the silo. It was taken to a high-tech FBI lab for further analysis. Unfortunately, due to backlogs and with no one injured in either fire, the wheels of justice turned excruciatingly slow for the town's people.

Margaret was quick to believe her husband was involved. She observed so much more than he realized. She kept the information to herself but knew the moment he was under suspicion, he would make life even worse than it was. She also couldn't turn him in, either. If she were wrong or if he got off on a technicality, she was as good as dead. And what about her children?

Colby was in good spirits. He may have been wrong about his wife cheating on him and he was relieved by that, but he was able to teach her a valuable lesson, too, and that made him feel prideful. He was confident she would never lie to him again. Colby believed he'd gotten away with his crimes. He effectively gave those who meddled in his marriage something else to wring their hands over. It was just after noon, and he was almost done tilling for the new crops of cabbage, cucumber, and tomato when he decided to head in for his lunch.

Sheriff Hackett drove up as Colby started up the porch steps. Margaret came out to greet their visitor.

"Good afternoon, Mr. and Mrs. Tye," he said, climbing out of his car.

"Sheriff, can I offer you some lemonade or tea?" Margaret offered.

"Oh, a glass of lemonade would be just fine. Thank you, ma'am."

"Tea for me, hon," Colby shouted at her when she walked back into the house.

Margaret could hear Sheriff Hackett ask Colby about his timeline again for the night of the fires and explaining his need for some additional clarification. She knew this was her moment. It arrived earlier than she anticipated, but if she didn't take it, she may never live to get another chance. She ran to where she hid the suitcases she packed up all week long in the coat closet. In two trips, she was able to get them out the back door and into the trunk of her car parked around back. The car was in plain view from where Colby was preparing for the summer crops, and she had been waiting for the next time he went into town. She ran back into the kitchen and poured each man their beverage and hurried back out front.

"Thank you, kindly," Sheriff Hackett said, as he reached for his lemonade.

"I was about to run into town. Do you need me to stay?" she asked the Sheriff.

"What's in town?" Colby asked abruptly.

The Sheriff looked at Colby and with a half-smile asked, "Is there a problem?"

Colby kept his eyes on his wife. "No. No problem. I was just surprised since she hadn't mentioned going anywhere to me."

Margaret let out a little laugh. "Well, I realized I need more laundry detergent. I'm on the last box and those boys will only be getting dirtier this summer."

The Sheriff was quick to let her know that he was fine just questioning Colby and she could get on with her day.

"I'll see you in a bit," she managed to say. She kept her eyes on him a bit longer than usual. "Love you," was the last thing she said before turning back into the house to exit out the back door.

Sheriff Hackett stayed a little longer. He asked Colby several questions like, where he gets his gas for his equipment and what his relationship with the Smithers was like. Colby was polite and answered all the Sheriff's questions with no problem.

He walked the Sheriff down the steps of the porch. "Oh, one more thing," the Sheriff said, turning toward him before he continued. "Can I trouble you for a cigarette?"

Colby smiled and started fishing in his pocket for his pack. He pulled out his cigarettes and handed one to the Sheriff.

Examining it, the Sheriff asked, "Is that your usual brand?"

Colby nodded and chuckled, "Ever since I was sixteen. I had no idea you smoke."

The Sheriff took the cigarette and tucked it behind his ear and said with a smirk, "I don't."

Colby was left baffled as the Sheriff tipped his brim and continued to his car.

Colby walked into the kitchen holding both empty glasses after the Sheriff's departure. He saw a plate with his lunch on it and sat down to eat, but he couldn't. He felt bothered. Something other than the Sheriff's visit was nagging him. The spotlight was on him, but he didn't care. There was something else. After a few bites of his lunch, the feeling was too overwhelming. He pushed it aside and went into the laundry room. The cabinet where Margaret liked to stock the detergent was filled with two large unopened boxes of the soap she used. Plus, the one sitting on the dryer was nearly three fourths full. She lied again. She sure as shit was not going to the store. He was determined to catch her in the act this time. Colby raced back to the kitchen and hit the redial button on the phone.

After one ring a tone played followed by an automated message, "Thank you for using Bell Tone. The current time is 1:13 pm."

He slammed the phone down on its cradle and went to grab his truck keys off the hook, but they were gone. He searched everywhere he could think of for his keys when the realization hit him.

"That fucking bitch!"

He ran to the file cabinet where he kept an envelope full of spare keys.

Margaret made her way to the front office of the middle school, gasping for breath in a panic.

The office secretary noticed and asked, "Mrs. Tye, are you okay?"

"My Boys. Call my boys for early dismissal please. There's been a family emergency."

"Do you happen to know which classes?"

"Uh, Darius is in eighth grade English. I can't remember his teacher's name. Oh! And Marcus is in Mr. Parks' class I believe, in the sixth grade math department," Margaret nervously said, trying to give as much information as she could to speed things along.

After a small eternity the boys made their way to the front office with their backpacks and confused expressions. Margaret spotted them and hurried to meet them, "Let's go. I already signed you out."

Marcus looked up at his mother, "What's wrong?"

She smiled as she rushed out the door, "Nothing. We're just going to get a jump on our summer vacation."

Darius was wary, "Where are we going?"

Margaret waited until Marcus was in the backseat before she lowered her voice and faced her eldest son, "Away from your father."

After topping off on gas and grabbing some snacks and drinks to tide them over, they hit the road to a town just outside Indianapolis.

Marcus made eye contact with his mother when she looked in the rearview mirror to check on them, "Mom, I'm sleepy."

"Hey, lie down and take a nap," Darius said as he climbed over the seat to join Margaret up front.

After a few moments of silence, she maneuvered the rearview mirror so she could see Marcus curled up across the seats fast asleep. The dull roar of the tires on the road had worked their magic.

Margaret gave a soft chuckle, "The car always did put your brother to sleep."

Darius treasured this time with his mom. They listened to the radio and sang along together to some of the songs they both knew. He felt happy and it confused him. He couldn't stop looking at her. He was unable to remember a time when she so freely laughed and sang.

They had a little less than half a tank of gas and were almost at the Kentucky/Indiana border after nearly two hours on the road. By now, she knew Colby was on to her.

"Mom?" Darius started, softly, "Can we stop for something else to eat?"

"Yeah, I need to get more gas and I'm sure your brother will need to pee when he wakes up."

She knew she could make it across the border on the gas she had left. Crossing the state line would make her breathe a little easier. She was honestly afraid to leave the safe cocoon of the car until she reached her sisters.

As the evening went on, there were a few cars on the road. Thankfully, none resembled Colby's truck. She convinced herself that she got her boys out of the woods and the big bad wolf couldn't reach them now. She made the decision to stop for gas near the small town of Corydon, Indiana.

As her boys used the restroom, she ran to the payphone by the cash register to call Shari.

"I had to leave today and we're on our way. Love you. See you soon," she said to her sister's machine. She noticed the time and realized her sister's family refused to answer their phone during supper.

She asked the boys to pick out one thing to eat and that they'd have to share a drink. Before she could tell the man at the register that she wanted to pump gas, he had already wrung up the snacks.

"Oh, um," she stared at the remaining seven dollars left from the thirty she siphoned from the joint bank account she used for groceries, "Boys, I don't have enough for that and gas," she said as she started to tear up.

She smiled at the attendant and handed him the seven dollars. "Seven dollars of gas please," she said, stumbling on her words.

"Are you okay, Ma'am?"

She smiled nervously, "Yes, uh, what is the most fuel-efficient way to Indianapolis?"

The clerk narrowed his eyes surveying the faded bruise on her face, "Are you in some sort of trouble?"

Margaret smiled wishing she didn't have to speak any further, "No sir, I'm -" she paused to tell Darius to take Marcus back to the car, "I'm just trying to get my boys to safety, and this is the last of the money I was able to get." She shook her head and laughed a little, "I really thought I took enough."

The man nodded. "Put that seven dollars back in your pocket book. I got you. Go ahead and fill it up," He reached for a bag to put the snacks the boys chose in it.

Margaret managed to smile through the tears, "Thank you so much!" she said, graciously.

As she put the money back into her wallet, she noticed a small smiley face sticker with the church's name on it she snagged the Sunday before. She had planned to give it to Marcus and completely forgot. She pulled it out of her wallet and handed it to the clerk. He smiled at the gesture and read the sticker, "Have a heavenly day! Well, thank you."

He peeled the backing off, placed it on the front of the register, and said, "This is the perfect spot for it."

Margaret smiled. "Thank you so much." He smiled back and nodded.

Heading back to the car Margaret allowed herself to feel hopeful again. She tossed the bag to Darius and told him to split everything up equally and went to top off the gas tank one last time. She made sure to wave at the kind man working alone and made a note to pay it forward.

The blue sky gave way to shades of amber and gold as the fiery sun began to set.

She spotted a familiar bend in the road and the memories came flooding back. She knew she was only a few minutes away.

After briefly watching Darius sleep with his head leaning against the passenger window and mouth breathing, she smiled at their sleepy innocence and knew she was doing the right thing for them.

Margaret was cautious as she turned into her sister's driveway. Approaching the house, she slowed to a stop and saw a bike leaning against a tree in the front yard. She exited the car and smiled when she realized her nephew, Caleb, was home.

He was a few years older than Darius. The last time she talked to her sister, she learned that Caleb had a job in town, and he rode his bike to work every day. She thought that he would be a good role model for the boys and would keep them entertained and motivated to do good things.

She opened the back door to the car, "Hey boys, we're here!" She said to two very sleepy faces.

Yawning and stretching, Marcus began rubbing his eyes, "Where are we?"

She smiled, "Your Aunt Shari's. Do you remember your cousin, Caleb?"

Darius shook his head no. Marcus looked over and said, "I don't either."

Margaret continued to smile, "It's been a few years. He is a little older than you. I think he's sixteen now, going on seventeen."

Chapter Seven:

Colby gave up on his search and returned to the farm as he had
seen no signs of Margaret. He went to all the places he thought she
would go. He even ran into the main grocery store in town when
he couldn't spot her car in the parking lot. No one working in the
store saw her that day. Plenty remembered her from a few days before though. He didn't let his time go to waste. He grabbed himself
a case of beer and sat on the porch to wait for her. He was confident
she'd return after the boys came home from school, but the bus continued driving past their residence.

He stood suddenly as a thought occurred to him. He ran to get
the checkbook they shared out of the kitchen drawer. He sat with
it at the table and looked at how much she spent on groceries when
she was there earlier in the week. He couldn't find the receipt to
match the transaction in the stack saved to reconcile the checkbook
weekly. It wasn't technically a lot of money he saw on the carbon,
but even without the receipt, he knew something was off. She was
so meticulous at showing him where every penny went.

"WHAT THE FUCK HAVE YOU DONE, YOU FUCKING
BITCH!!" He screamed in his empty house.

His head was spinning, and his world was crashing down around
him. He spotted his half-eaten sandwich sitting on a plate on the table and acknowledged he hadn't eaten since then. He picked up the
plate and threw it across the room in a rage.

"That goddamn cunt thinks she can leave me! She thinks she
can just take what's mine!" He ranted and paced. Colby reached for
another beer, realizing he drank more than half of the case in only a
few hours on an empty stomach and his blood pressure was probably on the rise.

He sat at the table with his head in his hands, "How dare her,"
he whispered hoarsely, "She will pay for this."

He looked over at the caller ID and remembered the first lie she
told him that week. There's only one person she can turn to now.

"She's taking the boys to her sister's," he said to himself.

The revelation breathed new life into him, and he knew he was on the right path. He had only driven there once many years ago and he was sure they hadn't moved since. He needed the address to properly map it out. He walked over toward a sideboard cabinet and opened the drawer. He fished around for a moment before realizing the address book was gone.

"Clever, Maggie. Very. Fucking. Clever."

He ran out to his truck and fished out the map he kept in his glove compartment and brought it back into the kitchen. Glaring at the map, he started to follow the route to the general area he believed his sister-in-law lived. He glared at the map until it became blurry, and he passed out just as he figured the best way to get to the town he knew his family was going to.

***

Shari and her husband, Aaron, were enjoying the warm evening on their small porch in their subdivision. After dinner, Aaron checked phone messages while their son Caleb helped his mother clean up. They knew to expect Margaret and the boys any minute now.

Shari turned when the front storm door opened to see her son walking out with his backpack on. "Since you're spending the night at Pete's house, can you set up your room for your cousins to stay in tonight?"

"I already have it set up for them," he said with a smile, "Do you want me to hang around a few more minutes to greet them?"

Before Shari could answer, she saw a car pull up into the driveway out of the corner of her eye.

"They're here!" She squealed and jumped down to greet them.

Caleb shared a look with his dad over their mom's reaction. The men were still smiling when they reached the car.

Aaron and Caleb helped with the luggage from the trunk, and the boys carried their backpacks into the house. Caleb showed the boys to his room and introduced them to his hamster, Bubba. Darius and Marcus were exhaustingly filled with uncertainty and didn't say much.

Caleb left to go to his friends while Shari warmed up leftovers for Margaret and the boys. After they ate, Aaron pulled out a board game for the boys to entertain them, while Shari and Margaret made up a bed in the living room and gathered towels and other necessities the three would be needing before settling in the family room to chat. The boys weren't used to staying up so late and Marcus had a hard time focusing, but his Uncle Aaron was kind and would gently remind him of the game rules or nudge him when it was his turn. They were intrigued by the TV in their cousin's room as they didn't have such luxuries in their own home. Aaron let them keep it on and planned to turn it off later after they fell asleep.

Chapter Eight

A pain shot through Colby's neck so violently it jolted him awake. His body didn't like the position he passed out in on the kitchen table. He rubbed his eyes and looked at the time.

It was just before 10 PM. He pushed away from the table and stood up. He grabbed a table knife and slapped some peanut butter on a slice of bread, and brewed coffee to wake himself up and clear the stupor he allowed himself to fall into. After feeling more like himself he examined the map one last time before deciding on his route to the town his sister-in-law's family resided in. He grabbed his keys and ran out the door without taking the extra time to secure it behind him.

***

The graveyard shift at the gas station was a lonely one. Most of the time, the lone employee kept busy stocking the shelves, taking inventory, cleaning, and prepping for the morning.

Colby stepped out of his truck for gas. He ran his fingers through his hair and rolled his shoulders. The coffee did its job to keep him alert, but he needed something to ease the dull ache the beer was doing to his head. He decided to head into the store to grab ibuprofen and a bottle of water.

The attendant had a scruffy beard and the gas station brand trucker hat he was wearing was barely holding his unkempt hair underneath.

Colby spotted his name tag, "Big John," and looked back up at his face.

"Uh, I need $10 regular on pump, uh-" Colby paused to look back at the pump he was parked in front of, "Pump 3, it looks like."

Big John nodded and asked, "Anything else?"

Colby looked back at where the cooled drinks were displayed, "Yeah, one sec," he grabbed a cold Gatorade and snagged a traveler's sized bottle of ibuprofen on the way back to the register. He twisted the metal cap until he heard the pop as the pressure was released. He opened the ibuprofen and chugged the electrolyte filled beverage when his eyes fell to something on the register that was familiar to him. He examined the sticker, and it was new. The edges had not been messed with and it was still glossy unlike the others around it.

Colby pulled out his wallet and produced the most recent picture he had of Margaret from almost six months ago and the school pictures of each boy.

"Have you seen this woman or these kids in here?" Colby asked, "It would've been in the past ten hours or so."

Big John looked at the photo, "Nope, are they missing or something?"

Colby stuffed the photos back in his wallet, "Or something. I'm going to grab a coffee. I think it's going to be a long night."

Colby looked toward the coffee and back at Big John, who just smiled and gestured for Colby to help himself.

Big John had a sense that if the woman and kids the man was looking for came through, it was well before his shift started. However, Colby's appearance and demeanor convinced Big John to give him as little information as he possibly could.

Colby walked over toward the coffee stand and poured a cup. He was convinced Margaret was in the store and that Big John was lying about it.

"Cream and sugar on the side with the lids," Big John offered when he noticed Colby staring into the black coffee he just poured. Something was off and Big John thought he should keep Colby talking.

"It's a good-looking bunch. Are they your family?"

Colby walked back to the register, "My wife and kids. She ran off with another fella. Took 'em with her."

Big John's eyes widened, "Damn, brother, sorry to hear that."

"Thanks," Colby started, "Don't forget pump 3." He smiled as a plan hatched. He believed John was pitying him and that made him angry.

"Must suck to work alone all night," he said, placing the hot coffee without a lid off to his left on the counter.

Big John scoffed, "It ain't so bad. There is plenty to do to keep myself busy."

Colby nodded and slowly grabbed the Gatorade bottle off the counter and turned it upside down in a tight grip.

Starting to get a strange feeling, Big John reached out and said, "Ya know, I'll throw that away for-"

Before he could finish his sentence, Colby pinned Big John's wrist against the counter and smashed the bottle over his head. The glass shattered. Big John started to stumble backward, looking for the shot gun under the counter when the piping hot coffee splashed in his face. He fell forward and hit his head on the counter.

Colby, still holding what was left of the glass bottle, grabbed John by the hair and stabbed him in the side of his neck, puncturing the jugular vein. Big John gasped and tried valiantly to fight off Colby, swinging his arms. His blood sprayed across the wall and window behind him and then pooled on the floor after he fell.

"You... fucker!" was all he could muster as he died.

Colby stared at the blood on his hands as the realization of what he did came over him. He knew he went too far but it was too late to go back. This was Margaret's fault. Big John would still be alive if she hadn't taken off. He reached for the bathroom key hanging on the other side of the counter after poking Big John's shoulder to see if there were any signs of life left and went to wash up before anyone else drove up.

He grabbed another case of beer for later and calmly walked back to the truck, pumped his ten dollars of gas and drove off into the night.

Chapter Nine

Aaron joined his wife and sister-in-law in the family room once he quietly closed the door to his son's room, leaving his nephews to drift off with the help of some good old-fashioned TV.

"We should take you to get a restraining order," he suggested, sitting on the couch next to his wife.

"Oh, I agree," Shari started, "A restraining order, a job, enroll the kids in school, find an apartment..."

Margaret gave a soft chuckle, "Can I just get through the weekend first?"

Aaron changed the subject to how impressed he was with the boys. He noticed that Darius was quick to help Marcus with the game they played and thought they displayed a special bond. The three talked until close to midnight when Aaron excused himself for bed, leaving the sisters to talk the night away.

Margaret was quiet for a while and then the crying started again as she tried to describe the physical abuse she experienced. She sat up from the couch and walked into the kitchen for a glass of water. Her sister followed closely.

"It's going to be okay," Shari offered.

Margaret shook her head in disbelief, "What if he comes here?"

Shari scoffed, "Do you think he's that stupid? Aaron's twice his size. It wouldn't be a fair fight."

"I appreciate you both so much, but..." She started to sob again. Shari rubbed her sister's back, waiting for her to regain her composure.

Margaret shook her head, "He's different now. I think something snapped in his head. He can be so cruel and hateful. I never would have believed he'd set someone's property on fire."

"Are you absolutely sure it was him?"

"I don't think I can prove it, but yes, in my gut, I am absolutely sure. Does that make sense?"

Shari squeezed her hand tighter, "Yeah. It does. Maybe something did snap. Maybe he will sober up this morning and realize he fucked up and will get help."

"No, he's well past that point. He'll come for us. I just don't know when."

Shari sighed, "Yeah. maybe. But not tonight. Tonight you need to rest."

Margaret wiped another tear, "I don't know if I can."

Shari smiled, "I have some tea for you that will do the trick."

She got up and pulled a chair up to the counter. Shari stepped from the chair onto the counter and reached in the far back corner of the cupboard, pulling out an old coffee can.

"What are you doing?" Margaret asked.

Shari turned with the coffee can in hand and pressed her finger to her lips, motioning for Margaret to be quiet. She handed Margaret the can to inspect as she climbed back down to the floor. Inside were small tea bags filled with something of a peculiar odor.

Margaret took a sniff, "What is that?"

Shari gave a devilish grin, "It's Cannabis tea."

"What?"

Shari laughed, "It's pot, Maggie. In tea form."

Margaret smiled, "Where did you get it?"

"A friend of mine went on a retreat in Northern California and came home with it."

Shari shook the can and cocked her head to the side.

Margaret thought for a moment and smiled. "Okay, yeah."

Shari, excited to share her stash, clapped her hands quietly and began brewing some tea as they continued to talk.

"It's more than the hitting, the possible arson, and how he treats the boys," Margaret started, taking the opportunity to tell her sister about the sexual abuse while her back was to her. She kept her eyes on the floor as she recounted the rapes, including the most brutal attack only five days ago.

Shari was motionless and let the words fall between her and her younger sister. Her jaw clenched and she wanted to throw things. She wanted to hunt Colby down and kill him herself. After a long silence, Shari turned to her sister and wrapped her arms around her, and they both cried.

A few minutes later the tea was ready and poured.

Margaret wrinkled her nose, "It's a little bitter."

Shari nodded, "Yeah it tastes like shit. More honey?"

The sisters made their way back to the living room where Margaret's makeshift bed was.

"You know," Shari said, thoughtfully, "Mom and Dad didn't like Colby."

"What?! They never said anything to me." Margaret was stunned.

"Dad thought he was obsessed with you. Like, he was happy that Colby was attentive, but before long, your friends were all replaced by him. You realize that now, don't you?"

"That doesn't make any sense to me, though. I always felt like I couldn't love him enough. I was always trying to prove that I wanted our marriage. I even insisted we try counseling last Sunday."

Chapter Ten:

Driving through a small Indiana town, Colby saw the time on a bank sign. It read, 1:06 AM.

The cuff on his right arm was still stained with Big John's blood and he started to shake again from the memory. He'd never taken a life before. Feeling sweat start to bead on his forehead and upper lip, Colby decided to pull over into an empty parking lot so he could calm down and catch his breath. All he could see was red, as he grabbed the road map, his hands shaking.

Closing his eyes, he focused on the trip they took years ago. Searching his memory, he recalled Margaret singing, "Two, four, six, pick up sticks."

His eyes opened and he said out loud, "Two four six, pick up sticks. One, three, five, something Gate drive."

He glared down at the map again and spied, "Irongate Drive."

Colby looked up from his map and searched the area around him for a phone booth. He walked across the parking lot to one and searched the phone book for his brother-in-law's name and found it.

"246 Irongate Drive, Ha!"

He ripped the paper out of the book and went back to the truck. Grabbing a pen from his glove box, he traced the roads from his current location to Aaron and Shari's and saw it wasn't far.

"Maybe a little celebration is in order." He reached for the case of beer he grabbed at the gas station and cracked one open. He could feel his entire body vibrating.

***

About an hour after the tea, Margaret and Shari were sitting in the living room of the small home on 246 Irongate Drive, laughing and feeling pretty relaxed.

Shari smiled and asked, "How are you feeling now?"

Margaret made a funny face, "Like I could close my eyes for days, so, pretty good, I guess."

The two laughed. Margaret yawned and put her head on Shari's shoulder.

"Thanks for calming me down, big sis."

Shari laid her head on her sister's, "Of course, anything for you."

They sat for a nice long moment and Shari could feel her sister falling asleep. Something caught her eye in the window across from them. She swore she saw headlights from a vehicle that seemingly slowed down, then continued on. Assuming someone was dropping off a neighbor, she closed her eyes for a moment. When she opened them again the lights were facing the house and disappeared just as soon as she saw them.

She started to get up and Margaret, startled by the movement, looked over at her. "What is it?"

"I'm not sure," her sister started as she was peering outside. It was too dark to see very far so she just shook her head, "I'm seeing things."

Margaret became paranoid, "What did you see?"

"I thought I saw someone pulling into the driveway," Shari said, turning away from the window.

Colby was on his third beer by the time he located the very long road of Irongate Drive. On his first pass through, he located it just as he passed it by. Nothing looked familiar to him. More houses had gone up since he was here last. He was frustrated, tired, and already getting a buzz from the beer because, once again, he forgot to eat. He'd grown accustomed to Margaret having his meals ready before his belly rumbled. Just another reason that bitch needed to be reminded of her place. He could feel the rage building up again. This whole night was ruined because of her.

Colby found a spot to turn around and drove past the house again. This time, he focused on the vehicles in the driveway. He saw his wife's car behind two others. He also noticed a light on in a room at the front. Someone was awake.

He knew he needed to make a plan and he tried to remember the layout of the house. Pulling into the driveway, Colby turned off the headlights before anyone would notice him. He needed to be swift.

Margaret jumped off the couch, "Shit! No! Shit!"

Shari tried to quiet Margaret, "Shhh, seriously, there's nothing out there."

Margaret slowly walked to the window and looked out.

"See? Nothing," Shari said as she went to turn the light off in the room for a better look.

Margaret peeked out of the window again and could see a familiar figure walking up the driveway.

"Shit, oh my god, he's here!"

Margaret backed away from the window and ran down the hall toward the bedrooms.

Shari then saw Colby as he stepped onto the porch.

"Oh, fuck!" She exclaimed. She felt herself grow cold with fear. "AARON!" She screamed, turning away from the window.

Margaret ran into Caleb's room and shook the boys awake. "Get up! Your dad found us; we have to go."

Darius bolted out of the bed and immediately started to get dressed. Marcus began to cry but did as he was told and put his shoes on. Shari met Aaron at the threshold of their bedroom. He was wearing his boxers, slippers, and carrying his shotgun with an expression she'd never seen before.

"GIVE ME BACK MY FAMILY!" Colby screamed while pounding on the front door with his fist.

Colby grabbed a big rock and attempted to throw it through the same window the women were standing at just moments ago. The glass was double-paned, and Colby was only able to cause a large chip in the glass.

Aaron yelled out for Shari, "Call the cops! NOW!"

Panicked, she ushered her sister and nephews into the master bedroom and picked up the phone.

"Phone's dead!" Shari screamed, running back to her husband to help defend in any way she could.

Huddled in the closet, Darius tried to calm and quiet his confused and scared little brother.

Aaron turned back toward the front door as silence fell over the house. The pounding stopped. He peeked out the window but couldn't see Colby anywhere.

A brick from the back patio was thrown through the kitchen door sending glass all over the floor. Colby stayed just to the side of the door, a blind spot from the inside.

Aaron ran into the kitchen with his shotgun in hand. After surveying the entire kitchen, he walked out of the shattered door to investigate further.

Colby surprised him and jumped from a crouched position, grabbing the barrel of the gun and lifting up just as it fired birdshot into the air. He used his momentum to knock Aaron off balance, causing him to fall back into the kitchen.

Able to wrench the gun from Aaron during the fall, Colby got to his feet, cocked the shotgun, and at close range fired a shot into Aaron's lower left leg. Birdshot pellets tore into his flesh, ripping through tendons and muscle, shattering his fibula.

Aaron screamed in agony as Colby cocked the gun again, stepping over him. Out of pure instinct to protect his family, Aaron grabbed onto Colby's leg as he tried to run out of the kitchen and into the rest of the house. Tripped up by Aaron, Colby's head hit the refrigerator and another shot went off, spreading small pellets into the wall and sending a wall-clock crashing to the floor.

Colby stood up and kicked Aaron in the head with his steel-toed work boots, knocking him unconscious.

He saw his sister-in-law running towards the hall and raised the gun to shoot only to realize that all of the loaded shells were already fired. She ran into Caleb''s room and Colby followed believing she was leading him to his wife and kids. He quickly caught up and grabbed Shari by her hair as she reached the door to the room.

Shrieking, she cried out, "RUN!"

Margaret and the boys bolted for the front door together out of the Master bedroom, which Colby had already passed.

Colby threw Shari onto her son's bed and struck her in the face with the butt of the shotgun, knocking her unconscious as well.

Escaping the house and running toward the car, Margaret twisted her ankle as she misstepped the final stair of the porch and fell. The boys pulled her to her feet, and she continued running with a limp. They reached the car only to see the tires were flattened. Colby sprinted toward them, and Margaret told the boys to hide. The boys fled into the darkness.

Out of breath, Colby leaned against a tree, "Time to come home, now."

Margaret shook her head, "No, Cole. We're done."

Colby wrenched his neck to the side with an audible crack, "You seem to think you have a say in this. I said now!" he said through clenched teeth.

Margaret was trembling and she cursed herself for it. She straightened her back and looked him in the eye.

"I said NO!"

Colby smiled in disbelief, "You have no idea what I went through, no, what you put me through tonight. You're coming home!"

He closed in on her so quickly she had no time to react. His hands wrapped around her throat. She clawed at his arms and tried to kick but darkness was forming in her peripheral vision, and she was slipping into a state of unconsciousness.

After a few moments, Colby opened the passenger door to his truck and removed the half case of beer, making room on the bench seat for his passengers. He tossed it into the back moving the rope he kept back there, aside. His eyes rested on some bundling twine and he used it to bind Margaret's wrists and ankles before placing her in the cab of the truck. He knew the boys did not go very far to hide.

"Okay, boys, I have your mom. Let's go home," he yelled.

He was willing to wait for them to emerge on their own and with the swift crack of the can, occupied his time with another beer and a cigarette. He heard sirens in the distance and his patience quickly ran out. Colby assumed someone heard the shots and called the authorities. He tossed the half empty beer onto the ground, took one last drag of the cigarette, and shouted into the darkness, "Get your asses out here now!"

It didn't take long to locate the scared boys. Marcus was still crying, and his sniffles gave away their position.

He looked up to see his father looming over him and asked, "Did you hurt Mommy?"

Colby reached for them and pulled them out of the bushes by their shirts. Margaret was not moving, and Darius could see she was tied up.

"We need to help mom," he whispered to Marcus.

Darius wrenched away from his father to face him.

Standing proud and firm, Darius said, "Promise not to hurt mom anymore."

Colby smiled, "Big man making big demands now?"

Darius stood his ground. "I mean it, Dad. Stop hurting Mom. Hit me if you need to, just leave her and Marc alone."

Colby looked down at his son and backhanded him across the face, "Oh, I will hit you, little shit, and do you know why?" He didn't wait for Darius to answer; as if he could. The boy was stunned by the force of the blow.

"Because you're weak and a pathetic little momma's boy. Both of you are." He said, shoving Marcus closer to the truck. "Things will be different. I'm not letting your mother raise little pussies anymore!" Colby said.

The sirens were getting closer, and Colby was feeling the rage take him over again. He picked Darius up, pinning his arms to his sides and threw him into Margaret. Marcus was too scared to move. Colby gripped a handful of hair on the top of his young son's head and directed him into the truck. Marcus' screams and cries were both amusing and irritating to Colby. He snagged a loose beer that fell out of the truck as he walked around to the driver side to head back home.

Darius grabbed the seat belt and secured himself and Marcus in together. The lap belt went over both of them nicely, but the shoulder part had to go behind Marcus' head. He reached over to hold his mother's bound hands and checked that she was still breathing.

His father raced out of the neighborhood and through the town. Darius wished he could get the attention of the cops as they passed by. Margaret, slightly slumped forward, started to open her eyes and she gave Darius' fingers a light squeeze.

She was able to slide one hand out of the binding while Darius kept his hand still over them in the hopes of blocking Colby's view. Marcus was still crying, and Colby was using his energy to focus on the road and if any of the flashing lights turned around to give chase. Once they were on Interstate 65, he'd be able to relax, but until then his body tingled between the alcohol and his blood pressure from all that took place in the past few hours. While Colby aggressively veered right around a bend in the road, Margaret jolted forward, grabbing the steering wheel. She tried to reach the brake pedal with her bound feet and at the same time put her weight onto their abductor, pinning him to the door. He lost control, sending the truck off the road into a drainage ditch. The truck skidded across the grass, flipping twice, it rolled back onto its wheels until it hit a tree with enough impact to send Margaret through the windshield. Marcus broke the passenger window with his head, causing a deep laceration. Blood was everywhere.

Colby, who was knocked out for a few short minutes, regained consciousness first. Seeing the blood and both boys laying still, he assumed they were dead.

He started pleading, "No, no, no."

The realization that Margaret was no longer beside him confused him. He saw the gaping hole in the windshield and the memory of what happened came flooding back. The dented driver's side door ached and creaked as he muscled it open. He stepped out and limped over toward her body on the ground beside the tree they struck.

Her breathing was labored and he couldn't tell where she was injured, but he did not care. She did this to his family. This was all her fault.

"You fucking bitch! You, whore!" he screamed at her.

He continued to rant and rave as he paced unsure of what to do. She was quiet and, for a moment, he thought she died but she started to moan. A calm came over him as he decided what needed to be done. He thought of the rope he had in the back of the truck and was able to locate it in the littered debris of his possessions scattered from the truck to the tree on the side of the Indiana road. He made quick work of the noose he fashioned and wrapped it around Margaret's slender neck. The street light nearby illuminated every movement.

He tossed the other end of the rope around a tree branch and started to pull her up, standing in the back of the truck for more leverage. She reached her feet and then started to lift off of the ground. With each tug of the rope the knot became tighter. Her already broken body was lifted higher and started to twitch. Her body then became still as her life left it.

Darius was completely unconscious from the back of his head hitting the metal part of the cab behind him. For a brief moment, a severely concussed Marcus was able to open one of his eyes. He saw his mother in the light flying in the branches of a tree. The light was distorted, and he saw his mother as an angel, while she hovered in the sky. The twinkling white light turns to blue and red streaks, floating across the trees. The lights reflect off of the treetops and collect on his mother's face.

"The angels are coming for Mommy," he murmured, "I want to go with you," he muttered just before passing out again.

Darius regained consciousness and crawled out of the driver's door and yelled at his father as he inched his way on the side of the truck, "Dad, stop! Please!"

Sirens stopped just as they pulled up to the scene. Darius, slowed from the accident, made his way to the front of the truck toward his mother's swinging body, unaware she was no longer alive.

"Drop the rope and get down from the truck bed," one of the cops instructed over the P.A. system of his cruiser. Colby pulled down harder on the rope and several pops rang out. He dropped the rope, sending Margaret crashing toward the ground. He lurched over the cab of the truck and then fell to his knees, noticing blood soaking the front of his shirt. Colby whimpered and died in the bed of his totaled truck.

Darius rushed to his mom and collapsed next to her, loosening the noose. "Mom! Mom, please get up. Say something! Mom, wake up!"

Two police officers rushed in to tend to Margaret as another officer swooped up Darius and pulled him away toward safety.

"My brother's in the truck. He needs help!" Darius yelled, trying to muscle away from the officer's grasp.

The officer handed him over to an EMT tech. "We are going to do everything we can for your family," he said to Darius.

The EMT was going over basic vitals on Darius when a gurney with his brother strapped on it was pushed into the back. His small head barely visible above the neck brace.

"I think I'm going to be sick," Darius suddenly said to the EMT, just before he vomited and passed out.

Chapter Eleven

A month passed and Aaron was recovering from surgery to put pins in his leg. He had a long road to recovery and his pain was barely managed. Shari's face was still swollen and bruised from her zygomatic injury. The butt of Aaron's gun hit her left cheekbone causing a fracture that reached the orbital socket. She also had a hairline fracture in her jaw which had to be wired shut for six weeks. She suffered from headaches and blurred vision that may or may not get better with time. Both Shari and Aaron were grateful that Caleb wasn't home that fateful night.

Their son became their main caregiver, and his girlfriend, Melissa, helped when she could. It was not the summer he deserved before going into his senior year of high school. He did his best for a kid who just turned seventeen and had his own plans shelved to care for his parents after his uncle destroyed their peaceful, quiet, and happy life. Instead of lifeguarding with Melissa and hanging out with their group of friends, his days were spent chauffeuring his parents to appointments, helping his mom move his dad to various rooms, household chores, and making most of the meals, stretching them as thin as they could.

Darius tried to help, but always seemed to get in the way. His family kept him at arm's length, and he missed his mom more than he let on. He was so used to keeping those emotions bottled up out of fear of his father's reactions. He slept on the couch in the living room and spent most of his nights staring at the area of the front window where the glass had chipped until he drifted off. Nightmares from that evening developed and sometimes Darius would dream of his mother. He would see her the way she was on that day, singing and laughing. In dreams, he would smell her perfume mixed with the minty gum she would chew. This olfactory memory would change to the visual of bright lights and sounds of metal twisting, glass shattering, and the way she was lying in wet grass with a rope around her neck. Waking up, sweating and crying for her, became a normal occurrence. Life was hard in Kentucky, but he preferred it to this.

The first time it happened, his Aunt Shari rushed to him. She did her best to soothe him. She'd fetch him a glass of water and sit, rub his back, and through her wire bound clenched teeth, hum. All he felt was guilt every time she showed up afterward, so he told her that he'd be fine. He didn't want to be babied. Their father's verbal objection to how their mother treated them still haunted his memory. Darius feared his uncle would hurt his aunt for the same thing. It was hardly a stretch of the imagination for him to come to such a conclusion. His uncle was no longer the kind and fun-loving man he was that night, playing games with him and his little brother. Darius blamed himself for his mother's death and didn't want this family to suffer the same fate. Caleb and Aaron seemed mad and tired all the time. It was only when Melissa came over to help, that attitudes in the house became lighter. Everyone was on their best behavior. All he really ever wanted to do was sit by his brother's hospital bed and talk to him.

Marcus had severe head trauma and was placed in a medically induced coma for two weeks due to brain swelling. His other injuries were a broken collar bone, a partially severed right pinky finger and a long laceration on the right side of his face that would leave a scar. After an additional week, he was finally allowed visitors. Darius never disclosed to his little brother what happened that night after he was told that Marcus may never remember much leading up to the accident. He didn't want those memories of fear implanted where they never belonged. If Marcus asked any direct questions, Darius would be honest. He just hoped his brother would forget with time.

Aunt Shari helped him explain that they lost their parents.

"Yeah, I saw the angels come and get her." Marcus said matter-of-factly. "When do I get to go home?"

"Uh, soon," Shari said, surprised but thankful she didn't have to relive that night again just yet.

Marcus was usually quiet during their visits. He only enjoyed talking to Darius. Eventually, his Aunt and Uncle stopped coming, and Caleb would drop Darius off when visiting hours started every day. The boys watched television and there was always a sympathetic nurse or two who would supply them with extra gelatine or a pack of playing cards. Marcus had to lay his cards on the tray and play them with his non-dominant hand. Darius noticed that his brother was usually calm, and it kept him at ease. For a few hours a day in the final week of his hospital stay, Marcus and his brother enjoyed each other's company, strengthening their brotherly bond.

The formal living room in the front of Shari and Aaron's house was now a makeshift bedroom for the boys. Privacy screens were placed from the front door to the wall separating it from the kitchen on one side and the opening from the kitchen to the family room on the other. The loveseat was too short for his growing body, so the extra twin mattress from Caleb's bunk bed was placed on the floor for Marcus to sleep on next to Darius, who was still sleeping on the couch. The family did what they could to accommodate everyone.

Shari, Aaron, and Caleb did their best to be kind and patient, but their lives were also turned upside down. The emotional and mental toll paired with the financial hit of copays, Shari's lost wages from her part-time job, and two extra mouths to feed weighed heavily on the household. The Tye brothers felt like outcasts in the home, so the boys spent most of their time exploring the woods behind the house.

Marcus' demeanor worried Shari. He was no longer a sweet boy who talked a lot. He mostly stared silently when Darius wasn't around. He also started sleepwalking in the middle of the night. It was unsettling to everyone but Darius. He figured out that the evening before a sleepwalking episode, Marcus usually complained of a headache.

Word eventually got around to all the neighborhood kids about some of the things Colby Tye did, as well as Marcus' brain injury, and the kids were cruel once the boys started attending school again. Marcus had a slow start. His brain injury was one thing, but he also had his writing hand still bandaged. The bus rides to and from school were torture for Darius. In the first week, he was already in two fights. One for calling his brother a derogatory term to imply he was slow and the other for saying something gross about their mother. Marcus seemed oblivious to it all. When kids would laugh at him, he would laugh back. They would call him crazy or psycho.

Darius found himself angry toward Caleb and felt his cousin should defend them. He thought the older boy was nice the night they arrived with their mom. Now, Caleb acted like he didn't know his cousins outside of the house. Even at home, he only talked to them when he needed to. Darius complained to his brother about Caleb, but Marcus seemed indifferent about it.

Darius thought he'd make at least one new friend in the neighborhood or at school but was frustrated that he hadn't. He missed the ones he had back in Kentucky and hoped to make it back there one day.

One unusually warm Saturday, in early November, the boys were in the woods behind the house playing, and Marcus said he had to go to the bathroom. As he walked toward the house, he could hear his aunt and uncle talking about him through an open window in the kitchen.

"We need to seriously discuss this. I know they're family, but we aren't prepared for this," Aaron stated.

Marcus heard his aunt sigh heavily. "I know," she said in defeat.

"I think we should consider turning them over to the state, Shari. There was no will, no life insurance policy. We've got nothing to help us financially."

"Maybe we can find a facility for Marcus?" Shari suggested.

Aaron scoffed, "Those cost a lot of money. Like, tuition for college."

Marcus decided to pee on the side of the house so he could stay hidden and eavesdropped some more.

"Look, we barely know them. I was behind helping her get away from that fucking monster, but I never wanted to raise them. Our son's almost out of the house and what about his future, huh?" Aaron paused to give his wife time to speak.

"It breaks my heart no matter what we decide. The holidays are coming and I'm exhausted. It's not like they want to be here anyway."

"Are you making your mind up now?" Aaron asked.

"Let's give it one more week, please? I need to figure out how we're going to do this. Maybe a new solution will present itself," Shari said, hopefully.

"Unless we miraculously win the lottery, I don't see how any of this works out for any of us."

"I was going to ask Caleb to have Melissa over for pizza and a movie. Maybe the four of them can start doing things together?" Shari said optimistically.

"Caleb has to field questions about those boys daily. I doubt he wants to be forced to spend time with them when he should be enjoying this year..."

Marcus had heard enough and left to rejoin his brother.

That evening their aunt made a big deal about "Movie Night." She rented a family comedy from the local video store, ordered pizza and popped microwave popcorn. Melissa came over with a few 2 liter bottles of sodas. Everyone gathered in the family room. Melissa joined Shari on the couch. Aaron took his usual spot in the recliner he sat in far too often recently, although he had to admit that it was a damn good and fortuitous investment. Caleb joined the boys on the floor when he returned from retrieving his hamster, moving inside a large plastic ball.

Bubba moved about freely on the living room carpet and Marcus found it irritating because he couldn't focus on the movie. Every movement the hamster made in the ball drew his eye away from the screen. Darius had a similar problem, but for him, it was Caleb's voice interrupting his focus.

"Come back, Bubba."

"Where ya goin', Bubba?"

"Did you wanna visit Melissa?"

Darius tried hard to ignore his cousin's constant interruptions about his rodent. He glanced at him hoping for Caleb to take the hint. Or, at the very least, he hoped someone else was as irritated and would ask him to stop.

"Is Bubba tired?"

"Oh my god, shut up!" Darius finally exclaimed.

"Excuse me?" Aunt Shari was incensed.

"I can't hear the movie with him talking to his rat every other minute," Darius complained.

"Can't we even get through one goddamn movie before you guys start bickering?" Aaron said under his breath.

"He's not a rat," Caleb cried.

"This is how our family gathers for a movie. If you don't like it, you can go back to your room," their aunt said in her own frustration.

Darius was embarrassed and angry. His room was a couch and a couple of privacy screens. He looked over at Marcus, and his brother was glaring at the large plastic ball with the hamster in it. Caleb was on the floor leaning against the couch between his girlfriend and his mother. Melissa picked the hamster up in his contraption and kept him with her just by Caleb's head. She noticed Marcus kept looking back at her, and poked Caleb in the shoulder to get his attention.

Caleb looked over. "He's so weird," Melissa whispered to him.

He nodded, patted her leg, and they continued to watch the movie.

The movie finally ended, and Caleb and Melissa gave each other a nod before Caleb stood up and announced, "Mom, I'm going to drive Melissa home now."

Darius and Marcus were quick to exit the family room. Marcus returned to their make-shift bedroom and sat on Darius' bed to wait for his brother to return from the bathroom.

Darius used the privacy of the bathroom to give in to the tears he wanted to release the entire night. It was times like this, he longed for the comfort of his mom. He wished more than anything he could call her and ask her to pick them up. He hated his cousin. He hated that Caleb had his own room with a TV and a phone. He hated that Caleb was allowed to have a pet. He hated Caleb for having a loving family that had no love left for him and his brother. He hated his aunt for chastising him in front of everyone, and he wanted to run away.

Caleb snagged his pet and put him back in his secure cage and closed his bedroom door.

Melissa put her jacket on and smiled over at Shari. "Thank you for having me over for the movie. It was really funny."

Shari smiled and replied, "I was happy you could join us tonight. You're welcome here anytime."

After walking out the door, Caleb stood on the porch with his keys in his mouth to finish putting his own jacket on. Melissa reached up to take the keys from his mouth.

"Dude, I'm sorry your family has to deal with your cousins after your uncle tried to kill everyone. This has to be hard on your parents."

"Oh, it's okay. I mean, Marcus got all stupid after his head injury and just creeps people out with his stares. I think Darius got his dad's temper. I'm just waiting for him to snap. If he tries to hurt anyone, I'll kick his ass."

Finished with his jacket, Caleb took the keys from his girlfriend and gave her a kiss.

"You know, I understand if you don't want to come around as often. We can hang out at other places together."

Their voices trailed off as they walked away toward the car and Marcus could no longer make out what they were saying from his spot near the window. When Darius came back into the room, he asked his brother how long it usually took Caleb to drop off Melissa.

"I dunno. They make out in his car for a while. I saw it once." Darius paused to make a face, mimicking them making out, "Disgusting."

Marcus excused himself to the bathroom. His aunt and uncle were still cleaning up and going back and forth from the family room to the kitchen, paying him little attention. He passed the full bathroom in the hallway that they shared with Caleb and checked the closed door to his cousin's bedroom.

A few minutes later, Marcus returned and laid in his bed, quiet.

Darius looked over, "What's wrong?"

"Nothing."

"Marc? Tell me. What's going on?"

Marcus shook his head. After a few seconds, he sighed and rolled over to face his brother.

"Caleb and Melissa were saying mean things about us, and I didn't like it."

"Screw them. When we get out of here, we don't ever have to talk to them again. Besides, I can't wait until I never have to hear him talking to his rat again."

Marcus nodded, "Yep."

Darius continued, "Once we graduate high school, we can start our own farm back home. We know how to do everything and we'd be good at it too."

Marcus closed his eyes as he listened to his brother talk of his pipe dream.

"We can raise chickens and sell the eggs to the local market. We can keep selling hay to Mr. Smithers and I bet others will want our hay, too. I already know how to drive a tractor and work the fields. We'll be set and won't need anyone. Just you and me."

Marcus smiled, "I like that."

A few minutes later Marcus drifted to sleep listening to the muffled sounds from his aunt and uncle's tv in their bedroom. Soon after, Caleb came home.

Darius looked over at his brother sound asleep. He could hear Caleb knock and then open the door to his parent's bedroom to let them know he was home and to wish them a goodnight.

Darius closed his eyes and tried to fall asleep when he heard a loud cry. It was a high-pitched screeching yelp which ended with a vocal, "NO!" followed by "WHAT THE FUCK!?"

Shari and Aaron rushed to their son's room. Darius was too curious to see what the commotion was and left his sleeping brother behind. By the time he was down the hall, he could hear his uncle ask, "What the hell happened?" and his aunt saying something soothing to her son.

Caleb rushed out of his room in tears. His eyes landed on Darius, and he immediately tackled him to the ground, throwing punches.

"I'M GOING TO KILL YOU!" Caleb screamed.

Aaron limped over and pulled a furious and sobbing Caleb off Darius, who screamed, "What the fuck did I do!?"

With his cousin secured in his uncle's arms, Darius peeked over into Caleb's room to see his aunt holding a dead Bubba. The hamster had a shoestring wrapped tightly around its neck on one end and the other had been tied to the top of the cage. When Caleb walked into his room, he saw his beloved pet hanged, suspended in air.

Caleb shouted toward Darius, "YOU FUCKING PSYCHO! YOU KILLED BUBBA LIKE YOUR DAD KILLED YOUR MOM!"

Darius turned to make eye contact with Caleb and said, "I never touched your stupid rat!"

Caleb lunged at Darius again, but Aaron held him back.

Marcus walked into the hallway and asked, "Why is everyone yelling?"

Caleb shouted, "Your psycho brother killed Bubba!"

Marcus looked at Caleb and flatly said, "No, he didn't. I did."

Chapter Twelve:

That night, Shari and Aaron attempted to rest in their bed with Caleb sobbing in the next room.

Shari finally broke the silence, "They have to go. I can't deal with this."

Aaron stared at the ceiling and stayed silent. He once held great affection for the boys, but now he was fearful of them and protecting his wife and son became paramount. The Tye brothers needed more than they could give them.

"I'm calling the State on Monday to get them into the foster program," Shari continued.

Aaron sighed, "Okay."

They did not sleep at all that night. Sunday morning came, and Aaron buried the hamster in the backyard. The brothers watched from the kitchen window as no one wanted to be around them.

Caleb stayed out all day afterwards with friends and Melissa. Shari and Aaron acted like the boys didn't exist and went about their day.

Marcus suggested they go into the woods as usual.

Darius sighed, "This sucks. I can't believe you killed that stupid hamster. Now they hate us."

"They hated us before. Now they're just honest about it."

Darius nodded his head, "Yeah, I guess you're right."

Later that day, Shari and Aaron decided to go out to dinner to get out of the house. The boys returned from the woods to find a note on the box of leftover pizza sitting on the kitchen table.

Boys,
Leftover pizza for dinner tonight.
We'll be back by 7.

Marcus opened the box to find a single leftover slice for each of them. They didn't mind the neglect when there was cold pizza to be eaten. Pizza delivery wasn't exactly a thing their family had the privilege of, nor was watching TV anytime they liked. The brothers actually felt giddy watching tv in the family room. It was how they wanted life to be for a couple of hours. Just the two of them doing whatever they wanted.

The next morning the boys ate breakfast after everyone else finished. Shari didn't make them their lunches as usual, and they didn't ask her for anything. The boys grabbed their backpack and went to the bus stop.

Shari drove Caleb to school so he could avoid riding the bus with his cousins. She dropped him off and headed to the courthouse to file a petition to have the Tye brothers removed from their custody and placed into foster care. Due to the situation, the state ruled it an emergency and the boys were placed in a state-run group home.

When they returned from school, Shari and Aaron were talking with two government workers in the driveway next to a van.

As the boys walked up the driveway, they saw the suitcases their mother packed in the trunk of her car many months before. Marcus walked up, absent-mindedly touching his facial scar, and asked the men what he was doing with their stuff.

The official turned around and asked, "Hey there! Are you Marcus or Darius?"

"I'm Marcus. That's Darius," he responded, pointing toward his brother.

"Hey Marcus, I'm Mr. Simmons and that's Mr. Johnson. We're going to take you to a new home."

Marcus smiled and shrugged. "Okay."

Darius shook his head, feeling rejected. He stomped toward the open van and climbed in.

He looked up to see Caleb's scowl and reached to slam the sliding door shut. He never wanted to have to see his cousin's face again.

Marcus climbed in on the other side and Mr. Johnson closed the door before heading up to Aaron and Shari with Simmons to have one final chat.

Darius looked over at Marcus. "They're sending us away. Fucking assholes."

Marcus shrugged again. "So what?"

Darius wanted to blame Marcus but knew it wouldn't help matters. He looked over and smiled.

"Just you and me, right Marc?"

His brother smiled at him. "Yep."

"Our innocence had been replaced by fear and we had become monsters. There was nothing we could do about it."

- Ishmael Beah
A Long Way Gone: Memoirs of a Boy Soldier

Simmons and Johnson silently drove the boys to their next destination. A home for kids like them, run by an older and unscrupulous couple, Peg and Harold. Everything they did for someone else was transactional only. They were married and owned the home but didn't live there. They bought the house to convert it into a bed and breakfast, but it was quickly turned into a state funded group home when the business failed due to lousy upkeep. The state would send their own sanctioned repair people and give them a break on the taxes if they would keep it as a group home. It was a deal they couldn't pass up, but it made them complacent, and they refused to do anything extra to keep the property nice.

It was a rat-infested slum.

The main level had a dining room, a living room with old musty used furniture, an 'entertainment room' with the only tv in the house, the kitchen, a powder-room, and two small bedrooms. The second floor had three large rooms with multiple beds in the front of the house, and two small rooms in the back, one of which the Tye brothers would occupy. The second floor also had the only bathroom with a shower that no one seemed to clean. The third floor had three tiny bedrooms that were clearly meant for one person. A bed and a small end table with one drawer were the only furniture in them. They felt more like large closets than bedrooms.

The sleeping arrangements were the least of their worries. There were holes in places on the main floor where you could see the dirt pad the house sat upon underneath. The bathroom sink had a pair of vice-grips fastened onto the control knob, where the handle broke off, for them to turn the water on. The hot water only became lukewarm at best, and the shower head had such heavy limescale build-up that the water flow felt like someone was peeing on you. There was a permanent dirt ring around the tub, which was never cleaned.

Food was limited. Everyone ate together at the large kitchen table at the same time every day. If you didn't make it in time, you didn't eat. The food was served buffet style, so if you were last in line, you only got scraps.

Despite all of this, they survived in the home over the winter, even with the heat seldomly working. Darius was still having nightmares and the dreams of his mom were becoming less frequent. Marcus could usually tell when Darius dreamed of her. His brother became moodier and prone to tears. Marcus was still recovering from his brain trauma and his sleepwalking episodes eventually stopped. Parts of his old personality would surface from time to time, so when Darius had an upsetting dream the night before, his brother took it upon himself to lighten the mood. He found his goofy side again but kept it closer to the vest. Things became better for them in March when a new kid showed up.

The boys were in the front room playing a card game but rushed to the window when they heard the van stop out front and a boy's voice.

"Oh, hell no. This place is a shit hole!" The boy said after the van door was opened for him.

Darius looked over at Marcus and back out the window.

"How old do you think he is?" Marcus asked.

"I dunno. Our age, I guess," Darius replied.

They watched as the boy walked toward the house with a bag of his belongings.

"Welcome!" Marcus said, with a genuine smile.

"Whatever," The new boy said without so much as a glance in Marcus' direction.

Darius saw the smile disappear from his brother's face. "He just wanted to say hi," he started. "There hasn't been another kid our age here in a while. What's your name?"

The boy stopped looking around and focused on the older Tye brother. He unclenched his jaw, closed his eyes and sighed, "Mike. My name's Mike Payne."

"Hey, Mike. I'm Darius Tye and that's my brother, Marcus."

Marcus, who walked back over to the table they were playing cards on, looked over and waved.

Mike narrowed his eyes at Marcus and said, "What's up?" turning back to Darius, "So, how is it here?" he asked.

Darius scoffed, "It sucks. We ran away like ten times since we got here in November. They're good at catching us and bringing us back, though," he admitted.

Mike nodded again while looking around. He spotted Marcus staring at a wall and touching the dark scar on the side of his face that disappeared into his hairline.

"Dude, the fuck happened to your face?" Mike asked, abruptly. "That scar is gnarly."

Marcus took it as a compliment and chuckled a bit but neglected to address the question.

Darius wasn't bothered by how frank Mike was. It was refreshing how up front someone could be without being cruel. Darius smiled and responded, "He had a brain injury from a car accident we were in about a year ago."

"Woah, that sucks," Mike responded.

Interrupting the conversation, Peg appeared with her arms full of linens.

Marcus asked, "Where are you putting Mike?"

Peg rolled her eyes, "He's going on the third floor." She turned to Mike, "Follow me."

Halfway up the stairs she reminded the Tye brothers to finish their homework.

Darius sighed, "Yeah, shouldn't we have a home to do homework in?" he asked his brother.

Darius and Marcus didn't see Mike again until dinner. He was late coming down and barely got any food. He sat next to the boys and sighed at the barren plate. Darius looked over at it and shook his head.

"Here," he said, handing him his roll.

Mike looked over, "You sure? You don't have much either."

"The meals are small, and I usually give most of mine to Marcus. He's hitting a growth spurt or something."

Mike looked over at Marcus who was in his own world, playing with his food and accepted the roll with appreciation and smiled.

The boys quietly ate for a moment until Mike asked how long they'd been in the group home.

Marcus answered without taking his eyes off his plate. "We got off the bus from school and the van was waiting for us at our aunt's house to bring us here. No one wants us."

Mike's eyes widened. Darius looked over and shrugged, "Pretty much."

Mike shook his head, "That sucks. What happened to your parents? If that's okay to... I mean, you don't have to-"

Darius was abrupt with his rehearsed answer, "Our dad was a monster and one day our mom had enough and took us to our aunt's. He tracked us down, shot our uncle in the leg, busted our aunt's face and killed our mom after the truck he kidnapped us all in rolled over. Marc's brain swelled, and he was in the hospital for over a month. The cops killed our dad and we had to live with our aunt and uncle. We were a burden on them, and our cousin hated us. Marc killed his pet, so they sent us here."

Mike was speechless at first and could only muster, "Wow!"

Darius nodded, "Yeah. What about you?"

Mike sighed, "My mom died when I was young. My dad raised me, he was mainly a fisherman and a hunter. I'd always gone fishing with him and I was just starting to go out with him to hunt. I killed my first buck two years ago." He paused and smiled at the memory, "Money started getting tight, so he decided to work the graveyard shift for my uncle at his gas station after I went to bed. One night, some asshole came in there and robbed the place. My dad was a big guy and knew how to defend himself but..." Mike trailed off.

Marcus blinked out of his stare, "Did he shoot him?"

"Nah, he sliced my dad's neck with a glass bottle."

Darius' eyes widened, and he swallowed hard. "Woah. When did that happen?"

Mike said, "End of May, beginning of June."

"Did they ever catch the guy who did it?" Darius asked, heartbroken, for his new friend.

"I heard from one of the detectives that they got him later that night, way north from where it happened, and get this," he leaned in closer to the brothers, "he was in the middle of hanging some woman in a tree!"

Darius made eye contact with Marcus and shook his head, willing his brother to keep his mouth shut. He wanted to make a friend so badly. If Mike knew that he was eating a meal with the kids of his own father's killer, Darius was sure he'd never want to speak to him again. He wouldn't blame him. The thought of losing another friend, especially due to his father's actions, caused his mood to worsen.

"How old are you?" Marcus asked without a hint of recognition to what was just revealed to them.

"Fifteen. You guys?"

"I'm twelve and Dari just turned fourteen."

The three boys became inseparable. They all shared the same bus from the group home. After it would drop Marcus off at the middle school, Darius and Mike would part ways at the high school and meet after their last class to rejoin Marcus for the ride home. All three boys would sit together in the entertainment room to do their homework. Darius felt more like himself now that Mike arrived. His grades were getting better, and he was finding that his nightmares lessened. None of them talked about their past anymore and would often talk about future plans. Darius talked about running the family farm and Mike wanted to do something around his favorite thing, fishing.

As the months grew warmer, the boys spent more time playing outside. There was a decent backyard with a rusted, tin-roofed tool shed. The padlock on its doors was just as rusted. Mike pulled down hard on the lock and it opened without issue.

Darius looked over at Mike and said, "Oh, shit! You think they'll notice?"

Mike shook his head, "Nah, they don't do any yard work. The state probably sends someone out. The yard's mostly dirt anyway."

Marcus, playing with some stones he found, chimed in. "Or maybe they'll get us to do it."

Darius and Mike looked at each other and agreed with Marcus. They were certain the three of them would be made to do it, with Peg and Harrold acting as though they were doing the boys a favor.

"Be thankful you can go outside for fresh air and exercise!" Mike imitated how the older couple would frame the chore.

Darius pulled open the rusty shed door. Inside were rakes, a push-mower, an empty can of gasoline, clippers, trimmers, wackers, and a plethora of other old and outdated yard tools. Mike spied a pair of tin snips and slyly palmed them, sliding them into the back pocket of his jeans.

Mike backed up out of the shed, tugging on his shirt and said, "Hey guys, let's close this up before they notice us playing in it. I don't feel like getting in trouble today."

Marcus was fascinated by everything, and it reminded him of the barn and all the chores he and Darius did. After a few more minutes of looking around, they closed the shed, and Mike set the lock back the way it looked before.

The next morning, Darius and Marcus sat at the table for breakfast waiting for Mike to join them. Peg and Harold made a surprise early morning visit and the boys watched as the older couple searched for Mike.

"You two!" Peg exclaimed, walking into the kitchen.

Marcus scooped up a huge fork full of his eggs and shoved them into his mouth, thinking that his meal was abruptly ending.

"Where's your little buddy, Mike?" she asked.

Darius was confused. He looked over toward Marcus who was still shoveling food in his mouth and noticed Harold walking outside, looking up the side of the house.

"I dunno. We were waiting for him to come down to eat."

Peg relaxed when she decided Darius was telling the truth.

She eyed Marcus, "No one's taking your food away from you. Take a breath."

Peg watched Harold through the window for a brief moment before asking the boys if Mike ever mentioned running away.

Darius shook his head and admitted, "He didn't say anything like that."

Peg sighed and said, "That little shit found a way to cut the fasteners from the bars on the windows."

Darius thought back to the shed, "We don't know anything."

Peg scoffed, "We actually came here today with some good news for him. A couple was willing to meet him. They're supposed to come visit him next week."

Darius and Marcus looked at each other.

"Did you tell them about Marc and me?" Darius asked.

Peg rolled her eyes, "Yeah, but they only wanted one kid."

Two weeks later the boys finished the school year in the third school district they'd been in since their mom picked them up and took them out of Kentucky a year ago. They barely passed. When they got off the bus, they recognized Harold's car out front, and Peg was waiting on the couch for them when they walked in.

"Pack up your things, boys. You've officially entered into the foster program."

Darius clenched his jaw and firmly stated, "I'm staying with my brother."

Peg shook her head, "You go where there's room."

The boys stood still. Their world was being turned inside out again.

Peg was irritated that they were pulling on her heart strings, "Look, I can tell you that the place you're going to tonight has room for both of you. I can't promise it'll continue. It's very rare to stay at one place together."

Darius shook his head in disappointment and stomped up the stairs. Marcus dropped his backpack and followed his brother to their room and packed up what little he still had.

The next morning, Peg went to their room to grab the linens, straighten up, and get it ready for new tenants whenever they arrived. An unusual odor was present the moment she walked in. Pulling the sheets from Marcus' bed, the odor became more putrid.

She groaned and put her hand up to her nose, attempting to block the stench. She knelt beside the bed to look under it. The first thing she saw was a large resealable bag. It was empty but something had been in it. The odor was present, and she saw what looked like fur and smears of red and yellow inside. Further under the bed she realized she was face to face with a rat. A dead rat. She screamed and backed away, yelling for Harold to come.

Harold looked under the bed, stood up, and lifted the small twin bed at the footboard, revealing a macabre sight. Six rats with their necks broken and string wrapped around each of them. They were hanging from a wooden slat running the width of the bed.

"Oh God!" Peg gagged and ran from the room.

Chapter Fourteen:

Early June 1997

The brothers endured a chaotic few years, constantly moving from one home to another. It seemed like they could never settle down in one place for more than six months. As a result, they had given up on the idea of making any new friends, as they were never anywhere long enough to establish any meaningful connections or relationships. However, they found solace in each other's company and that was enough to keep them going. Every time they were placed in a new foster home, they faced a fresh set of challenges. It was disheartening to realize that most of the families they stayed with didn't genuinely care about their wellbeing. In fact, it seemed like each new family cared even less than the previous one, and the boys stopped bothering to learn anyone's name.

The majority of these families were neglectful, and some were even abusive. The boys were used as ashtrays or punching bags in some places. The routine of ER visits to police station interviews happened far too frequently. Eventually, they gave as good as they got, and Marcus was always sure to leave an impression after he was gone. No one seemed to care enough about dead wildlife. At least not enough to report these incidents to the authorities. Especially the foster parents with things to hide.

School was no picnic, either. The kids were cruel by mocking them for being dirty and needing assistance with school lunches. Marcus was picked on for being in the special education classes. They spent more time in detention than not. Darius became a decent pickpocket and knew exactly how to get back at the more affluent kids. He saved every dime he stole, and worked any odd job he could get after school and on weekends. Darius remained focused on the two most important things to him, money and his brother. Nothing and no one else mattered.

Darius turned eighteen and managed to graduate. He secured a full-time janitorial job at a state park, and got his brother a part-time, after-school job. They were finally able to pull the trigger on their first big goal. Darius had saved enough to get a small apartment and a used truck. He was completely independent after aging out of the foster care program. He was not about to leave his younger brother and applied to ask the court's permission for custody of Marcus. He was denied.

Marcus stayed at his brother's apartment most of the summer, and they would focus mainly on working and saving money. The foster parents didn't care that Marcus was out of the house. The dad was a truck driver and rarely around. The mother, a waitress who had her own side hustle in the house, had strange men showing up at all hours of the night.

Darius tried to challenge the foster parents for custody of Marcus again, but they decided it was worth the courthouse visit to hold onto Marcus after losing half of the money they were getting before Darius was of age. Darius argued that they were neglectful, and he was asked to prove it, but he could not. It backfired and strengthened how much the fosters were doing to put food on the table. The entire system was broken.

As the new school year approached, Marcus knew he'd have to go back to spending his nights at the foster home. It didn't weigh heavy on his own mind, but he could tell his brother didn't want him to go back. He watched as Darius exhausted every avenue to get custody of him, to no avail. His brother told Marcus how powerless he felt, and it resonated with him. They'd never had any power over their lives. Besides, he really loved how the summer went, working and living with his brother in their own place. Marcus didn't want any of it to end either.

A few weeks later, they had no choice but to adapt to a new routine once Marcus was back in school, staying most nights in his foster home. School became worse for him now that his older brother was no longer there. Darius would pick him up at the school in the afternoons to go straight to work, and on Fridays, he got to stay with his brother until Sunday night.

His foster mother's drug habits progressed to smoking meth during the summer and the effects were taking a huge toll on her already small frame. Marcus noted when each john came to the house, and even noted the repeat customers. The noises that came from her bedroom at night made sleep very difficult. Some of the men were rough and abusive, and even though he never particularly liked his foster mother, he loathed the men that showed up even more. She stopped working her regular job and Marcus never saw the truck-driving foster father after the second summer court date.

On a Friday afternoon in late September, Marcus stood in front of his school, waiting for Darius. As soon as he pulled up, Marcus opened the creaking door of the truck and jumped inside.

"I stayed at your place last night if anyone asks."

Darius looked at his brother and grinned, "But, you did stay at my place last night." He tossed Marcus a bag from a fast-food place. "Eat."

He didn't ask for any details. Darius had his brother's back with unwavering loyalty. One of the last things they did in the park before clocking out was replace trash bin liners. To maximize time, this was the only job they did separately. It was a fairly large park so one would go to the west end while the other went to the east end and they met in the middle. Darius had made it to the middle and noticed Marcus wasn't even nearby. He walked the path Marcus would take until he spotted him talking with a man. Darius continued walking, eyeing the stranger until he noticed a badge. It was a detective. He quickened his pace to join the conversation.

"Excuse me, this boy's a minor. Can I help you?" Darius said when he reached them.

"Hey there. Mr. Tye's not in any trouble. I'm Detective Willis. He may have witnessed something last night and I was told I could find him here by a..." He paused to look over his tiny notebook, "Hector Rodriguez."

Before Darius could ask who that was, Marcus looked over to his brother and said, "He's your replacement at the home. Showed up last week."

"So, what do you hope my brother can help you with?"

"Right now, we're just trying to piece together a few things that led up to an unfortunate event," Willis stated.

"Foster mom's dead." Marcus offered the information to his brother while the detective danced around it.

"I take it you didn't like her too much?" Willis asked.

Marcus questioned, "What's there to like?"

"Detective, may I speak with you over here?" Darius interrupted and walked a few feet away. Marcus went back to work as Det. Willis followed his brother.

"My brother had a traumatic brain injury a few years back. You're not going to have a normal conversation with him."

"Ah, I knew something was off. I was about to put him on the long list of suspects."

"Long list?" Darius felt relief.

"Well, the foster kids, current and past, are all on there to be cleared, of course."

"Right. What about her husband or the johns?" Darius tossed out other possible leads in the hopes Willis would stop looking at the foster kids.

"Did you say, John or johns?" Willis asked.

"Johns. Her customers. She had to get paid in other ways to support her meth habit. It may have even been an overdose?"

"Meth didn't put that rope around her neck," Willis offered.

"Oh, shit!" Darius could not hide his surprise and he looked over at his brother. "I'm so glad he stayed with me last night, then."

"Oh. You mean he doesn't stay in the foster home every night?"

Darius seized an opportunity, "You've just learned his foster mother was a whore with a meth habit. Would you want to sleep there?"

Detective Willis nodded and had to admit that he wouldn't, but he still needed to ask the boy a few more questions.

"Marc, I know you stayed with your brother last night, but can you remember anyone threatening her or coming around more often?"

Marcus managed a smile and told the detective about every man he observed in the past few weeks, their descriptions, and frequencies. He was nearly giddy giving him all the information from memory.

Darius didn't ask his brother any of the many questions he had until they were both secure in his apartment. He went to the kitchen and grabbed a couple sodas and a bag of Marcus' favorite cheese curls before collapsing on the couch next to his brother.

"Okay, I need details. What the fuck did you do?" he finally asked.

"I did one thing, and it was simple."

"Oh yeah, what was that?" Darius asked as he popped a cheese curl in his mouth.

"Made it so you can get custody."

Chapter Fifteen:

The brothers spent the next decade doing what they always did. They stayed and worked in Indiana for a couple more years. The case of the murdered foster mother went unsolved. During their time in the area, two more women were found dead with little to no leads. The boys grew into men who developed a mistrust for any government or authority figure. Darius closed their bank account, and they moved all around the region working for cash. They had become accustomed to squalor. Marcus and Darius started working as janitors again but this time at an outlet mall. They found it easy to slip into crowds, especially during the holidays to pickpocket and snag unattended purchases. The food court was their favorite spot. Marcus enjoyed taking food from abandoned trays.

They made connections at the mall with the same type of unscrupulous people they encountered at the park in Indiana. They learned about firearms, street drugs, and fake IDs. They would bounce between Tennessee and Kentucky for the winter months looking for work. Rent was still due and sometimes they had to find other means to pay it. Darius excelled at breaking into cars and stealing radios for cash but had not yet perfected hotwiring. Marcus would sell stolen bikes and yard tools after breaking in, and ransacking sheds and garages.

Darius decided to scope out a convenience store across town. He observed how they took the money from the registers on Tuesday night and put it in a lock bag in the safe for Wednesday morning's deposit.

It was clockwork, and by his estimation, Darius figured they would have at least three thousand waiting for deposit. This would be an easy score that could keep them afloat for a few weeks.

The plan was for Darius to drop Marcus off at the front and drive around the back of the store. Marcus, donning a hunter's neck gaiter and baseball cap, would walk to the fridge in the back and grab a soda. Once the place was empty, Marcus would pull the gaiter up, brandish a gun, and demand the lock-bags in the safe. From there, he would lock the employee in the office, after dismantling the phone, and escape out the backdoor to Darius waiting for a quick getaway.

The brothers went over the plan several times. Marcus even wore a gaiter on his neck and a cap in the store a few times to get a feel for everything.

The day of, Marcus put on a different cap and gaiter and even wore different shoes and a jacket.

No one was in the store and the clerk barely looked up when he walked in. Marcus navigated toward the back and grabbed a different brand of soda than before and even grabbed a candy bar. He stopped at the magazine rack and snagged some smut that he placed under his arm, and he headed toward the counter.

Suddenly, the bell on the door rang and a man with a gun drawn, and bandana over his face, stormed into the store screaming, "Hands up, NOW!"

Marcus stopped cold, assessing the situation.

The gunman pointed the barrel toward Marcus and said, "Don't be a hero. Move your ass over there."

Turning his attention, and the gun, back to the clerk, the gunman demanded, "Money, let's go!"

Marcus cocked his head in recognition of the man holding up the store. The store that he should be robbing. There was something familiar about him.

"Mike?"

The gunman looked over at Marcus, back at the cashier, and back at Marcus again. His eyes widened as he saw a paler but familiar scar coming down from the baseball cap on the side of Marcus' face. The very thing the gaiter would have helped conceal.

Mike kept the gun on the cashier, "Marcus? Damn, man, you got big!" Mike started to laugh, "Jesus Christ! Where's your brother?"

"He's around."

The cashier, with his hands still raised, looked back and forth between the reunited men.

Mike turned back to him and said, "Don't let our conversation keep you from filling up my bag."

"You should also get the money from the safe in the back," Marcus suggested.

"Thank you, Marc. That's a great idea. Let's go back to the safe."

Mike directed the employee and Marcus to the back.

After a moment, the nervous cashier managed to get the combination set. There was a loud click and the heavy door swung open. Inside the safe were five lock bags filled with cash.

Mike looked on in amazement, "Holy shit! How much is there?"

The cashier surmised, "Five, maybe six thousand."

A loud gunshot rang out, causing Mike to jump back and drop his gun, believing the cops arrived.

He looked over at Marcus, who was holding his own gun. Mike's ears were still ringing as he looked back at the cashier, dead on the floor.

Marcus closed the space between him and Mike quickly.

"Why the fuck did you shoot him? Why do you have a gun?"

Marcus answered, "Same reason as you. You actually interrupted me. I killed him because he heard our names, and I wasn't disguised. Well, actually," he let out a little laugh, "I didn't need a reason. I was gonna kill him anyway."

Marcus picked up Mike's gun from the ground and used it to shoot the antiquated video recorder connected to the security cameras around the store. He reached inside his jacket and pulled out a large dark green garbage bag and made Mike put everything from the safe into it. Marcus took it and directed Mike towards the back door and out to where Darius was waiting.

"Mike?" Darius asked through his opened window.

"Your brother just killed a guy." Mike blurted out as a greeting.

"We gotta go before the cops come," Marcus said, getting in the car, ignoring Mike.

Darius looked back at Mike. "The fuck you doin' here?"

Mike shrugged, "Guess we had the same idea."

"Let's go, now!" Marcus demanded as he secured himself in the passenger seat.

Darius was stunned to see his friend after so many years. He had questions.

"Get in the back," he said to Mike, flatly.

"What the fuck, man?" Marcus was stunned.

With sirens getting closer, Mike jumped into Darius' car, and they sped away with Marcus and Mike bickering.

Once they were parked across town, Darius pulled into the back area of a crowded parking lot. He had missed Mike but had zero trust in anyone and he wasn't about to let his old friend know where he was living.

Marcus kept the gun on Mike the whole time and he had no intention of stowing it away now that they were away from the cops.

"Start talking," Darius said to Mike.

"What do you wanna know?" Mike asked.

"Why didn't you tell me you were running away?"

"Because you would've wanted to come."

"No shit!" Darius exclaimed.

"Would you have left your brother?"

Marcus looked from Mike to Darius and back at Mike. He wanted to shoot him in the face now more than he did back at the store.

"With three of us, we wouldn't have made it very far. Hell, two of us would've been hard enough. I knew you wouldn't leave Marc and, honestly, I did want you to come with me. I just couldn't ask you to choose so," Mike sighed before continuing, "I made the choice for you."

Darius was quiet before finally asking, "How much did you get?"

"What do you mean?" Mike asked, confused.

"You robbed the cash register. How much did you get?"

"Oh, um," he took the wad of bills out of the bag he shoved in the pocket of his hoodie, "About $150."

"Okay. Marc?" He turned to his brother, "How much did you get?"

Marcus didn't take his eyes off of Mike as he reached into the garbage bag on his lap and pulled each lock bag out one by one until there were five spread out.

Darius noted the loot and gave a low whistle. He instructed Marcus to feel each bag and to give the one he believed had the least amount in it to Mike.

"Why aren't we splitting everything 50/50?" Mike asked, annoyed after Marcus handed him the bag he chose.

Marcus pointed his gun at Mike and said, "We could take it all."

Darius turned to look at his friend again, "We won't be able to take you to your car. You understand."

Mike concealed his portion of the stolen money and got out of the backseat to make the long walk back across town.

Finally home, the brothers empty the contents of the bags onto their kitchen counter. They made quick work of the locks and dumped all the bills out. In total, they scored $4,563, a nudie mag, one candy bar and a soda.

"Wonder how much more we would've had with the bag you made me give Mike," Marcus mused.

Darius looked over at Marcus. "Seriously? He knows who we are. The cameras in the store definitely caught both of you. Oh, and you killed a guy."

There was a tense silence before Darius continued, "We haven't seen Mike in a long time. We can't trust he's not going to say anything to the wrong people about us."

"Not if we killed him, too."

Darius did a doubletake, "The fuck is wrong with you?"

Marcus hated that question. He gritted his teeth and went back to looking at the money they counted.

"I'll tell you what. Next time you go in, and I'll wait in the car," he finally said before turning on his heel to take a shower.

Unsure if a tracking device was in any or all of the lock bags from the safe, Darius poured bleach all over them in the hopes of destroying anything that could trace them back to him or his brother. He asked Marcus to join him in scattering the bags all over town, but his brother wanted to lay down after his shower complaining of a headache coming on.

The next morning, Darius woke up on the couch where he passed out the night before, watching television. He could hear his brother humming in the kitchen. The melodic tune and the aroma of bacon gave him a feeling of nostalgia, but Darius couldn't quite place what he was feeling nostalgic for. He looked out the window and noticed it rained overnight. His stomach rumbled in reaction to the fragrance Marcus was creating in the next room once the brewed coffee joined in the array of scents. He couldn't help but smile as he imagined himself floating into the kitchen like a cartoon as though the fragrance were a cloud he could ride on. Darius loved watching cartoons with his brother while their mom made breakfast on

Saturday mornings. Before, of course, the demands of their father for outdoor chores took that time away from them. That sudden reminder dulled his good mood which was hindered further when he spotted muddy footprints leading into the kitchen bringing his thoughts back to the present.

He looked down and noticed Marcus wearing boots with wet bits of grass and foliage that clung to mud around the soles.

"Were you outside?" Darius asked, pouring himself a cup of coffee.

Marcus looked down at his boots, acknowledging the mess, "Whoops. I went for a walk."

"Well, your little walk made a mess. You tracked all over the place."

Marcus started to feel anxious and visibly jumped at a loud pop from the sizzling bacon.

"You okay?" Darius asked.

"Right as rain," Marcus responded sharply, at first. "Actually, I should clean it up now before it sets. Do you mind?" He motioned for Darius to take over the cooking duties.

Marcus took his boots and grabbed a trash bag from under the kitchen sink along with carpet cleaner. He walked around the corner, out of sight from his brother, stripped naked, and placed everything in the garbage bag and tied it. He was no longer feeling panicked. The anxiety was replaced with calm and laser focus as he moved with ease and speed.

"Hey, do you remember watching cartoons on Saturday mornings?" Darius yelled out to his brother.

Marcus had raced to put on a towel and get back to the kitchen after spraying the carpet cleaner in the living room.

"Nope," he said, kneeling to clean the tiled floor.

Darius was thoughtful as he finished making their breakfast. His brother scrubbed the spots on the carpet and quickly showered and redressed before sitting down to eat.

"Wanna explain the garbage bag?" Darius asked.

Marcus swallowed some coffee before answering calmly, "No, but it's gonna need to be burned."

Chapter Sixteen:

____

2010 - Spring

Early Spring arrived and the brothers were down to their last few hundred dollars. Rent was due in two weeks and legitimate work wouldn't pick up again for another month.

"We need a quick score," Darius said after counting what was left of their money.

Marcus asked, "What do you have in mind?"

"The store on the corner of Fifth and Market. Let's hit it tonight," Darius suggested.

Marcus held up a finger, "Hold on a sec," walking toward his backpack on the couch. The notebook he pulled out was filled with notes from their past robberies and lists of future targets. Marcus kept notes of various money drop times, when the stores were the least busy, and what kind of security systems they had, including ATMs, which usually had cameras. Keeping notes helped Marcus remember details. Darius was thankful for this quirk as it made them sharpen their skills and prepare for any inevitability. They even had escape routes and backup routes planned. When they weren't desperate for cash, they still focused on getting it. The brothers would spend time in all the places they grew accustomed to hitting. Darius was usually the one in and out of these places during the day since he was more comfortable talking to others. It also helped that his looks were plain and unremarkable. Marcus put people off by his blunt remarks and the wicked looking scar on the side of his face was a little off putting. After chatting up and flirting with one of the cashiers during the day, Darius learned the store's owner preferred to put his money in a cheaper system and added less expensive fake cameras to make the place appear more secure. Marcus took the information from his brother and did his own reconnaissance to find out which cameras were fake and which ones they needed to avoid.

"Okay, "Marcus started with a huge smile, "Get this. It looks like we should wait to hit it between three and four in the morning." Darius shuffled over toward him, and Marcus handed him the notes as he continued, "Check it out, they do the most business on Wednesday mornings. Tonight, they have the ATM guy come in and restock."

Darius finished the thought, "So, they'll have the most cash in the safe and ATM with only one person there until the banks open."

The men spent the next few hours into the early morning going over a plan before making their move on the convenience store. Marcus, with his gaiter already covering most of his face, walked around the front of the building, wearing a hoodie with a pistol in the front pocket, leaving Darius waiting in the car, positioned for a quick getaway.

Darius had the windows rolled down and could hear two pops of the gun. This was according to the plan to scare the cashier. What wasn't part of the plan, was the patrol officer who happened to be driving by at that exact moment.

"Fuck!" Darius said to himself as he focused on the police cruiser in the rearview mirror.

The police officer pulled off to the side, turned on his lights and jumped out of the car. He made his way to the front door of the store, calling in the robbery using the radio on his right shoulder.

"Sir! Drop your weapon and come out with your hands up!" He yelled out, keeping his gun trained on Marcus while pulling the door open with his left hand.

Marcus remained perfectly still with his gun and eyes on the clerk.

The cop repeated his command, "Drop your weapon!" The radio on his shoulder made a sound followed by a loud pop.

The officer dropped to the ground unable to answer his radio. Darius came up on his left side and made sure he was down.

He continued inside and said to his brother, "Grab the cash from the register and let's go. I can already hear the backup coming."

Marcus forced the clerk to finish emptying the register before shooting him between the eyes.

"Fuck Marcus! You didn't have to do that!" Darius cried.

"He saw your face. He could identify you!" He yelled at his brother, pushing past him.

The cash they got was far from what they were hoping to get. Darius couldn't stop thinking that if they waited a few minutes before going into the store, the cop wouldn't have heard the shots, and they'd be counting more cash. He watched as his brother furiously jotted down notes in his notebook, occasionally reaching to scratch at the hair growing back in on his head. Marcus began shaving his head on a regular basis and was constantly changing his facial hair. The television was tuned to the local morning news and the story they were expecting began.

"Police are putting together a profile on the two men that held up a convenience store in the early morning hours leaving two dead. One, a fifteen-year veteran of the police department, was gunned down just outside the store. He leaves behind his wife, who is expecting their second child, and a four-year-old daughter. Police say the two men made away with an estimated $200. The two men are believed to be from the area, and police are asking for tips from the community. In other crime news, the police are also asking for the public's assistance regarding the women found hanged --"

Marcus turned the television off and tossed the remote aside.

Darius felt irritated. He turned to Marcus and said, "That fucking cop shouldn't have been there. He'd be home with his family right now."

Marcus scoffed, "Whatever. He chose that job, and you did what you had to do. Besides," he started as he got up to get a drink from the kitchen, "You probably did his wife and kids a favor. I know you did me one."

Darius caught the soda his brother tossed him and winked at him, "I got you, baby bro."

Marcus punched Darius in the shoulder hard, "Don't ever fucking call me that again."

The Tye brothers were surprised by a brisk and sudden knock at the door. Quick to cock the guns next to them, Darius crept to the door to look out of the peep hole as Marcus prepared to shoot if necessary.

It was Mike.

The brother's shared a look before Darius pulled the door open and Mike walked in.

"You guys have been busy. I see you made the news," Mike said, putting his hands up and stopping abruptly. Marcus kept his gun on him and refused to uncock it.

"How'd you know to come here?" Darius demanded, now standing behind his old friend.

Mike took a breath to calm himself before explaining, "Well, ever since I found out you were in town, I've been keepin' an eye out for you. And one day, I saw your car and followed it here. I've known you've been here for a bit."

"Who've you told about us?" Marcus asked just itching to put a bullet in him.

"Not a goddamn soul! Look, would you please just put the fucking safety back on?" Mike pleaded.

Marcus shook his head. "Fuck off, Mike," he said.

Mike looked back at Darius and saw his gun was drawn and pointed at him, too.

"I came here to help, but if you want, I'll go fuck right off," he said defiantly. To prove he meant what he said, Mike dropped his arms and glared at Darius.

"We're cool, Marc," Darius said, dropping his gun he turned and locked the door. Mike continued past Marcus and sat down on the couch.

"I gather you have less than twenty-four hours before the cops figure out who you are."

Darius clenched his jaw. "How do you figure that?" He asked.

Mike smiled, "Well, they know your height, weight, shoe size, what car you drive. You killed a cop and they can see enough of your head on one of the cameras, so they won't rest until you're caught. It's only a matter of time before someone looks outside and says, 'Hey, that car looks like the one from the news,' Want to take bets on when that's going to happen?"

Darius rubbed his face and shouted, "FUCK!"

Marcus was suspicious. "How do you know what the cops know?"

"Let's say I got a promotion since you last saw me," Mike said with pride, "But look, I have something you guys might want to consider. It's in Kentucky."

Marcus and his brother shared another look.

Darius asked, "What's in Kentucky?"

Mike smiled and replied, "I have this contact named Jobusch. Well, Joe Buscemi, but we call him Jobusch. He's building a team of guys to act as muscle and I think you two would be perfect."

Darius looked confused, "Like, bouncers?"

Marcus interjected, "Who the fuck cares, Dari?! Let him tell us all about it while we pack up some stuff. We need to leave now."

Mike nodded in agreement, "Joe works for a family as a book-keeper, he's called The Accountant, in the organization, and he needs to find guys who don't mind getting their hands dirty as collectors and enforcers. There's only one problem."

Darius shook his head, "What?"

Mike sighed, "You need the heat to cool down first. You're gonna have to lay low for a bit."

"Couple months?" Darius asked while his mind raced.

Mike nodded, "Couple months."

Darius looked over at Mike, "What are the details?"

Mike smiled, "I'll get them to you. In the meantime," he said, as he held out a wad of hundreds and fifties to Darius, "I suggest you find yourself a motel for a few days. Get rid of your car, STAT. And, here's the card of a guy who will set you both up with fake IDs. Tell him it's a favor to Buscemi. Can you remember that?"

Mike proceeded to stand up and headed toward the door. Marcus stopped him. "How do we find you?"

"I'll find you. Don't worry."

Mike continued to walk past them and toward the door, "Clock is ticking, boys," he said as he walked out.

They torched their car after moving it to an empty cul-de-sac with plots marked for a brand-new neighborhood. Darius grew a full beard and started parting his hair differently. They stole cars from a small airport and crowded mall parking lots all along the border of Tennessee and Kentucky. It was a means of money and transportation. The locations they chose to steal from almost always guaranteed some time would pass before the vehicles were reported stolen. The brothers would sell any after-market stereo systems to pawn shops, and the rest of the cars they lifted were sold for parts at chop-shops they'd gotten familiar with. This kept them going while they waited the next few weeks out in small cash-only motels just south of Bowling Green. Sometimes, they had to share a bed, but they didn't care. It was a roof over their heads and only temporary until Mike got in touch with them again.

Chapter Seventeen

"Alright, Mike, have a seat," Joe Buscemi said to his trusted employee. "I hear you have some guys in mind for our Securities and Collections agency?"

Mike smiled, "I do. They're a bit rough around the edges and one of them, Sir, is scary as fuck, but they're both smart as fuck, too."

Joe laughed trying to light his cigar, "Oh, Mike! This is why I love you, man, you just say whatever the hell's on your mind in the funniest fucking ways. Okay, so explain to me how they're so smart first, and I want examples. Then, you can explain to me why they're so scary."

Mike went on to explain how the brothers had only ever dealt in cash transactions and that they constantly moved around and changed their identities often. He acknowledged that the only job that ever went sideways made them cop killers. He argued that the brothers would be willing to take less pay in order to have the full protection of the family.

"Bottom line, Sir, these guys put in the work in every situation. They can't account for every single variable, but they adjust their game each time. They make quick decisions when something happens that they didn't plan for, and I gotta admit, those decisions never fail. The issue with the dead cop," he paused to take a deep breath, "was an unfortunate situation. But, if Dari hadn't done what he did, we wouldn't be on the cusp of getting two badasses on the team."

"Now, is Dari the scary one?" Joe asked.

"Nope. He's a pussycat. Marcus, on the other hand, lacks a soul. I'm sure of that."

"No shit. The pussycat killed the pig, huh?" Joe laughed at his own joke. "Alright, give 'em my card. I want Dari to call tomorrow at noon and slip 'em some money for gas. No hiccups, Mike."

"No hiccups, Joe."

***

The next morning, Marcus woke up to find an envelope slid under the door. Inside was a fifty-dollar bill and a card with a phone number and a message that read:

Dari has to make the call at noon today or no deal.
Don't fuck this up.
Use the $ for gas.
-M

Darius picked up the phone at 11:59 am and called the number that Mike gave him.

"This is Joe," a man's voice said over the line.

Darius stammered, "Uh, is this Joe Buscemi?"

Joe replied, "That depends. Who's this?"

"My name's Darius and a guy named Mike Payne gave me your information. Said you were looking for some guys and that me and my brother would be a perfect fit."

"Mike Payne, huh? Well, I'm willing to meet with you and your brother. I'll decide if either of you are a perfect fit or not, so don't get ahead of yourself," he said, chuckling, "I'll tell you what, you sound motivated. Where ya located?"

"Just south of Bowling Green, Sir," Darius replied.

Mike smiled at the respectable tone in the young man, "I'll arrange for someone to meet you. There's a motel called The Blue Star off of route one-eighty-five. Now, there's a diner on the property. Be in the diner on Friday at 9 AM."

Darius confirmed, "Friday, Blue Star, diner, outside Bowling Green, on one-eighty-five, by 9 AM. Got it. Thank you, Sir."

After hanging up the phone, He turned to Marcus and asked, "Did you hear that?"

Marcus nodded, "Yep. That's in three days and only a few hours drive from here. We should leave first thing in the morning, scope it out, and leave nothing to chance."

Darius agreed. They spent the day locating and stealing one more car and scrapping the previous one. Marcus made one stop for ibuprofen and water when he felt one of his headaches coming on. They parked it behind a fast-food restaurant close to the new motel they checked into once they secured their new ride.

That night, Darius heard a noise and rolled over to face the couch Marcus slept on and slightly opened one eye. He noticed Marcus standing in front of the couch, motionless. Normally, he'd simply ask his brother what he was doing, but Darius couldn't speak or move. Something told him to wait. He chose to pretend to be asleep. He rolled back over and listened as his brother unzipped his backpack to retrieve something, grabbed a jacket and walked out the door, quietly closing it behind him.

Darius threw off the covers of the bed and rushed over to see where Marcus was headed. He looked out the same window his brother stood in front of moments ago and spied Marcus talking to a sex worker on the corner under a sign for a restaurant.

"Trying to get some ass? Now?" Darius scoffed, "This fucking guy."

He watched as they walked in the opposite direction of the motel. Darius quickly put on his pants and shoes. He was pissed that his brother would waste their money and he decided to follow them and put a stop to the transaction. He grabbed his gun and put it in his waistband under his shirt.

Darius thought he'd lost them when he heard a noise and was surprised to notice a trail leading into a wooded picnic area.

"What the fuck?" Darius asked himself as the path continued into thicker woods. He stepped over old beer cans and bottles littering the area. It was clear that this was not a family friendly hidden oasis but a place where teens could get high or wasted and fuck around.

He hurried down the dirt path until he heard hushed voices. He couldn't make out what was being said, but he recognized his brother's tone. Then, there was silence. Darius walked down the path a little more when he saw Marcus with his hands gripped around the young woman's neck. She struggled with all her might, but he slammed her against a tree, pinning her. She attempted to scratch at his arms, and he tossed her to the ground. As she writhed, choking, and attempted to put distance between herself and her attacker, Marcus grabbed a rock to knock her unconscious. He rolled her over and straddled her to continue choking her.

Darius stood paralyzed watching his brother. The way he moved when he attacked the woman was all too familiar.

Marcus pulled out a rope from inside his hoodie and wrapped it around her neck. He knelt over her to make sure she was still alive. He preferred that the women didn't leave him until he had them secured.

Darius felt like he couldn't breathe as he continued, completely transfixed, watching his brother as Marcus started to softly sing.

"Sweet mockingbird fly.
"Higher and higher in the sky where the angels fly."

Marcus held onto the other end of the rope as he looked for the perfect branch. If she regained consciousness, he'd feel her through the rope, tugging.

"Golden rain falls onto your wings as the sun rises high."
Oh, sweet mockingbird fly."
The shadows are near, don't you cry."
Clear your eyes and fly real high."
Sweet mockingbird fly."

Satisfied with a thick lower branch, Marcus hoisted his new victim up. Her toes were mere inches from the ground. He stayed near her, singing and stroking her hair until he heard the death rattle. She swayed back and forth as the rope creaked against the wood. Marcus wiped sweat beaded on his brow when he looked up to see someone approach him.

"Dari?"

Marcus was knocked backward by his brother's fist slamming into his jaw.

Darius waited to see what his brother would do in retaliation. He stood firm, ready and waiting for any sudden movement of aggression. Marcus recovered his balance and stood in silence. He kept his head hung down as he instinctively rubbed the left side of his jaw, but he made no move against his brother. Darius felt anger so when the lump in his throat grew and the tears began stinging his eyes, he was confused.

"Why?" Was all Darius could manage to get out. His voice gruff and barely above a whisper was caught by a sob.

Marcus stared at the ground and shrugged his shoulders. He felt ashamed the moment he realized his brother saw how he scratched his itchy brain.

Darius waited for an explanation that would not come from his brother. He stared at Marcus until the sound of the engine brake on a semi-truck coming off an exit in the distance reminded him they weren't the only ones up at this hour. Darius turned and walked back to the motel leaving his brother to follow a short distance behind.

Back at the motel, Darius could barely sleep. He found himself looking over at his brother soundly sleeping on the couch like nothing happened. When dawn broke, he decided to give up on sleep and get a shower.

They left the motel to get breakfast, but it was a quiet meal. Marcus knew his brother was processing, and Darius could only do just that. After their somber meal, they returned to their room and Darius watched TV to disrupt the silence.

He stopped on a show with several women holding shiny metal briefcases which caught his attention. Blankly watching, he realized he was starting to count how many beautiful women were on the screen. Darius' mind started to imagine rope around their necks. Finally, his thoughts came full circle back to his brother.

"How many women, Marc?" He finally asked in a quiet but firm voice.

Marcus was not one to play coy and he respected his brother enough not to play dumb. He knew the number Darius wanted.

"Four, I think."

Darius grabbed the remote and turned off the TV. Sitting up on his bed, he asked, 'What do you mean, you 'think,'?"

Marcus sighed and looked up at the ceiling. He tossed his notebook on the small side table by the window and turned in his chair to fully face his brother.

"Sometimes, I have flashes of women, their faces, in my brain. They're like dreams or maybe memories. There's definitely four who I remember every moment of." He attempted a smile, "You met number four last night."

Darius had his own memory tugging for him to acknowledge, "The morning you tracked mud through our apartment -"

"Shit! Five. Forgot that one."

"Aw, fuck, Marc! You wanna take a moment to think real fucking hard on this? So, five maybe more? Is that what we're dealing with here?"

Marcus looked down and shrugged at the ground, feeling ashamed again. Darius ran both of his hands down the length of his face and took a deep breath.

"Do you remember who and where the first one was?" he asked his brother, bracing himself for the answer by gripping the back of the chair placed by a narrow desk.

"Do you remember our last foster mother?"

"Her?" Darius was incredulous, "But that was over a decade, you were just-" He stopped and stared at Marcus who maintained eye contact. All this time, he believed his brother witnessed something he wanted no part of in his last foster home.

"Wait, YOU killed her? So, you were just a kid when you became a serial killer? Is that what you're telling me?"

Marcus appeared to be staring off into space as he absentmindedly stroked the ridges of his scar. He continued to stare as he finally spoke, "I never thought of myself as one of those before."

Darius believed he could adapt quickly to just about any situation, but this came out of nowhere and he felt like he took a hundred gut punches from a prize fighter. He knew the accident changed Marcus in scary and sad ways, but this was on an entirely different playing field all together.

"Is this how it is now?" Darius asked for confirmation.

Marcus nodded and Darius took that as his admission he couldn't stop himself.

Darius swallowed hard, "Okay. We don't want to fuck up this opportunity tomorrow. Can you keep your ass in the motel tonight?"

"I'm fine for a while." Marcus responded.

"Alright then. We'll just pivot like always."

Chapter Eighteen:

The morning of the meeting, the Tye brothers grabbed their backpacks and duffels and went to the diner early and ordered breakfast and coffee. They secured a corner booth with Marcus facing the front entrance and Darius kept an eye on the kitchen that had a rear exit. Just before 9 AM, Marcus clocked a black SUV with three men inside, pulling into the parking lot. He reached down to touch the hilt of his boot knife and quietly alerted his brother. Darius turned in his booth to see a fairly tall man, older than them, in a dark suit and wearing aviators stepping out of the passenger seat. The driver stayed in the SUV while the other gentleman walked into the diner and made a beeline for the two men in the back corner booth.

"Hello, Marcus and Darius. I'm Liam Stacey. Let's go for a drive."

He laid a fifty-dollar bill on top of the check the waitress set down on the table, turned around and walked out. The brothers exchanged a look and then scrambled to follow Liam.

The driver and a man from the backseat were also well-dressed. Both exited the vehicle, patted the brothers down, and placed their belongings in the back. The boot knife and a gun from Darius were taken and placed in a lock box.

"You knew exactly where we were in that place. How?" Marcus asked fearlessly once everyone was in the car, the well-dressed man from the backseat now sat between him and his brother.

Liam smiled as he waited for the driver to pull back onto the main road and head into town, "Deductive reasoning," he started, "Why were you there at that time and why did you follow me out?" Liam quizzed back.

Darius answered him, "We did as we were told, Sir."

"Excellent answer, young man!" Liam said, with praise. "Now, one of you, give me a 5-digit number," he demanded, holding the lock box with their weapons on his lap.

Marcus quickly said, "1-2-3-4-5"

Liam smiled and quipped, "That's the same combination on my luggage!"

He looked around for a reaction to his joke that never came and shrugged it off.

Liam Stacey loved the sound of his own voice. The brothers spent the better part of the next two hours listening to his military stories and how he got his job in the family. His hubris was in full display, and it rubbed Marcus the wrong way. When Liam wasn't talking about himself, he was texting or taking and making phone calls. He never stopped talking. Darius focused on the road signs to determine where they were, and surmised they were headed somewhere toward Louisville. They finally pulled into a parking garage by a building in a small downtown area of a river town not far from the brothers' childhood home. In fact, Darius remembered riding through this town several times with his parents when he was a boy. It had changed considerably since the turn of the century.

The five men walked from the garage to a dry cleaner. The brothers followed Liam and his goons to the back of the humid shop, and into an air-conditioned office where a man sat behind a desk, reading a paper and smoking a cigar.

"Joe, I got the Tye brothers here for you," Liam said, when Joe failed to lower his newspaper at his entrance.

The paper lowered, revealing a man with a cigar in his mouth and the smoke from his cigar swirled above his round face. Darius couldn't help but imagine Joe dressing up as Santa Claus for neighborhood children.

"Thank you," Joe said, dismissively.

Once Liam left the room and the door closed, Joe asked the brothers to have a seat. He looked at each brother.

"You must be Marcus. And you," he said, pointing at Darius, "Must be our cop-killer."

Darius visibly winced at the moniker.

"Look, kid, it's a hiccup and I don't like those. Luckily for you, I do like your buddy, Mike. I trust him and he vouched for you two." He snuffed the cigar before continuing, "As you can tell, we're very careful with who we bring on into our little organization." He motioned for the brothers to look around the office they sat in.

"This room is only for me to use to meet with people like you. There's nothing in here," he said as he pulled out drawers to prove they were empty. He stopped and looked up at the brothers, "I tell you this to keep the good folks in the front business safe. You won't find anything about any of us or the organization here. Do you understand?"

"Yes, Sir," Darius said, followed by his brother.

"I got two jobs for you. We collect dues from businesses we protect. I'll give you a list and an amount and you go to those places and collect that amount. Easy, right?"

Darius agreed. "Sounds easy enough. What's the other job?"

Joe nodded and answered, "It's kind of a smorgasbord. We may need you guys to rough some people up, send messages, watch people, and report back. Stuff like that."

Marcus asked, "We gotta kill anyone?"

Joe leaned back in his chair and folded his arms, "Not today. But, I get a feeling if we ask, you won't have an issue with it," he said, keeping eye contact with Marcus.

Marcus quickly answered, "Not a one."

Joe's smile faded some before he added, "You do not kill anyone without the organization's say so. Do you understand that?"

Marcus nodded and Darius said, "Yessir."

"Great! You're hired. You'll need new IDs, cash, phones and a place to stay. No more boosting cars. We'll give you one."

Darius nodded, "That's great. Thank you."

Joe walked to the door and asked Liam to come back into the room.

"Anything else?" He asked the brothers.

Feeling overwhelmed, Darius shook his head.

Joe took a step closer to the brother's, "I want to make this very clear, right here, in front of a witness," he paused to point at Liam, "You two are low-level. You do as you're told, like good soldiers, you'll move up in our organization. You make zero demands. Zero. Mistakes are human and accidents do happen, but do not go out of your way to fuck anything up. Do we have an understanding?"

The brothers nodded.

"Okay guys, let's go." Liam clapped his hands and walked away.

The brothers were driven to an apartment complex that was much better than any place they'd ever stayed in before. Their balcony backed up to a community park that reminded Darius of the first job he and Marcus had in high school. Before leaving, Liam handed them a manila envelope filled with cash, and set the lock box on the kitchen counter.

"You now represent some very powerful people. I highly suggest you clean yourselves up. Get a haircut, freshen up the look a bit and buy some clothes. This is what that cash is for. You'll also find a card for our guy to get you legit IDs for whenever you may need to have one with names already pre-approved."

He pointed to the lockbox and continued with a smile, "The 5-digit code you chose earlier is the combo. You can keep the lockbox, and these are now your keys," Liam finished, handing them two sets. One for the apartment, and one for the SUV they traveled in that day. He walked out and Marcus watched from one of the bedroom windows. Liam reached the parking lot and got into the passenger seat of an identical SUV driven by the same man as before.

His brother was looking over the list they needed to collect from. The note told them to report back to Joe at the end of the week. They were instructed to text Liam when they were ready, and he would collect from them.

"What do you say we tour the town and locate these businesses on the list?" Darius suggested.

Marcus looked at the stacks of cash on the kitchen counter, "Maybe we can get a TV and hit a grocery store while we're out?"

By the end of the week, they had collected nearly half a million dollars. Liam checked the lists and counted the cash. He handed over 5% of their collections and a new list for the following week.

"Twenty-five grand?" Darius asked.

Liam misunderstood, "Yeah, you guys aren't gonna make as much as the rest of us yet. You still have a lot of heat coming from Tennessee that we've stayed ahead of up till now. Plus, you know, every job has a probationary period." He laughed at his attempt to pretend they were working a normal job.

Darius was still reeling from the amount he held in his hand. He had a difficult time masking his surprise that, one day, it would be much more.

Liam left and the brothers decided to do the same thing as the week before. They tracked down all the listed businesses beforehand to familiarize themselves and then bought whatever they needed.

***

Detective Diego Muñoz settled his 5'10" frame into his worn leather chair, the unsolved case weighed heavily on his shoulders. He rubbed his sore, arthritic knee, and the reason this was his last big case. He adjusted himself and kept writing notes trying to ascertain any connection between the victims. The mountain of paperwork in front of the soon-to-be retired Tennessee detective seemed insurmountable. The constant reminder of lives tragically cut short as haunting images of the three women, their bodies suspended from trees, lingered in his mind. The frustration fueled his determination to bring their killer to justice. Diego believed more victims were out there that went unnoticed before the first girl was found. He sent a message to neighboring states, to share information.

His tired eyes wandered to the corkboard on the wall, adorned with a tapestry of hints and clues. Each piece of evidence meticulously arranged, forming a mosaic of possibilities. Weather reports, carefully pinned alongside photographs, provided a glimpse into the fateful moments when the victims lost their lives and when they were discovered. The estimated time of death, painstakingly calculated, added another layer to the intricate puzzle that Diego was determined to solve.

With a heavy sigh, the old detective glanced at the clock on his desk. Time was slipping away, and he had yet to find a break in the case that was looking more and more like a serial killer. Frustration gnawed at him when his phone rang, shattering the focus. He picked it up swiftly, his voice filled with a mix of anticipation and authority as he answered, "Muñoz."

The voice on the other end relayed urgent news of yet another victim closer to the border over the state line in Kentucky. Without hesitation, Diego responded, "Send me the location. I'm on my way." His tone was resolute, a testament to his unwavering commitment to protect and serve.

The earth was damp under his feet as Diego made his way past litter on the trail through the wooded area that had been sectioned off by the town's sheriff.

The older detective spotted the officer in charge and introduced himself.

"Detective Muñoz, I was told to expect you. Officer Robert Hoyt," the officer said, as he shook Diego's hand, and continued with the business at hand. "We believe the victim is a local prostitute, based on what's left of her clothing and style of shoes." The officer looked at his notebook to rattle off the other information, "Seems to be approximately mid-twenties and there are possible signs of a struggle, but with weather and predation..."

Diego rubbed his stubbled chin and completed the officer's sentence, "Crucial evidence is probably gone or tainted." He let out a heavy sigh as he made his way on the trail.

"Has the coroner estimated how long she's been out here yet?"

"A week, maybe two," Officer Hoyt answered.

They walked closer to the crime scene and the officer continued as he volunteered information, "She was found by two teenagers."

As Diego entered the clearing, he saw the victim being rolled into a body bag from the ground before it was lifted onto a waiting gurney. He turned to the officer and asked if she had already been cut down.

"No, Sir. The amount of time she'd been out here, plus the vultures..." The young officer took a moment before continuing, "The neck's gone. There's really not much left of her. She was found kind of crumpled on the ground under the branch."

Walking closer to the body, the stench hit Diego like a giant punch in the throat and the sound of flies made it worse. Diego gagged. He never did get used to this part. The officer introduced the detective to their coroner, Dr. Grace Thompkins.

Diego placed a handkerchief he kept in his pocket over his nose and mouth and asked, "The rope, is it one-inch braided cotton Manilla?"

Dr. Thompkins nodded in confirmation. "We believe so, but I can't confirm until we get it to the lab."

"This isn't my jurisdiction, but will you send your report to me when you've finished your exam?" Diego asked, handing the coroner his card.

"Absolutely. You've seen this before?" she asked.

"Maybe. My gut says this is the same guy that killed a few women in Tennessee."

"Tell you what," Grace started as she zipped the body bag up, "Let's share info. Maybe my eyes will see something in the collective of victims."

Diego was happy for the help. Within moments the remains were loaded into the coroner's van, and it was off to be examined, leaving others to continue collecting anything believed to be evidence.

Officer Hoyt was making sure any footprints he found were marked for casting when Diego joined him and the two made their way back to Detective Muñoz's car.

Diego stopped suddenly as he looked across the street. On the other side of the road was an old, dilapidated motel. Further down the road he noticed a tavern.

Hoyt followed Diego's gaze and asked, "What are you looking at?"

"I'm looking at the place she probably picked up her johns and the place she would've taken them to. I think this guy may have just taken a shit a little too close to where he eats."

"I don't follow."

"The other women were found with the clothing intact and no sexual activity," Diego volunteered, seemingly talking to himself more than to Officer Hoyt.

Diego took a step forward and turned to look back in the direction of where the victim was found.

Officer Hoyt was perplexed watching the older detective work something through in his mind when Diego suddenly started walking toward the motel.

Diego introduced himself to the man with long unwashed hair behind the counter of the motel and asked if anyone had stayed there overnight and not by the hour.

The clerk scratched his head in thought. "Yeah, two guys stayed here for a day about ten days ago."

"Did they use a credit card?"

"Nah, Cash. Sorry."

Diego looked at Officer Hoyt and said, "This man needs to sit with a sketch artist. Have it sent to me when you get it."

Feeling as though he was on the cusp of a break in the case, Diego raced back to Tennessee.

Chapter Nineteen

Darius and Marcus spent a lot of their down time getting to know the county around the town they were now calling home. Darius remembered the counties of central and west Kentucky from his childhood. Jefferson, Bullitt, Hardin, and Meade counties would scroll across the bottom of the TV screen while he sat in front of it, hoping for a snow day.

Now, he and Marcus would explore those counties to look for anything they felt would be fun or useful to them. One such place was a strip club called Marlon's Dollhouse. It wasn't anything spectacular, but it was just out of the way, and fun.

The Tye Brothers cleaned up their look, but they refused to wear suits, choosing comfort over style. Darius would argue they were in style as the 90's grunge look never vanished. Once they had fresh haircuts, the brothers got their new emergency IDs. They were reminded to only use them if they were ever pulled over and to never reveal the names to anyone outside the organization. The identifications were meant as a safety measure from their real names going in the system.

The third week's list was shorter. It was a list of gas stations owned by the organization down route 60 and along route 42. They were easy since there was no one to intimidate. However, the last business, a bakery, was marked, "Liquidate All Assets."

"What the hell does that mean?" Marcus asked his brother.

Darius shrugged, "Your guess is as good as mine."

They repeated the routine of the past two weeks visiting the businesses on the list to plot their route for efficiency and to counter any foreseeable issues. While out, they noticed their favorite strip club was only a few miles away. They drove into the empty gravel parking lot of the Dollhouse and parked on the side. Marcus stepped up the front steps and found the door securely locked.

"I guess thinking a strip club would be open before noon was a longshot, huh?" Darius said from behind.

Marcus replied, "I figured they'd serve lunch."

Darius laughed and said, "You craving clam sandwiches or fish tacos?"

Marcus laughed at the dumb joke and shook his head, "Man, anything at this point. I'm hungry."

"Well, you're in luck. Liam just texted back and wants to meet at the coffee shop on Fifth in twenty."

The brothers went back into town and ordered cold brews with ready-made sandwiches and sat in the outdoor café wearing sunglasses. They watched as Liam walked past without a word. He went inside to get his own coffee and joined them.

As he sat, Darius slid over the list and pointed at the "Liquidate All Assets" next to the name, Jimmy Ryan, at the bakery's address.

"So, what does this mean?"

Liam smiled, "I can see why you have questions. This means you get to destroy all of his property at this address. Go crazy, kids!"

Darius asked quietly, "So, it's not a hit?"

Liam laughed, "Nah, those lists come in a different envelope. If I need you for assistance, they'd be coming from me or above, and you aren't there yet."

"Is Marlon's Dollhouse going to be on any of our lists?" Marcus asked.

Liam Stacey's eyes widened, "So, something you boys should know. Mr. Bandoni has a strong opinion about those types of establishments."

Darius was quick to ask, "I take it his opinions are more on the negative side?"

"That's putting it mildly. Look, you're free to visit those places all you want, but don't talk about it. He shows little respect for those who frequent them."

After a few moments of awkward silence, Liam Stacey nodded and slapped the table, "Welp, I'm going to go enjoy this coffee elsewhere. You guys have fun collecting," and he walked away, disappearing around a corner.

***

That night, Darius and Marcus headed back over to the Dollhouse. The parking lot was about half full, which was pretty good for a weeknight. The music thumped in their chest as they walked inside. The lights were bright at the bar and stage but were dim everywhere else for the patrons. A woman was swinging around a pole on the stage doing a typical dance for the lonely men surrounding her.

Marcus looked around and nodded. "I like this place."

Darius shot Marcus a half-smile, "Yeah, me too."

They continued to look around as they made their way over toward the bar. A beautiful brunette with blonde streaks around her face, wearing tight black shorts and a black top with a plunging neckline, turned toward them to take their order. Her name tag was pinned near her left breast and read, "Beks."

She smiled, "What can I get you?"

Darius smiled with as much charm as he could muster, "Actually, Beks, we'd like to speak with the owner if he's around."

"He is. I'll call for him," she said as she picked up a cordless phone from the counter behind her and dialed.

Darius turned towards the entertainment while he waited.

"She's damn good!" Darius said to his brother who was already watching the very limber dancer wow the small crowd.

Marcus nodded and then turned his attention to a thin, lanky guy, who looked barely old enough to work there, walking up beside them.

"Did you request to speak with the owner?" He asked.

"Yeah," Darius responded, standing straighter.

"I'm Josh. Marlon asked me to bring you to him," he said, before turning to lead them down a hall to a closed door.

Faintly over the thumping of the music, a voice on the other side of the door yelled, "Come in!" to Josh's knocking.

Once inside, after the door closed, the audible difference between the music in the club and the quiet office was instantly noticeable to the brothers. Marcus moved his jaw to pop his ear and eventually heard reggae coming from a small speaker on the desk from across the room.

A stubbled, bald Jamaican man looked up from his computer, "Yeah?"

Darius asked, "Are you Marlon?"

"Yep," Marlon replied.

"The owner?"

Marlon narrowed his eyes at Darius and turned toward his employee, "Josh, you can go, but before you do, can you check the sign out front? I'm worried it no longer says, "MARLON'S Dollhouse.""

Darius and Marcus moved out of Josh's way as he left, but neither reacted to Marlon's jab.

"Can I offer you boys a drink?" Marlon asked as he pulled the cork from his private stash of Bumbu rum to refill his glass.

"No. Thank you," Darius responded for the two of them.

Marlon looked from Darius, to Marcus, and back to Darius, "Does he talk or is his job to just look mean as fuck?"

"I like your place," Marcus said abruptly, before his brother spoke for him again.

Marlon's grin widened and he beamed from the praise, "Thank you!" he exclaimed.

"Is there more to it? Other rooms?" Marcus asked with genuine curiosity.

Marlon addressed the questions, "Well, there's the main stage area and bar out front. We have a smaller stage in the back for private bachelor parties, or the occasional old rich white guy who doesn't want the missus to know and is willing to pay the rental fee."

"Lower level? From the outside, it looks like you have a basement," Marcus continued.

"Uh, well, yeah. This building does have a basement, but I use it for storage. Wow," Marlon continued dryly before looking over at Darius, "He's way chattier than I thought he'd be. May I ask why you're so interested in my club?"

"You should consider being open during the day and offering lunch specials," Marcus firmly suggested.

"Buddy, if I could afford to be open 24/7, I would. Times have been tough," Marlon admitted, taking a huge sip of his drink.

"We may be very useful to one another," Marcus thoughtfully said, looking around the office.

"What does that mean?" Marlon asked Marcus before turning to Darius and asking, "What does he mean?"

"It means we'll be regular customers," Darius, who was just as confused, answered for his brother again.

Marlon smiled, "I hope you're generous tippers. My staff works hard, and I can't afford to pay them what they deserve."

***

On the way home, they stopped for a bite. Marcus was in a rare, but considerably good mood. The waitress came over to take their order. After writing it down she looked up at the television in the corner and asked, "Oh, you guys hear about this? It broke about two hours ago. Pretty crazy." She raised the volume using the remote control in her apron.

"... found in Woodburn, KY. Police have released a sketch based on one eyewitness account of two men. Officials are calling them, 'Persons of Interest' at this time and ask the public to call the 800 number listed at the bottom of the screen if you've seen them. The victim's identity has yet to be released, but sources say that there may be some similarities to the unsolved cases throughout Tennessee. We will keep you updated as this story unfolds."

The sketches of two men displayed on the screen with the 800 number disappeared as the news segment switched to traffic. Marcus was still squinting his eyes and kept his head cocked to the side as the waitress left to put their order in.

Darius looked over at Marcus and rolled his eyes.

"Is that what I look like?" He finally asked.

With a laugh, Darius replied, "Either the witness was blind, or the sketch artist flunked out of art school." He got quiet before seriously asking his brother, "Who do you think the witness was?"

After their meal, the brothers headed back to their place. The apartment door had just closed when someone knocked on it. Marcus was reaching for the lock and paused, looking at his brother who already had his gun pulled, trained on the door. Marcus looked through the peephole and back over at Darius. He rolled his eyes and walked away as he pulled the door open an inch.

"If you don't want to shoot your buddy Mike, put the gun down," he said as he walked past his brother.

Mike pushed open the door and walked into their apartment looking around, smiling big.

"Did your boy hook you up or what?!" he asked, reaching to shake hands with his old friend, Darius.

Darius was all smiles, "Where the hell have you been, man?"

"Ugh, they got me out of town a lot doing what I do. I have the week off, so I thought I'd swing by and see what you guys were up to. How are you liking it so far?" Mike asked, excitedly.

Marcus grabbed a few bottles of beer from the kitchen and joined them in the living room. He watched his brother and Mike catch up and discuss the organization. He closed his eyes and relaxed.

"Marc!"

Marcus jolted awake, surprised he fell asleep so easily. "What?" he asked, looking around to make sure he hadn't spilled the beer he forgot he was holding.

Darius chuckled, "Mike said he'd like to join us on our trip to the bakery. You cool with that?"

Marcus took a sip of beer and grimaced before saying, "You don't think we can handle it?"

Mike looked to Darius for direction. When all the older brother did was shrug, Mike threw his arms up in defense, "Hey, man, I didn't mean that. We just thought it'd be fun if I joined you guys."

Marcus looked over at his brother who only raised his eyebrows at him.

"Sorry. Head wasn't cleared yet," Marcus said with a tight-lipped smile.

Mike continued, believing he still had to convince Marcus, "Look, the higher ups aren't gonna care if I'm there. You'll get paid the same. I just wanted to hang."

"It's cool Mike, really." Marcus stood up and handed his unfinished beer to his brother. "You wanna finish this? I'm going to bed."

"Well, we were thinking it would be better to go to the bakery tonight?" Darius clarified for his brother who slept through most of the conversation.

"Man, I am beat. Can't we do it tomorrow?" Marcus asked, halfway down the hall to his bedroom.

"Don't worry about it, Marc. I'll help Dari," Mike suggested.

Marcus stood there and wondered why Mike was pissing him off so much tonight. He smiled again and said, "Cool. G'night," before leaving the other two men to do the job.

Darius stared at the bottle his brother handed him, "I have an idea," he said to Mike.

Marcus woke up the next morning and went about his own daily routine. He walked into the kitchen expecting to see the counter littered with empty beer bottles and was pleasantly surprised when there were none. He looked around the corner, back into the living room, and didn't see any bottles in there either. He shrugged and went about making breakfast for himself and Darius. A soft noise made Marcus stop in his tracks. He reached for the largest knife in the block on the counter and waited. The deadbolt on the apartment door turned, and Mike strolled in carrying a large flat box with the name "Snyder's "printed on it. Marcus' grip on the knife tightened and he imagined stabbing his old friend and claiming self-defense during a break-in.

Mike smiled when his eyes met Marcus', "I brought doughnuts," he whispered loudly, as he continued to walk through the apartment to join his friend in the kitchen.

"I was making breakfast," Marcus said in protest, holding a package of bacon.

"No one's stopping you, Bud," Mike retorted. "Is your brother up yet?"

Marcus was feeling irritable again, "I haven't seen him," he started, "Don't you have your own place?"

Marcus turned to start the coffee and continued his routine.

Darius emerged from his room and after seeing what Mike brought, started laughing.

"Got a craving, huh?" Darius finally asked once he recovered.

"Yep, just out of the blue. Did you tell Marc yet?" Mike asked, sitting down and helping himself to an eclair from the box he brought.

"Tell me what?" Marcus was unsettled that his brother was keeping something from him.

"We took care of the bakery last night," Darius answered, grabbing a coffee mug.

Marcus continued making his breakfast as he endured the other two men recounting the story of how they destroyed the place. They talked over one another and laughed at each other's accounts of making Molotov cocktails and transporting them. Darius was genuinely relaxed and jovial. Marcus gritted his teeth and regretted going to bed early the night before.

"I wish I could do this with you guys permanently," Mike announced.

"It would be cool if you were around more," Darius admitted. Marcus did not agree with his brother and found himself counting the days when Mike had to leave again. Once his meal was ready, he walked past the other two men and sat on the couch in the living room, grabbed the remote, and turned on the TV to drown out their voices. He got lost in weather and traffic reports while he ate.

"We have breaking news from overnight, a local bakery was destroyed sometime around 2AM when a vehicle crashed through the store front. Fire and rescue say no one was injured and the cause is under investigation."

Marcus looked up to see his brother and Mike paying attention to the report. They seemed so proud of themselves. Darius looked away from the TV long enough to view the text he received.

"That was Jobusch," he said after the news went to commercial.

Mike looked over after walking back to grab coffee for himself and asked, "What does he want?"

"To meet with me and Marc in an hour."

"Where?" Mike asked while Marcus sat quietly.

Darius shared the address that Joe texted to him, and Mike was surprised, "No shit! You guys made an impression if he's inviting you to his home so early."

A few moments later, Mike gets his own text from Joe. "Welp, he wants me at his place, pronto. Maybe I'll see you guys there." He put the coffee cup in the sink and left.

The brothers made their way to Joe Buscemi's home which was nestled in a beautiful, gated community. Joe's home was at the far end of a side street, the entire lot was outlined with a tall wrought iron fence that became a heavy gate at the end of the driveway.

Darius pulled up to ring the buzzer through his opened window.

"Name?" A voice came over the speaker.

"The Tye brothers."

A moment later the gate opened, and they were instructed where to park. They were met with security guards and their automatic rifles. They gave their names again and asked to retrieve the duffel bags of money from the backseat which were then searched by the same guards. Once they were satisfied that the men were who they said they were, one of the guards asked the Tye brothers to follow him into the house.

Inside, it felt more like a home than a compound. Portraits of many family members and pictures of various gatherings and social events cluttered the walls. They continued through the foyer, past a formal sitting room until they reached Joe's office.

Joe was at his desk, ending a phone call when they were announced.

"Hey fellas, I saw the fire on the news," Joe said with a huge smile. "Beautiful work."

Darius smiled as he sat down in the chair designated for him, "Thank you."

"I must know how you did it," Joe demanded. "But first, can I get you guys anything? Coffee, water...?"

"No thank you, Sir. We just finished our breakfast when you texted," Darius answered.

"Excellent! I see you also brought this week's list of collections with you. I must admit, I didn't expect you to be so efficient. Now, tell me, how did you pull last night off?"

Darius explained and was honest about Mike's involvement.

"So, you came up with using a stolen car and Molotov cocktails in the middle of the night when no one would be at the bakery? Am I hearing this right?" Joe asked.

Darius became nervous, unsure if he made a mistake, "Yes, Sir. Everything we did was my idea," he declared, willing to accept accountability if he upset the organization.

"And my scout, Mike Payne, helped you?"

"Yes, Sir."

"Where were you?" Joe now focused on Marcus.

"Asleep," Marcus said flatly. He was uncomfortable and saw Joe react to the quick answer. Marcus looked at Darius who gave him a look that made him realize he needed to say more.

"I had a long day with collecting and I haven't been getting a lot of sleep lately. So, I was lucky that our buddy, Mike, stopped by and took it off my plate." Marcus hated giving Mike any credit, but if they did something wrong, then maybe he could place the blame at Mike's feet.

"I love how you guys just get shit done. And speaking of Mike, he has brought good news for our cop-killer," Joe said, pointing a finger at Darius.

"It seems that the video footage the cops had on you has gone missing and they have zero leads. So, unless you have an ex-girlfriend in Tennessee with an ax to grind, you should be in the clear."

Darius was relieved but wondered why Mike hadn't told him earlier. "That is good news. Thank you."

"You boys keep performing like this and you will be rewarded, handsomely," Joe said with a smile.

"So, even though I sat out of the bakery thing last night, we're good?" Marcus asked, needing clarification.

"I know your history with Mike. We don't have the luxury of trusted friends too often in this line of work. He vouched for you and I trust him. He proves himself time and time again. Now, you two have impressed not only me, but the head of our organization, E. I. Bandoni, as well."

The head of the Bandoni Family being impressed with them, filled the brothers with pride.

Mike was waiting for the brothers at their place again. Marcus was annoyed at first, but his spirits lifted when Darius said, "This fucking guy," under his breath.

"Dude!" Darius barked. "We were together all fucking night!"

Mike, clearly confused, responded, "Yeah. We were."

Marcus opened the door and the three men went inside before Darius continued, "It didn't occur to you to tell me about the video disappearing?"

"Oh!" Mike started with a laugh. "Against the rules. Sorry."

"What rules?" Marcus interjected.

Mike sighed and plopped down on the couch, "When I have to find info for or on another employee, I have to keep that info to myself until I report back to Joe or anyone above him."

Darius was immediately contrite, "Oh. Sorry, man."

Mike laughed, "No worries, brother. I wanted to tell you, but I could lose my job."

"I understand, man."

"I do have some news that Joe's letting me tell you, though."

"What's that?" Marcus asked, still reeling from Mike calling Darius 'Brother."

"As soon as I find someone to take my place as Joe's scout, I can live in the area full time and do more jobs with you."

Mike went on to explain that it would take some time to find the right person that Joe was comfortable with, "Plus, I'd probably be with them their first time or two out to make sure they know how to go about certain things."

Marcus wasn't pleased.

Chapter Twenty:

Late February 2011

The winter was worse than years before. The organization brought on a new scout who was simply known as Dave. Eventually, Mike moved to live in northern Kentucky full time and would often join the brothers on their jobs. For months, the brothers did their weekly lists with no issues and were always ahead of schedule with the money drops. The higher ups in the organization took notice. They used the money to each get their own cars for personal use. They made sure to ask permission to use their aliases on the purchases and it was granted. They also learned much more about the organization and who their powerful enemies were, other than the FBI, of course.

One early morning, the brothers and Mike received texts to meet Liam in the bustling Benedict Park at noon.

The weather was much warmer that day, and food trucks were lined up for those working in the buildings surrounding the park to grab a quick bite during their lunch hour. The four men found each other after ordering their own lunches and grabbed a table in a less populated area.

"Well, Marc," Liam started as he unwrapped a freshly made burrito, "Now's the moment you've been chompin' at the bit for."

"Oh?"

Liam nodded and gestured for him to guess.

Marcus wasn't about to play a guessing game with the egotistical prick and took a large bite of his taco to avoid talking anymore.

"You're no fun, you know that?" Liam asked before continuing, "I need help with something."

Liam pulled out a large black envelope for the others to look at while he ate.

Darius asked, "The son?" What did he do?" after he finished reading the dossier on Mannix O'Connell's eldest son, Robbie.

"I don't know and I don't ask questions. The problem is that he's protected and difficult to get to," Liam explained, looking around to make sure no one is listening.

Mike asked, "Do you have a plan yet?"

Liam smiled, "I'm all ears for suggestions, fellas."

Mid-March 2011

Robbie O'Connell slid into the back seat of a black town car, idling in its usual spot in the parking garage next to the elevator. His weekly meeting ended at its usual time, and he was headed home to change before meeting a date for dinner. He flirted with his date over text while his driver navigated the car through the twists and turns of the five-story parking structure. Robbie's bodyguard sat in the passenger seat and noticed a car pull out behind them after they reached the second level.

"You're too paranoid, my good man," Robbie chided, jokingly.

"I'm paid to be paranoid, Sir."

Robbie barely looked up from his phone to smile at his father's employee when he said, "Your boss is too paranoid. Hey, you gotta see this." He leaned up to show a picture his date sent of herself in lingerie.

The driver started to inch out of the garage when a car on the road stopped in front of him, blocking the car from moving forward. The windows on the passenger side of the car blocking them were down, and loud pops rang out. Robbie's driver tried to put the car in reverse but the vehicle behind him made it impossible. They were trapped. His bodyguard opened his car door to get a clean shot of one of the passengers in the car on the road. He was brought down before he could squeeze a shot off with a bullet to the back of his head from Liam's gun in the car that blocked them from the rear.

Marcus, from his position in the backseat of their stolen car on the road, continued firing into the windshield until he was satisfied the driver was taken care of. Mike rushed to the back door behind the driver as Liam opened the back passenger door and they both unloaded their guns into Robbie. While Mike readied a Molotov cocktail to toss into the stolen car he and Liam had been in, Liam grabbed Robbie, who was still holding his white pearl-handled six shooter, out of the car and dumped him on the ground. Robbie was knocking on death's door when he tried to get a shot off. Liam placed his foot over the dying man's hand and relieved him of his gun. Robbie was rolled over and a coin fell out of his pocket, rolling under the car and away, hitting Marcus in the foot as he got out of the car to yell it was time to go. The coin had the O'Connell family crest on it and Marcus decided to pocket it.

Liam was pleased to see that in a second holster, an identical white pearl-handled six shooter waited for him to take and join its twin.

He heard Marcus yell, "Let's go!" and followed Mike, after snagging a photo of the body, to the car Darius and Marcus waited in. Once they were out of the city limits, the four men took off their gloves and masks and abandoned the stolen car on a quiet road. Mike tossed the last Molotov cocktail in the car, and they split up. Liam and Mike headed to Bandoni's estate, and the Tye Brothers were given a location to meet back up with them after Bandoni handed over payment.

Darius and Marcus drove to the abandoned farm where they were supposed to meet Liam and Mike. They turned down a familiar stretch of road and couldn't believe their eyes.

"Marc? Do you recognize that silo?" Darius asked his younger brother.

"Are we really looking at the Smither's Farm right now?"

Darius didn't say a word. Instead, he accelerated the car up the road until he was in front of the house he had dreamed of returning to.

Marcus looked at the house and back at Darius. "Is that?"

Darius answered, "Yep."

They turned down the driveway of their childhood home and stopped to look around.

Memories came flooding back over both of them. Darius stepped up onto the porch and heard the weathered wood cry with each step. Marcus followed behind and headed over toward the window missing its glass. Only tiny bits of shards remained on the ground. A family of raccoons skittered through holes in the walls to hide.

Marcus looked over at Darius and said, "We're scaring the poor homeowners."

Darius refused to walk inside the house. Instead, he turned and sat on the porch steps. Marcus followed suit, feeling compelled to join his brother. He had some memories of his parents and their childhood before the accident, but he knew his brother was impacted by many more.

"The place never looked better, huh?"

Darius scoffed, "I wanted to come back here and start the farm back up."

Marcus nodded, "I know. I remember the plan."

"It's not the plan anymore, Bud." Darius swallowed and stood back up. "We better head back to the meeting place."

"Good work guys, thank you," Liam said, getting out of the car with a duffel bag of cash.

Marcus asked, "What's up with the ghost town?"

"Well, according to Joe, about fifteen years ago or so, there was a town just down the highway." Liam stopped to look around, and then pointed, "In that direction. There was nothing but farms out here. So, people were moving out, and no one was moving in. Then, a developer started buying up the land and then went bankrupt."

Mike chimed in, pointing at the silo, "That's kinda sad. It looks like people really only come out here to fuck around and burn shit."

"Yeah, there's a church down that way that's partially gutted. It actually creeps me out," Liam admitted.

"So we got paid?" Darius asked curtly to change the subject.

Liam nodded, "Yessir!"

Darius gestured toward his brother, and Liam tossed the bag to him. Marcus peeked inside to see it was full of money. He tried to mask his surprise at the sheer volume of bills. It was more than they had ever pulled in before.

Later that evening, Mike visited the apartment with a six-pack of Guinness to celebrate their first hit together. Darius had been noticeably withdrawn during the meet-up and his friend wanted to cheer him up. Marcus wasn't a fan of the dark brew and volunteered to make a run for more beer and snacks leaving his brother and Mike alone.

"I thought we'd kill some more Irish tonight?" Mike said, pouring the dark ruby red stout.

After some time, Darius gave in to his friend's prodding. They sat on the balcony, in the cool evening air. Darius told Mike about how they realized where they were earlier today for the meeting. He went on to talk a little bit more about their sad and fearful childhood.

Mike listened and when Darius went silent again, he decided to approach his friend with an idea they used to talk about in the group home where they first met.

"I have a proposal that may cheer you up."

"What's up?"

Mike's eyes gleamed with excitement as he shared his plans of moving out west and starting a charter fishing company. He had been saving up a substantial amount of money, and his childhood dream was never far from his thoughts.

"I don't think Marc is up for another change, man."

"Dude, he's a grown man. If he wants to stay here and keep working for the family he can. You don't have to live together the rest of your lives."

Darius worried that if he wasn't there to help Marcus, his brother would become a nationally known serial killer. There was no way to explain that to Mike. No one could know.

"Wouldn't you like to change the direction of this merry-go-round?" Mike began, "To run a legitimate business you built? We have the money. We'll hire people to run the boats and be the brains behind the operation."

"Fishing?" Darius asked, his voice laced with doubt.

"I'm tired of just surviving brother, and I know you are too. Let's live for once, and have something more, I don't know...normal." Mike could feel Darius was considering the idea and he decided to double down. "Instead of looking over our shoulders, we could find wives, settle down, have barbecues..."

They both turned to hear Marcus in the kitchen.

In a whisper, Mike skipped to the final thing he wanted to say to Darius, "You deserve more, my friend. It's time to forge a new path for yourself."

Darius looked out to the brightly lit park below them and knew his friend was right, but his brother could not be left to his own devices. He ran his fingers through his hair as he realized he was his brother's keeper, but he didn't want to let Mike down, either.

"What's your time frame to pull the trigger on this venture?" Darius finally asked, deciding there was no harm in living in the fantasy for a little while.

Mike took a moment to consider before answering, "Next year, at the earliest."

Darius nodded and smiled and then he responded firmly, "He can't know," just as Marcus came into view walking towards the sliding glass door separating him from his brother.

"You guys wanna go to the Dollhouse tonight?" Marcus asked as he joined the others on the balcony.

"Not in the mood, Bud," Darius answered.

Mike scratched his head and with a sheepish grin admitted that he did, but was too tired.

"I was just telling Mike about our old house."

Marcus smiled, "Oh, I was wondering why you guys looked so serious."

Darius excused himself to use the bathroom and Marcus took his seat outside.

"So, did you ever find out the name of that guy?" he asked Mike after a few seconds of silence.

"What guy?" Mike asked, confused.

"The guy that murdered your dad."

Mike was taken aback, "Oh, um, actually, I haven't thought about that, like, ever," he stammered.

Marcus was pleased that Mike was visibly knocked off guard, "You never looked into it?"

Darius rejoined them, "Look into what?" he asked, leaning on the balcony's railing.

Marcus gave Mike a look to encourage him to speak, "Um, my dad's death," he answered, staring at the park.

Darius was incensed and glared at his brother.

Marcus kept the smile on his face, "Well, I'm going out for a bit. See ya," he announced, and he walked back through the apartment and left through the front door.

Darius cleared his throat, "You okay?"

Mike looked up at his friend who continued to stand rather than take the vacated chair, "Yeah," he started, "I'm just kinda pissed."

"Look, Marc doesn't do well socially. He didn't mean-"

"Oh, no," Mike interrupted, "Not at Marc. I'm pissed at myself for not looking."

***

The evening turned into morning. Darius woke up to the sound of his brother returning home. He picked up his phone to see what time it was. 4:13 AM.

"Shit," he said under his breath as he ripped the covers off and ran to confront his brother wearing only his boxer briefs.

"Please tell me you didn't do anything to the chicks at the club. Please!" He demanded, pushing his way into his brother's room before Marcus could close the door.

"The fuck?" Marcus said backing up into his room, surprised by his brother.

"If you did, we have to leave," Darius continued.

"I didn't go to the club!" Marcus snapped.

Darius stood there feeling anger towards his brother. "Where did you go?" he asked, pointedly.

Marcus started to get undressed for bed when he said, "For a drive."

"I thought you went to the Dollhouse."

Marcus sighed, "Nope," he said as he got into bed.

Darius gave up and went back to his room. Marcus made it very clear he was done talking, but Darius was determined to get answers to his questions. He resolved to wait until later to get them. Brother's Keeper, indeed. Darius knew the moods of his brother better than his own. He planned to wait until the moment presented itself.

***

It was a lazy day. Something they referred to as, "A No Bones Day." They relaxed and tried to do as little as possible. Evening rolled around and Darius started to prepare dinner.

"Hey Marc, Mike said to turn on channel 5 news," Darius reported the text from the kitchen while he continued cooking his new favorite meal, stir fry.

Marcus came in from enjoying a beer on the balcony and grabbed the remote.

"He said that there's gonna be a story on the O'Connell hit," Darius said, reading another text and simultaneously plating the food.

"Man, I wished we had seen the breaking news yesterday. It's a commercial now, do you want me to pause it when the news comes back on?"

Darius walked over to the couch with the plates, "Nah. Dinner's served."

"Oh, dinner and a show," Marcus quipped.

And now, more information is in on that stunning and frightening event that took place at a parking garage downtown yesterday evening. The three men killed have been identified as Derek Montrose, 37. Jered Young, 45, and Robert O'Connell, 34.

Four suspects ambushed the vehicle carrying the victims, concealing their identities and the two vehicles driven by the suspects were both stolen. Due to the identity of the victims, there is concern that this may be the beginning of a rival gang war and innocent bystanders will be caught in the middle.

Darius got up to retrieve the drinks he forgot about as the newscast continued to a different anchor behind the desk.

In other public safety news, a woman was found hanged in the woods of New Albany, Indiana this afternoon -

Marcus muted the TV and continued eating while Darius stood still with cans of soda in his hands, staring at him.

Chapter Twenty-One:

The gang war predicted by the local evening news was slow to start. The Bandoni Family owned a few civil servants who didn't appreciate the low pay they received from the government. Mannix O'Connell knew his son was murdered on Bandoni's order, but he had to be careful how he proceeded. Evidence went missing from that day, so he knew justice was not going to be on his side. He wanted to hit the smug Italian with everything he had. Patience was one thing Mannix knew was his greatest strength. In the meantime, he mourned his son and kept his surviving relatives closer. He chose to gather information, stay quiet, add to the security at all of his properties, and wait. Mannix felt it in his Irish soul that Bandoni's day was going to come. He just hoped he'd be alive to see the day.

***

Several weeks passed since the hit, and Darius was busy making sure Marcus didn't get caught for his latest excursion. They continued their routine in collecting and visited The Dollhouse regularly. Mike showed up one day with a gift for the brothers, matching knives engraved with their initials.

"What the hell is this for, man?" Darius said, after he opened his.

"I'm the happiest I've ever been and it's all because of you guys," Mike shyly admitted.

Marcus awkwardly thanked Mike for the gift. He really liked the knife and rarely received gifts. Darius playfully slugged Mike in the arm.

"This is awesome, man, thank you!"

"You're welcome, brother. Thank you." Mike responded to his best friend.

Hearing Mike call Darius by the term of endearment, again, made Marcus immediately want to plunge the knife into Mike's throat.

"Also guys, I just spoke to Jobusch, and he's got an urgent job for us."

Darius glanced at Marcus, then back at Mike, his interest was piqued.

"What kind of job?" he asked.

"The Liquidate All Assets kind of job," Mike began, "Alright, there's this guy named Seamus McDowell who owns a warehouse on the edge of town. It's filled with valuable possessions belonging to the O'Connell family. Joe wants us to burn it to the ground like the bakery."

Darius asked, "When does he need it done?"

"Tonight. We got intel that it will be guarded but not heavily. We just have to stroll in, make some noise, and stroll out. Then, collect some much-needed money." Mike raised his eyebrows at Darius with the last thing he said, and Marcus caught it.

"Sounds too easy and I don't trust it. We need more time to plan," Marcus stated flatly.

Darius nodded in agreement. "We'll scope it out beforehand."

"It just has to be done tonight," Mike implored.

The three men headed down toward the warehouse to look around. There was a truck out front with men loading several crates inside.

Marcus turned to Mike, "What exactly are these valuable O'Connell possessions?"

"Drugs and weapons, boys."

The three men watched from a safe distance.

"Should we liquidate around the same time as before?" Darius asked.

"Absolutely. It'll give us time to get what we need now that we've seen the size of the building." Mike responded as Darius pulled onto a road and headed back into town.

They grabbed a quick bite to eat and then went to a hardware store. Darius watched as an employee of the store nodded at Marcus in recognition.

"You know that guy?" he asked his brother.

"Not personally," was all Marcus said.

They each carried purchases to different cashiers. Marcus bought the gas cans, and Mike bought the duct tape. Darius went back outside to wait in the car.

Before heading home, Darius pulled into a gas station and filled the gas cans Marcus bought while Mike went in for some cheap beer in glass bottles.

The drive back to the warehouse was quick with no other cars on the road. Darius killed the headlights and put it in neutral once he got closer to the back of the seemingly vacant warehouse.

"Okay, we go in the front and secure it first, then torch it and get to the car, and after that, we celebrate boys," Mike reminded the brothers.

The three men walked towards the building as quickly as possible in a wide arc on either side. Marcus on the left and Mike stayed with Darius on the right.

Two guards stood out in front of the building holding semi-automatics. They were smoking cigarettes, relaxed. They never had a chance. Marcus nodded to Darius as they were attaching silencers to their barrels and within the next second, they both squeezed off muted shots. The guards dropped. The three men continued walking swiftly in a crouched position to enter the front. Marcus opened a backpack with one of the gas cans in it and started to pour gasoline on the crates.

Darius and Mike headed toward the back when two more guards they did not expect, spotted them.

"Hey, who are you guys?" One yelled out to them.

The other looked back to the front and saw the body of one of the guards from the front and yelled, "Intruders!" as he dove for cover.

Gunfire erupted in the warehouse. Mike and Darius jumped in opposite directions and scurried behind crates to take cover.

Darius couldn't see where either of them had gone. Marcus already set fire to the crates in an attempt to draw the other guards to him, and the smoke was starting to dull visibility.

"Cover me," Mike said to Darius when he saw one of the guards turn back to the front. Darius fired in the direction where Mike pointed and then heard a few shots fired off, followed by silence.

Darius called out, "Marcus?"

Marcus replied, "Yeah, it's me. Saving your ass."

Marcus had taken care of the guard that came towards him with ease. As he tracked the other one, he watched as Mike readied himself to take a clear shot of the other guard occupied by Darius' position. Ever the opportunist, Marcus saw a solution to his problem and made a quick decision. He timed his shot beautifully.

Darius looked over at Mike just as the smoke rolled thicker in between them.

Marcus quickly moved to where his brother stood, "Where's Mike?"

Darius, still looking where Mike once stood, yelled, "Mike? You okay?"

Mike did not answer.

"Dari! The fire! Go out the back door and get the car. I'll look for Mike."

"I see him!" Darius yelled, rushing to the spot where he saw his friend. Mike laid on the ground with blood coming out of his neck. He was trying desperately to speak, but the bullet did too much damage.

"No, no, no, no, no. You can't be hit. C'mon, man. Mike!" Darius pleaded, trying to pull Mike up.

Marcus came up behind his brother, "Dari, go out the back and get the car. I'll grab him. Go!" Marcus shoved Darius away from Mike. His brother nodded and started running to the back of the warehouse.

Marcus bent low to Mike's ear, "The name of the man who killed your dad was Colby Tye. He was our father, and Darius knew all along," he whispered cruelly. Marcus sat back to view Mike's face as he made sputtering sounds.

"Would you look at that? Fatal neck wound? Like father, like son, eh? Oh, and thanks for the gift. My brother and I will cherish them. Darius is my brother. Mine. Do you understand? I need you to know why I put this bullet in you."

He continued talking as he placed one bag of Molotov cocktails near Mike's head and carried the other to the backdoor, "Well, hopefully you're dead before the fire gets ya."

He took one, lit it, and placed it next to the bag before racing out to intercept Darius from running back in.

"Dari, he's dead," Marcus said as he wrapped his arms around his brother to keep him from running back into the building after he parked the car. Seconds later, they felt the heat from the explosion near the door and a second explosion from somewhere in the middle where they knew Mike was.

Marcus had Mike's blood on him as he drove back to their apartment. He could see it on the right side of his neck and jaw every time he glanced in the rear-view mirror. The acrid smoke odor lingered on their clothing. Marcus looked over at Darius who alternated between sobbing one minute and staring silently the next.

***

"How the hell did this happen!" Mannix O'Connell yelled at his right-hand man, Bryan "Sully" Sullivan.

"We're not sure how, Sir," Sully began to answer, "We feel confident it's Bandoni again, but-"

"But no evidence, right?" Mannix interrupted.

Sully scratched at the stubble on his pock-marked face. With his short red tuffs of hair around his male pattern baldness, and a scar that went from his left eyebrow across the bridge of his nose and ended on his right cheek, Sully resembled an evil leprechaun.

"Is it the same crew that killed my Robbie?" The Irishman asked.

"We believe it is, although they are down a man. We just received word that there were five bodies recovered and we only had four men in there at the time."

"Good. I hope he suffered," Mannix snapped. "Did we lose everything?"

"We did, Sir."

Mannix O'Connell looked up at his trusted employee and admitted, "I'm getting too old for this shit."

Sully sighed, "Should we retaliate this time?"

"It's retribution I want, Sully. Retaliating is just going to get more O'Connell's killed."

***

"I should've been with you guys," Liam Stacey said to Marcus when he joined him at the Smither's farm the day after Mike's death.

"Dari barely eats. I've never seen him like this," Marcus volunteered.

"Mike was a great guy. The organization loved him."

Marcus smirked, "I guess you guys didn't know he was planning on leaving, huh?"

Liam was surprised and he did not like surprises, "What the fuck do you mean?" he asked.

"He was trying to convince my brother to leave and create their own business," Marcus said, nonchalantly.

"What kind of business?" Liam asked.

"Some childhood pipe dream he had, "Marcus started, "Revolved around fishing or something."

"Oh," Liam relaxed and then laughed, "He was a nice guy. It's a shame, really."

Marcus didn't offer any emotion or agreement. "So," he started, "Is Bandoni happy with what we accomplished otherwise?"

"Yep," Liam reached into his car for a bag of money, "You took out four guys and severely crippled their business. This bag is heavy. Plus, Mike's portion is in there. Maybe that can bring some solace to your brother."

Liam left moments later, and Marcus decided to go for a drive around the roads he knew as a child. He didn't have much memory of the area, but Darius told him a lot about their time here the night after Robbie O'Connell's hit. Marcus found himself in front of the church. The once beautiful stained-glass windows had huge holes from rocks thrown in the years past. He noticed scorch marks from a fire. He assumed the fire department arrived quick enough to save the building. The trees and vegetation surrounding the church seemed to protect the structure. He made his way inside to look around. The wood cried under his feet, and he desperately wanted to remember or at least feel something about the area. Marcus saw how their childhood home affected Darius, but it did nothing for him. After a few more moments of exploration, Marcus walked back outside and felt drawn to an area of tall grass, until he came upon the old well.

Marcus was finally struck by a memory of his father's angry voice, *"God damnit! I said be careful. You fall in that well and no one will ever find you,"* and he instinctively stepped back from the well, uncomfortable with the feeling of anxiety he got standing there. Marcus promptly walked away and back to his car.

***

Detective Diego Muñoz looked over the emailed images of the latest Tree Girl victim from Indiana. The printed report had been faxed hours earlier. He sat at his desk comparing the notes on the report to the images. With a huge sigh, Diego stood up to face his link analysis map and placed a red pin in the small river town on the southern border of Indiana.

"So, we're moving north, are we?" he said to himself.

Diego went back to his desk and sent all of the new case information to Dr. Grace Thompkins, the medical examiner he met in Kentucky nearly a year ago. Satisfied that there was little else he could do but wait, he left his desk for more coffee and to walk around. If he sat for too long, his stiff knee would get worse. After he made his way back to his desk, he saw the doctor's response.

Forgive me if you've already done this, but have you considered looking at cases where female victims were found with rope around their neck indoors? Hanged or otherwise? Our killer started somewhere. His first victims may not all be, "Tree" girls.

Warmest Regards,
Grace

Knowing he'd have to look at cases state-by-state, he mumbled to himself, "No amount of coffee is going to help." Diego went straight to work, looking for any female victims in Tennessee that met the criteria in the past decade.

Chapter Twenty-Two

Weeks went by and the days began to blur for Darius. He drank alone on the balcony more and rarely went out, unless he was working. He felt comfort in his usual routine of getting lists, collecting, reporting, and getting paid. Marcus would try to engage him with their favorite card games.

One night, he had had enough of his brother's sullenness and practically dragged Darius to the Dollhouse.

"Is this place looking shittier than usual?" Darius asked, as they sat at a table near the back.

"I don't know. Maybe," he said as he looked around, "You know I have noticed I'm not seeing some of the girls I liked anymore."

"You didn't kill 'em did you?" Darius said flatly, without looking at his brother.

Marcus chose to ignore his brother's question. They spent the next hour watching the dancers, and Marcus paid for his brother to get a lap dance from a very eager dancer.

Marlon walked through the club and saw Marcus by himself. He wasn't particularly fond of the scary man, but Marlon was at a crossroads and needed help.

"How's it going tonight?" he asked, taking the seat Darius vacated.

Marcus gave a genuine smile to one of the few people he didn't mind being around, "Good and you?"

Marlon sighed, "Not great."

"Oh. Why's that?"

Marlon gave a light chuckle and said with a nervous smile, "I'm losing my business. I have to do a bunch of repairs and still pay my girls. Well, the girls I have left, and I really don't have enough money."

Marcus remained silent. Marlon was trying to gather the nerve to ask for a favor but failed to find the words. He stared at the table in a rare moment of utter speechlessness.

Marcus sat thoughtfully for a moment when he suddenly smiled, "I think I have an idea that will make everybody happy."

Marlon was still nervous but welcomed a fresh solution, "What's your idea?"

Darius made his way back to the table, interrupting the conversation.

"That was quick," Marcus said wryly.

"Fuck you," Darius said, grabbing a chair from a nearby table and setting it down between his brother and Marlon.

Marcus turned back to Marlon and continued what he was saying, "You let me and Dari set up underground poker games in that basement of yours and we'll front you 50 grand."

"Wait. What?" Darius asked, confused.

"Seriously?" Marlon asked, staring in disbelief at the younger Tye brother.

Marcus nodded, "You give us complete access to that basement. We'll use our own money to set it up. You give the two of us free drinks and food. You'll get zero profits from whatever we make so don't ask, but you," Marcus made a point to look at his brother, "and all of your employees will be under our protection. Once your Dollhouse starts making a profit again, we'll collect our 50 G's plus interest. Does that sound like a deal?" he asked, looking back to Marlon again.

Darius remained quiet, completely transfixed.

Marlon was short-sighted with relief as he shook Marcus' hand with a big smile. "My girls are off limits and free food and drinks are only for you two, not just anyone who comes to play poker and it's a deal."

Marcus nodded in understanding. "The only access to the girls we require is as paying customers, like always. We won't make you feed anyone who comes to join a game. We will keep your establishment separate from our business except for what we've already agreed to. Now, are we all in agreement on terms?" Marcus asked.

"I can live with that," Marlon admitted. He left to let his bartender and wait staff know to no longer charge the Tye Brothers for drinks and food.

"What happened? Couldn't get it up for Coco?" Marcus chided his brother when they were alone again.

Darius gave a half smile and snickered, "I appreciate what you're trying to do, but she ain't my type."

"Funny. I thought Coco was everybody's type," Marcus quipped while taking a drink.

"She liked the sound of her own voice, and that breath was rank."

Marcus choked on his beer giving his brother an opportunity.

"How long have you been thinking about this underground poker shit?" Darius asked, changing the subject.

"Since the day we walked into his office."

"Oh, wow!" Darius exclaimed, blindsided that his brother kept it from him for nearly a year and a half.

"I like it here," Marcus said thoughtfully, "Kentucky, not just this strip club."

Darius laughed as the waitress brought over two more beers wearing little more than a smile.

"It is the longest we've stayed in one place." Darius admitted.

"This underground poker and casino will bring in a lot of money, Dari."

"Oh, it's a casino, now, too?"

Marcus gave his brother a sheepish grin, "It always was. We own Marlon now. I'll determine his interest rate on how fast he realizes that. We're gonna do whatever the fuck we want."

"For fifty grand up front, this better make us money."

"We can afford it; besides I have another plan if we need it. You and I are going into business together, and this is going to be better than some fantasy fishing bullshit."

"What the fuck did you just say?" Darius demanded.

Marcus noticed his morose brother lost the smile he had just found. "Your little secret charter fishing business?"

"How?" Darius started, "That was months ago," he said, defensively, searching his memory of that day.

"When were you going to tell me? While you were packing your fucking bags? 'See ya, Marc. Mike's my brother now."

"Oh, fuck this," Darius said, as he got up and walked out of the club. He had to get away from his brother. A brother that could not comprehend grief. A brother who almost had him feeling better about life before dropping a bomb.

Marcus chugged his beer and followed his brother out into the parking lot.

"I know Mike didn't tell you!" Darius yelled, as he continued to the car, feeling his brother close the space between them.

"Nah, your boyfriend wouldn't betray you. Oh! Hey, maybe that's why Coco's not really your type?" Marcus goaded.

Darius turned and grabbed his brother. With fists full of Marcus' shirt, Darius slammed him against the exterior of the Dollhouse.

"You don't have a clue what you're talking about," Darius said through gritted teeth.

Marcus remained calm when he said, "Enlighten me, brother."

"You overheard," Darius verbalized his realization.

He let go of his brother and stood back. "That night, you went to get beer. How long were you listening before you let us know you were home?"

Marcus straightened up and smoothed his shirt, "Long enough."

Darius stared off into the distance, deep in thought.

"Then, you brought up Mike's dad, why?" he finally asked.

"I was toying with the idea of telling him the truth," Marcus admitted flatly.

"Jesus Christ!" Darius said, still trying to remember the sequence of events that night, "Then, you left. I thought you came here, but..." The next realization hit harder. "Holy shit, is that why you did that chick in Indiana? Because you got your feelings hurt? Fuck me!" Darius paced in the empty parking lot.

Marcus leaned on the building and waited for his brother to calm down.

Eventually Darius went over to their SUV and sat on the bumper. He put his head in his hands and gave a heavy sigh, "You wanna know what the craziest thing about this is?" he started to ask, "I was never even going to do the fishing thing with Mike. I don't want to stop doing this with you."

Marcus instantly let go of the anger he had held since that day. "Really?"

"Yeah, really." Darius looked up at his brother, "Just ask me about shit before flying off the handle like that again, okay?"

Marcus nodded and said, "Okay. I want to get home and plan out our new venture. We're gonna need new IDs and Marlon has to keep his mouth shut. Can we stop for ice cream on the way?"

"The Devil may hold the cards, but it's up to us to play the game."

-Lilith Saintcrow
Working for the Devil

Chapter Twenty-Three

Winter 2014

The two and a half years that followed their impromptu agreement with Marlon flew by. The brothers continued their routine for collecting from businesses under the organization's protection and took on any side jobs the family gave them.

Marcus continued his habit of writing in his journal about their jobs and noted how to improve. He recorded anything he thought was important enough to remember. Darius found that his role of brother's keeper was easier now that they were busy every single day with a multitude of important things. He also noticed that as long as Marcus was busy and positive, he didn't sneak out for any extra-curriculars, and the "Tree Girl Killer's" cases were getting colder.

The basement renovations of the Dollhouse took longer than expected and cost more than the brothers estimated. Marcus set his contingency plan into action. He figured he and Darius could capitalize on the reputation they had with the family of being dependable and trustworthy foot soldiers. He had Darius mention to the more lucrative businesses that dues would be going up soon and was instructed to act like he was doing them a favor with the heads-up.

The following month, those businesses were overcharged without the knowledge of the family, between $500-$1,000, which the brothers took for themselves to put into the casino without touching any more of their own personal funds. After a few months, Darius would claim the family changed their mind and collect the original dues from those businesses and scam another group. He would come across as empathetic and heroic to the very people he victimized, honing his skills as a con man.

Once the gambling den took off, the brothers were not short on success, and they managed to amass a staggering 1.5 million dollars in profit with no sign of it slowing down. Amidst their rise of financial success, the Tye Brothers knew all too well that unwanted attention would threaten their newfound wealth. They set up a system to get to the casino through Marlon's Dollhouse and every player was properly intimidated to keep their mouth shut.

Everyone knew the reputation of the Tye Brothers. Except one poor loser who didn't want to part ways with five grand, mentioned it would be a shame if Bandoni found out about the casino. He was found in the river by fishermen a few days later, slit from neck to scrotum with rocks stuffed into his chest cavity.

Additionally, the brothers maintained their other clandestine operation of randomly and discreetly charging businesses extra fees during their collections for Buscemi. They didn't need the extra cash, but they got a nostalgic adrenaline rush from it that they hadn't felt since they were in Tennessee.

With their hidden schemes and strategic moves, the Tye Brothers were able to maintain a tight, anonymous grip on their flourishing empire for some time. Their ability to keep their gambling business under wraps from Joe Buscemi, coupled with the extra funds they siphoned from their unsuspecting bosses, gave them the upper hand in the cutthroat world of gambling. As their wealth continued to soar, so did their ambitions. The brothers dreamt of expanding their operations even further, envisioning a future where their gambling empire would reign supreme, all while keeping their secrets locked away, hidden from prying eyes.

Chapter Twenty-Four

Philip Elio owned and managed a successful restaurant in the historic section of downtown, where most buildings were turned into eateries and high-end clothing shops. The Cucina Italia specialized in authentic Italian dishes, specifically, Sicilian. It was Joe Buscemi's favorite place to dine. After the restaurant became successful, Buscemi offered protection at a discounted price because he was a regular. Eventually, the Cucina Italia found its way to the list of new places for Marcus and Darius to collect from. When they would come for the dues, Philip was usually out of the restaurant, but he made sure to have the money in an envelope ready to hand over to them by his kitchen manager.

"Cucina Italia's the last place, right?" Darius asked, referring to the list of businesses they had to collect that day before heading to the Dollhouse.

"Ah, yes, the Italian coochie," Marcus answered with the sense of humor of a fourteen-year-old boy. His brother laughed just before Marcus added, "I wouldn't mind a little Italian coochie from that hostess."

"Dude, she looked barely legal," Darius admonished. He was becoming uncomfortable talking about women with his brother, and It was bad enough working in the basement of a strip club. Darius found himself constantly doing inventory on Marlon's dancers. He couldn't trust the word Marcus gave to protect them. It wasn't that he cared about the dancers, he only cared about his brother getting caught.

"You're no fun," Marcus retorted, his good mood unaffected by his wet blanket of a brother.

Philip stood behind the bar to wait for Joe Buscemi's collectors. He chose to meet the men who told his kitchen manager that the dues would be going up. Something wasn't sitting right with the message relayed to him and, although he saw the man in his establishment a few times since, Philip didn't want to involve Mr. Buscemi until he had his facts straight. The collectors were scary and Philip was nervous, but his livelihood and restaurant were precious to him. He had his usual dues of $2K in an envelope under the bar while he busied himself helping the bartender prepare it for when they opened.

The Tye Brothers parked in back and knocked on the kitchen door to be let in. The kitchen manager smiled at the brothers and informed them that the owner was in front of the restaurant waiting to finally meet them.

Philip glanced up when he saw two men emerge from the kitchen and walk toward him. He knew who they were, and seeing the scar on one of their faces confirmed it.

"I have the money right here," Philip said, as he reached under the bar. Marcus instinctively put his hand on the grip of his gun.

Philip caught the motion and quickly said, "I abhor violence, my friend," as he tossed the bag of dues onto the bar in front of Darius.

"It smells amazing in here," Darius offered to keep the nerves calm.

Philip's eyes didn't leave Marcus' hand as he thanked the other brother for the compliment.

"$3,500 right?" Darius asked.

Philip's eyes flew to Darius when he countered, "Jobusch and I agreed to $2,000."

"We left a message with your kitchen guy about the dues. They went up," Marcus said, keeping his hand on his gun.

Darius noticed the restaurant's owner referred to Joe Buscemi as Jobusch, and started to think this wasn't the right place to scam. Before he could squash it, Philip raised his hands and asked for a few minutes to get the rest of the money from his safe.

He locked the door to his office and reached for the phone. He watched the feed of his security cameras, focusing on the brothers waiting at the bar.

"Joe, it's Phil, from Cucina," he said into the receiver.

"Hey Phil, how's business going?"

"Business is great. I wanted to invite you for a special dinner tonight at my place. I'd like the opportunity to talk with you about something important. On the house, of course."

Ecstatic, Joe responded, "Delizioso, my friend! I accept!"

"Great, I'll have your favorite table reserved. Bring your beautiful bride. Tonight at 6pm?" Philip asked as he shut the door to his safe and palmed the extra $1500.

"She'll be happy to join me. Six, it is!" Joe Buscemi confirmed.

Philip handed the money to Darius and escorted them out of the back. He thought to inform his kitchen manager of the special meal to be prepared for their guest that evening, when he noticed Darius put the extra cash in his pocket rather than with the rest of the dues.

Later that evening the bold fragrance of tomatoes, onions, garlic, basil, and pesto, surrounded by undertones of rosemary, oregano, and olive oil wafted throughout the downtown streetscape of the Cucina Italia. Failure to secure a reservation on a Friday or Saturday night would have you waiting at the bar for close to an hour. Business was very good for Philip Elio and he was one of the very few businesses beloved by the organization that protected it.

Joe Buscemi and his wife, Mazie, arrived and were immediately seated in his reserved corner booth. Philip took a deep breath and made his way to greet one of the most respected members of the Bandoni crime syndicate. If he did authorize the increase in dues, Philip was prepared to accept that.

"Philip! I see business is doing well," Joe said as he saw him approach.

Philip clasped his hands behind his back. "Yes, indeed. I have fresh Arancini as an appetizer for you," he said as the server placed a warm plate of the fried risotto in front of the couple.

Joe smiled and nodded when the waiter waited for permission to pour the accompanying wine.

Philip continued, "In a few moments, you will enjoy small bowls of Ribollita followed by the main course of Pasta alla Norma and if you still have room, my pastry chef's cannoli are simply to die for."

Joe and Mazie were over the moon with their dinner plans and impressed by the treatment and effort Philip made for them.

"This meal sounds amazing, Phil. Thank you."

"My pleasure and, if you don't mind, may we talk later? Perhaps over those cannoli?"

"Of course. Better conversations are had over a full belly, if you ask me."

"Yes, Sir. I agree."

After all of the dinner dishes had been cleared from the table, Philip walked up with a beautiful ornate carafe of Grappa, along with two tulip shaped glasses. His server placed a plate of two large cannoli with chopped pistachios sprinkled on top.

"Thank you, Lorenzo," Philip said to his server, "I'll pour for our guests. You may go."

"Uh, Lorenzo," Joe called out, "would you bring an extra glass so that your boss may enjoy this with us?"

The waiter smiled and nodded and hurried off to fetch another beautiful piece of stemware.

"Now, what's on your mind?" Joe Buscemi asked.

Philip nervously smiled, "I just wanted to confirm with you the amount of dues we agreed on."

Joe Buscemi leaned forward as the smile faded from his face, "This is about your dues?"

"Have they increased?" Philip asked bluntly.

Joe was confused, "No. Care to tell me why you believe they have?"

Philip took a breath and a sip of his Grappa before explaining how a month ago, his kitchen manager was given the message of an increase. Before he could continue, Joe interrupted.

"A month ago, you were told this was going to happen?"

"Yes, Sir."

"And you didn't call me? Hell, you've seen me in here a handful of times. Why did you wait until now?"

"Forgive me, Joe, um, Mr. Buscemi, it's just that, since I was given the information secondhand, I thought it wise to make sure of it for myself before bothering you," Philip said, feeling his face become flushed.

"No. I can respect that. In fact, thank you for considering that my time is not to be wasted," Joe said to calm his friend, "Now, please, continue your story."

Philip explained how the brothers not only demanded an extra fifteen hundred, but that it was not placed in the envelope with the rest of the dues.

Joe smiled at Philip, "You gave them the extra money before or after you called me today?"

"After, Sir. I thought it was best to give them what they wanted and talk with you face to face as soon as possible."

"Nico!" Joe summoned one of his guards from a nearby table. As Nico made his way over to his boss, Joe counted out $3,500 from the large billfold he carried his jacket.

"I will fix this," Joe started, as he handed the cash to Philip. "For your trouble. No dues this month. Plus, the $1500 that my collectors clearly stole from you."

"Thank you," Joe said, looking at the money in astonishment. "I will leave you to enjoy the rest of your dessert. Good evening." He bowed his head towards Mazie before taking his leave.

"Can you tell me, where are Darius and Marcus Tye right now?" Joe asked Nico.

The man smiled briefly and said, "They're probably at the Dollhouse, Sir. They've been spending a lot of time there recently."

Buscemi scoffed, "That dirty strip club? Figures. They need to get a fine woman in their lives," he said, patting his wife's leg and giving her a loving smile.

He looked back at his guard, "Go retrieve them and meet me back at my office in an hour."

The man nodded and walked away.

"I guess this means you'll be dropping me off and going back to work. Should I stay up?" Mazie asked her husband of twenty years.

Joe gave her a kiss before answering, "I will do my best to get home to you before you fall asleep."

***

Nico pulled into the overflowing parking lot of the Dollhouse and searched for a spot. He was amazed at how busy the place was for the middle of the week.

He walked into the club after the doorman checked his ID and looked around. Based on the number of cars and the volume of people he saw, he became confused. Nico knew that in a place like this, the bartenders were usually in the know. He kept his eye out for one or both of the Tye brothers as he made his way to the side bar.

He smiled at one of the two bartenders to get her attention while he stood off to the side. Beks made her way over to the tall man, "What can I get you?"

Expressionless, Nico said, "Marcus and Darius Tye."

Beks smiled, "I'm not sure who you mean."

Nico looked unamused as he said, "I know they're here. I saw their car outside."

Beks sighed, "Okay, but I said nothing. They're back there, but you'll need the pass phrase to give to the bouncer at the door."

Nico glanced in the direction she motioned to and turned his attention back to Beks.

"What's back there?" Nico asked.

"Again, you didn't hear anything from me," she waited until Nico nodded in agreement before continuing, "They have an underground casino going."

"Care to give me the pass phrase?" he asked.

Beks sighed and said, "Seymour Butts wants a slice of Rhubarb pie."

"Excuse me?" Nico asked, stifling a laugh.

Beks repeated the ridiculous phrase and said, "It's not the worst they ever came up with," before walking away to take a drink order.

Nico turned and headed toward the back. When he came up to the bouncer he sighed and repeated the phrase, and the bouncer opened the door to the basement.

He navigated down the dimly lit concrete steps into the Dollhouse's basement. The heavy bass-filled dance music from the club above was heavily muted once the door behind him was secured, and he was able to hear the softer music in the basement. The set up was quaint. There were six round poker tables, a blackjack table, and a roulette table surrounded by people.

Marcus was unsuccessfully flirting with his drink girl while she poured him a bourbon as he noticed Nico. He made his way over to his brother and together they walked over to him.

"Hey," Darius said, approaching him.

Nico, still taking in the atmosphere, said, "Nice place. You guys put this together yourselves?"

Marcus responded, "Yeah."

"Does Joe know about this?"

Darius narrowed his eyes, "No."

Nico nodded and said, "He asked me to come get you. Something's come up and he wants to talk to you both."

Darius reached back to the gun hidden in his waistband.

Noticing his posture, Nico continued, "You know, if I don't return with you guys, he knows where we are and he'll send more. I assume that would be bad for your little business."

Darius stopped reaching and showed his empty hands.

Nico smiled, "Good. Let's go. I'll drive."

Joe Buscemi was not in good spirits. When Darius and Marcus entered his office, he quickly turned to them and said, "The money from Cucina Italia, where is it?"

Darius responded, "In the bag with the rest of the collections to be delivered to you tomorrow."

"How much did you collect from that owner?"

Darius lied, "I have no idea. I need to look at the list."

Joe pulled out a piece of paper. "I kinda expected you to say that. Here's the list!" he said as he balled it up and tossed it at Darius.

Uncrumpling the paper, Darius began to speak, "What is this all ab-"

"Just read the amount, Darius!" Joe interrupted.

"Two thousand dollars."

Joe nodded, "Two grand."

"Yeah, two," Darius confirmed.

Joe rubbed his chin, "Then why did you collect thirty-five hundred?"

Darius asked, "Thirty-five?"

Marcus rolled his eyes, "Yeah, we took thirty-five from him. Our mistake."

"Damn right, your mistake!" Joe exclaimed.

After a long quiet moment, Joe looked over at Nico and said, "Ya know, people don't die often enough. Know what I mean?"

Nico nodded.

Darius glared over at Marcus who rolled his eyes, unfazed by the entire exchange.

Joe leaned in closer to Darius and asked, "Before I get to waste my precious time tomorrow, contacting all of our businesses on your lists to see if you made more mistakes, I'll ask you this one time, have you over-collected from anyone else?"

The Tye Brothers looked at each other briefly and Joe picked up on it.

"For fuck's sake. Are you skimming from me?" Joe demanded to know.

Darius looked at his brother again who kept his eyes on Joe.

Joe hits an intercom button on his desk and begins to speak. "Hey, I need so-"

Marcus, knowing that it would only be bad news from here, intervened.

"We can pay you all of it back."

Joe paused in mid-sentence and let go of the speak button.

A second later, "You okay? Boss?" a voice on the intercom asked.

Marcus continued, "Fifty thousand. We can pay it back tonight."

Joe pressed the button again, "Yeah. We're all good here," he confirmed to the voice before facing Marcus, "Fifty?"

Marcus nodded.

Joe asked, "You can get me fifty tonight? How?"

Nico chimed in, "They have the cash in a nice little underground casino setup down at the Dollhouse."

"What's this now?" Joe asked.

Darius clenched his jaw, afraid that everything he worked for was going to vanish into thin air.

Marcus looked over at his brother and saw how visibly upset he was and looked back to Joe Buscemi.

"We'll show you," Marcus said.

Darius' eyes widened and he looked at his brother in disbelief. Marcus nodded as a plea for his brother to trust him.

"Yeah, It's true. We started the casino about a year ago and it's successful," Darius offered, now confident his brother had a plan.

"How successful? Do we not pay you enough?" Joe asked.

"Startup costs were more than we expected," Darius volunteered.

Marcus quickly said, "We've made three hundred thousand."

The brothers had twice that amount in the Dollhouse alone.

Joe stood from behind his desk and waved a gesture for the men to leave. "Let's go take a look."

He pressed the intercom button on his desk, "Get my car. The big one. Have Rocco meet us. There will be four of us in the back."

Nico escorted Marcus and Darius out of the office and down to the car, already waiting out front.

They got in the back with Joe Buscemi while Nico climbed in the driver's seat. A fifth man, Rocco, appeared and climbed in the back next to Joe. He opened his jacket, exposing a handgun. He made eye contact with Marcus and grinned.

Marcus was not intimidated in the least. He took note of the gun and winked at Rocco.

Nico shifted the car into gear and pulled away, taking them back to the Dollhouse.

Chapter Twenty-Five

With Spring approaching, the next morning was beautiful. Frost melted under the sun as it warmed the earth. Opening the doors to his balcony and taking a deep breath of the crisp morning air, E.I. Bandoni decided to have his breakfast on his patio with his morning newspaper.

Two men approached him as he sipped his cappuccino, waiting for him to acknowledge them. Bandoni looked up and nodded. One of the men, he recognized as Gerry Carpe, an officer on his payroll.

Bandoni gave the worried looking man a smile, "Gerry! How is your mother's rehab going? I heard the hip surgery went well."

Gerry wasn't a fan of being reminded that everyone was corruptible, including himself. He was raised by a wonderful single mother, and she was so proud when he entered the force. Unfortunately, after she took a nasty fall, his salary wasn't enough to help her, and Bandoni swooped in.

"She's well, Sir. Thank you."

Bandoni took his cloth napkin from his lap and wiped the corners of his mouth on his large round face, "Well, spit it out, son. I'm a very busy man."

"I'm afraid I have bad news."

Bandoni looked up from his paper. "Bad news? What kind of bad news?"

Gerry took a steadying breath before blurting out, "Sir, Joseph Buscemi was killed."

"Joseph? My trusted accountant?"

"Yes, Sir. I saw this in an evidence bag," Gerry said, handing over a small coin. "It was found a few feet away from the car."

"Car?" Bandoni said, as he stood up examining the coin. "Exactly how did Jobusch die?" he asked, starting to feel sorrow for his old and trusted friend.

Gerry handed over the initial report for him to go over and he left as soon as he could. Bandoni was insistent on seeing the crime scene for himself, reading the report in the car on the way.

Buscemi's car was still down the road from a secluded rock quarry and miles away from any main roads, neighborhoods, or retail areas and other public attractions. The vehicle was set ablaze, left to burn out. Bandoni's car pulled up as close to the caution tape as his driver could get, and the crime boss stepped out of the car. Liam Stacey followed behind him. The air still smelled of burnt rubber, petroleum, and cooked flesh. The crime scene crew was busy collecting more evidence and coordinating the effort to move the half-burnt vehicle from where it was left. The bodies were already on slabs at the morgue.

The report said that there were three dead inside the car. Bandoni recognized the men from their aliases on the list as Nico, Buscemi, and his personal bodyguard, Rocco. They had all died of gunshot wounds before the fire was started. Luckily, the blaze did not burn for very long and the report also indicated that Rocco was missing his weapon. Nico's piece was on his corpse. He never had the chance to pull it from its holster. The preliminary estimated time of death was between 10 and 11 the night before.

Liam twirled the coin that displayed a crest with the word O'Connell on the bottom. He quietly handed the coin back to his boss. Bandoni said a silent prayer before taking the coin back.

"Let's go. I need to call a meeting," He finally said, walking back to his car.

***

Darius and Marcus headed to the Dollhouse to get their money from the previous night's games. Marlon was still on the premises, in his office. He made a habit of opening all the doors when he was alone so he could see inside each room or hall. It was based on his own fearful superstitions of being alone late at night in a place with many places to hide. Marlon heard a noise from the basement and went to investigate with his favorite baseball bat gripped in his right hand. He saw the lights had been turned on and he walked down the steps to see the Tye brothers. Darius was bagging the money from their safe while Marcus was cleaning up the tables.

"Jesus, have you guys been down here this whole time?" Marlon asked. "I turned the lights out an hour ago." He looked at his watch and saw it was just after 2 AM. Marlon knew for a fact his last employee had left nearly fifteen minutes ago.

"Yeah," Marcus said bluntly.

Marlon knew he was lying but didn't care why. He smiled and walked back up to his office. Marcus and Darius shared a look.

"Should we?" Marcus asked, showing his gun and looking up in the direction Marlon went.

"Nah. Not yet anyway. You made him our alibi if it comes to that. Just keep going," Darius said, throwing more bundles of cash into his bag.

Marcus chuckled, "I actually have a regret."

"Oh yeah, what's that?" Darius asked.

"I made a reservation for us at that Italian place and now we won't get to eat there."

Chapter Twenty-Six

Despite their differences, the families unanimously agreed the local library, within the sanctity of knowledge, was the best place to meet. It was a shared understanding that learning was a sacred entity that deserved safeguarding rather than manipulation or ownership.

Within the library's walls, these families found solace in conducting their clandestine gatherings and discreetly exchanging vital information without the threat of anyone brandishing weapons due to the metal detectors at the entrances.

Bandoni, a prominent figure among them, took initiative to ensure the utmost secrecy by reserving a conference room tucked away in the library's secluded depths. Shielded from prying eyes, this sequestered chamber became a haven for their confidential discussions, allowing them to strategize and communicate without fear of detection.

Several of Bandoni's men stood by the door to the conference room. Mannix O'Connell strutted into the library with several men of his crew.

One of Bandoni's men stood and said, "You can take one man in with you. The rest wait with us."

Mannix looked over at his right-hand man, Sully, who opened the door to the conference room to find Bandoni and Liam seated at the table.

Bandoni looked stoic in a custom fitted Italian suit, with his hands folded on the table in front of him. Liam sat by his side with his blazer closed and his arms folded across his body.

Sully pulled out a chair for his boss. Mannix unbuttoned his jacket, exposing his button-down shirt neatly tucked into his blue jeans, secured with a belt and a buckle with the family crest. His right-hand man remained standing behind him.

"What's this all about, Eustachio?" Mannix asked.

Bandoni leaned in, shifting his shoulders over his elbows, looking Mannix O'Connell in his eyes. "My accountant and two of his men were killed yesterday."

Mannix scoffed, "Sorry to hear that. I'll send flowers."

Bandoni leaned back and produced the coin from his palm and slid it across the table. Mannix trapped the coin with his hand and examined it. As he gazed at the family-oriented token, Bandoni revealed, "This was found near their bodies."

Mannix recognized his son's coin and passed it to Sully. He looked it over and gave it back to Mannix, saying "I believe that was the coin Robbie kept on him."

Bandoni glanced at Liam who he put in charge of the hit on Robbie.

Liam noticed the look in his peripheral vision when he asked Mannix, "Where's Robbie now?"

Mannix raised the coin and asked, "Do you mind?" while motioning to his shirt pocket. Bandoni gestured for him to keep it.

He slid the coin into his shirt pocket and said, "Here's the thing fellas, my boy, Robbie, has been residing in the Willows Grove Cemetery for two years now."

Liam reacted, "My condolences to your family. I'm sorry for your loss."

Bandoni shook his head and said, "Shame. Such a shame."

Mannix knew Bandoni was behind the hit on his son, but chose to keep the accusation guarded for now. He was thoughtful before saying, "Now either, A: one of the souls taken yesterday is responsible for my boy's death, or B: the same arse who killed my boy did your guys and wants to place the blame at the feet of the O'Connell's. So, your guy - was he family, this accountant of yours?"

"No. Well, not immediate family. Joseph Buscemi was the son of a friend of my father. I considered him to be family as well as, my oldest friend."

Mannix nodded, "Buscemi. I recognize the name. They called him Bush, right?"

Bandoni nodded. "Jobusch, yes."

Liam leaned back. His blazer jacket opened revealing two empty pistol holsters.

Bandoni wiped his face in frustration. "I can guarantee Joseph did not have a hand in your son's death. He never had anything to do with that and his men were loyal to him. They'd never do anything he didn't know about." After defending his men, he asked, "So, are we in agreement we're looking for the same killer?"

"I suppose we are." Mannix reluctantly agreed.

Bandoni admitted, "I was really hoping you had more information."

Mannix quickly replied, "You were hoping to blame my Robbie."

"Truth be told, yes. I did suspect one of your men," Bandoni explained, "If it had been, this would be over by the end of the day."

Mannix nodded with a grimace when he stood up from the table and said, "Sorry to disappoint you."

The other three men began to filter out of the door. Bandoni walked past Liam and instructed, "Go get the car."

Liam shuffled past the two families waiting in the library and headed out.

Both Bandoni and Mannix address their men, quietly inside the library. Mannix whispered to Sully to go get their car ready as well.

Sully left his boss' side to navigate the bookshelves and headed toward the front door. He started down the front steps where he spotted Liam pulling the car around. He watched closely as Liam stepped out of the driver's seat and holstered both of Robbie's pearl-handled guns.

Liam noticed Sully's glare. He smirked and shot him a wink as he slowly buttoned his jacket, nonchalantly leaning on the car, waiting for his boss.

With new insight, Sully decided to return to the library to talk to Mannix.

Mannix turned toward Bandoni as they slowly made their way out of the library, "If you do come across the man who killed Jobusch, would you please do me the honor and allow me to question him about Robbie. I'd extend you that favor if it were your brother's boy, Brenden."

Bandoni knew Mannix tossed his nephew's name out as a veiled threat but chose to continue playing this chess game they started in the conference room.

"I appreciate that. I do consider Brenden to be more of a son than a nephew."

Mannix asked, "How old is he now?"

"Twenty. He's going to be twenty-one in a few short months."

Mannix smiled, "Ah, I remember twenty-one. Boy those were fun days."

Sully approached and whispered in Mannix's ear. His expression changed from a smile to a scowl. Mannix glared at Bandoni.

"It appears your man, Liam Stacey, was just seen in possession of my son's custom pistols," he stated. "Tell me Eustachio, how did he come upon them? Have you just spent the last 30 minutes lying to me? Or are you an ignorant bastard?"

Bandoni glared at Mannix and said, "I will not be spoken to in such a manner."

Mannix gritted his teeth, "You better fuckin' explain yourself."

Bandoni took a deep breath and rolled his shoulders. "I have the right to question him first. You know that," he started, reminding Mannix O'Connell of the pact they had. "Now, I will find out how they came to be in his possession and will message you promptly."

He pointed to his men and motioned toward the door. Mannix asked his men to stand down and let them pass.

Liam spotted Bandoni and the other men exiting the building. He walked toward the back passenger door to open it for his boss. Liam looked to the other men who were behind Bandoni, and none made eye contact with him. He looked to the front of the library and noticed the O'Connell's all staring at him. Liam closed the door and quickly walked around the car to the driver's seat.

He looked in the rearview mirror and was met with his boss' eyes.

"Take me home, Liam. We need to have a discussion."

Bandoni remained silent the entire ride home, and opened his own car door, stepping out before Liam could walk around to let him out.

"Is everything okay, Sir?" Liam asked.

Bandoni looked over to the SUV pulling up and waited for his other men to exit.

"Disarm him, now!" Bandoni ordered one of his men, Luca, to take Liam's weapons. Luca took possession of the pearl-handled twins while another reached down for the knife Liam secured to his leg under his trousers.

"You," Bandoni said to the one holding Liam's knife, "Hold onto that for him. And you," he gestured to Luca, "Follow us. Let's go."

Liam had never been more afraid of his boss than at that moment. His knees were shaky as he willed his legs to move him up the steps and into the grand home.

He entered the front door and proceeded upstairs, down the hall, and into Bandoni's office several paces behind Luca, who was still carrying the guns he took from Robbie's corpse.

Liam stepped into the office just as Bandoni, swearing in Italian, gestured for the guns to be placed on his desk. He grabbed a letter opener and threw it in the direction Liam was standing.

"Get in here and shut the goddamn door!" he shouted.

Sweat rolled down Liam's back as he shut the door, and he noticed that Luca had unbuttoned his jacket and stood in the corner facing him. Liam knew by that stance, Luca was preparing to shoot him if given the order.

Bandoni, with an inferno of anger, grabbed Liam by his shirt and threw him to the floor.

"Get up!" Bandoni commanded.

Liam stood again. Bandoni, significantly shorter, looked up at a trembling Liam Stacey.

"You stole Robbie O'Connell's guns?" He spoke in a softer tone.

Liam swallowed hard and nodded. Bandoni started pacing in front of him in thought.

"Why?! Idiota?!" Bandoni shouted as he quickly walked up on him, causing Liam to fall back into a chair. Bandoni struck Liam in the face with the back of his right hand. The signet ring he wore cut Liam's cheek with the swift blow and caused a trickle of blood to roll down, dripping from his chin.

"WHY?!" Bandoni asked again, demanding an answer.

Liam fumbled with his words, "I... I didn't know they'd be recognized."

"Ritardato mentale! They were custom guns! Now Mannix wants your head and I'm inclined to turn your sorry ass over to him."

"I'm sorry, Sir. I didn't know!" Liam pleaded.

Bandoni struck him again with the same hand. "You... Didn't... Think!" He reached into his inside pocket and pulled out his handkerchief and tossed it at Liam.

"If you took the guns, you must have taken that coin."

Liam's eyes widened, "I never saw a coin when we hit him. I swear it to you."

"I'm supposed to believe you? His guns weren't the only thing taken from him, Liam."

"I swear, I only took the guns. There was no coin." Liam was openly weeping.

"Clean yourself up," he said.

Liam wiped the blood from his cheek and lip and gave Bandoni a teary-eyed look as his lip quivered, "Just make it quick, please," he softly begged.

Bandoni scoffed, "I am not going to kill you." He turned and looked out his office window. "I will replace you, and obviously your pay will be cut. I do not believe you are worth the good money I put into your bank account. Or the good money you put up your nose, but you still have some value."

Liam tasted the blood from the cut on the inside of his cheek.

Bandoni turned around and asked, "Those brothers that collected for Joseph, they assisted you several times, yes?"

Liam nodded, "Yes. Including the hit on Robbie. They're smart and quick, but you won't be able to separate the two. Darius and Marcus Tye are a package deal."

Bandoni nodded, "Smart and quick, you say. Well, I guess that makes them exponentially better than you, huh?" Bandoni walked back over to his desk and gazed upon the six-shooters. "Then, I will use them both. You can do their job until you are ready for field duty again. In the meantime, you should grow some brains."

"But -" Liam started to object. Bandoni snapped back, "You don't get to protest anything! You are reckless and very lucky I can not afford another dead man right now. You will collect, capisci?"

Liam nodded as Bandoni continued, "You will report here, to me, every day. I will send you out to the businesses and you come back for your next assignment. As a matter of fact, you will do everything I say. If I tell you to wipe my ass, YOU WILL WIPE IT! Capisci?!"

Liam gulped hard. "Understood, Sir."

"Get out of my sight!" Bandoni said, dismissing him.

Liam started to walk out when Bandoni added, "I will tell Mannix O'Connell you bought your guns at some pawn shop. If he wants them back, you will deliver them. If something happens to you, it happens. I will not retaliate or feel anything for your loss."

Liam nodded and walked out with Luca following behind.

Bandoni called his personal assistant, Dante, in to take dictation. Dante pulled out a notebook and pen and said, "Sir, I'm ready when you are."

Bandoni nodded, "Mannix, I am writing to inform you that I have questioned my man, Liam, about the guns and the coin. He came across his new weapons at a local pawn shop and purchased them outright. I wish you the best of luck finding the party responsible. As promised, if I find them first, I will contact you."

He waved Dante off and said, "Bla-bla-bla signed me, you know the rest and have two men deliver the message."

As Dante started to walk away, Bandoni called out, "Oh, and set up a meeting for this afternoon with the Tye Brothers."

Bandoni sat and swiveled in his chair toward his desk to continue working on the daunting task of finding a new accountant he could trust.

Chapter Twenty-Seven

A car approached the O'Connell estate. It was smaller than Bandoni's but seemed more secure. They had stone walls surrounding the property and cameras.

As Bandoni's men approached the gate they saw a speaker on the side with a call button. After speaking with someone to state who they were and why they were there, they proceeded down a cobblestone driveway toward the home. Two guards approached the car with semi-automatic weapons and motioned for them to get out.

Mannix stepped out of the house and headed down the front steps with Sully close behind him.

The two men stepped out of the car and the passenger approached Mannix.

"Mr. O'Connell, we have a message for you," Bandoni's man began.

Mannix listened to the message, given exactly as Bandoni dictated and he became hung up on one phrase.

Mannix looked over to Sully and narrowed his eyes. He faced the messenger again and asked, "Local pawn shop?"

The man reading the message nodded.

Mannix turned to Sully, "How many local pawn shops are there?"

Sully replied, "Two."

Mannix nodded and asked, "You sure?"

Sully nodded with a slight smile and confirmed, "Oh, I'm certain."

Mannix pursed his lips and cocked his head to the side. "How can you be so sure, Sully?"

Bandoni's messenger shuffled his feet awkwardly and glanced at the driver before looking back at Mannix O'Connell.

Sully's smile widened, "We own both the pawn shops in town."

Mannix clasped his hands and said, "Well shit! We own them?"

Sully nodded, "Indeed, we do."

"So, tell me, Sully, do you think the owners of the pawn shops would recognize Robbie's guns?"

Sully nodded, "Oh, they certainly would."

"And do you think they would let me know if anyone came into the store to sell the guns?"

Sully nodded again, "I'm certain they would."

Feigning astonishment, Mannix asked, "Really? How are you so sure?"

Sully replied, "Well, one is run by my son. The other, is run by Robbie's best friend, Jimmy."

Sensing their message was not received well, the messenger started to back away towards the car.

The expression on Mannix's face became dark. "I have a message for Mr. Bandoni."

"Yes, sir. What's the message?" Bandoni's messenger asked.

Mannix gave a subtle order to his armed guards, and they opened fire. The messenger was riddled with bullets and the driver scrambled for his gun but was hit in the side as he attempted to crawl under the car.

Mannix walked up to the injured man holding his own 9mm, "Well shit, I guess we'll deliver the message ourselves," and he fired a fatal shot to the back of his head.

***

Freshly showered after power naps, Darius pulled up to the Bandoni estate with Marcus. They announced themselves and were let onto the property. Dante met them and escorted the brothers to the patio where they found Bandoni already seated at a small table with a carafe of coffee.

"Gentlemen, please have a seat with me and enjoy some coffee," Bandoni said as soon as he laid eyes on them.

Bandoni's waiting servant poured the coffee as he began to talk.

"So, I have asked you to come here to share some terrible news about your boss Joseph Buscemi, or Jobusch, I believe you called him."

Marcus gave Darius a quick glance before asking, "What about him?"

"Unfortunately he has passed away."

Darius hoped he looked shocked, "That's terrible, do you know what happened?"

Bandoni answered, "Unfortunately, I do not have all the details. But, I also wanted to share some good news. I am promoting you from collection to enforcement."

Marcus sat up in his chair and asked, "So we're working with Liam Stacey now?"

Bandoni took a small sip from his hot coffee and said, "No. Not exactly. You will be replacing him. He is going to be the one in charge of collecting. I am looking for his boss right now, but for the time being, You and Liam will be switching roles."

Darius nodded, "Understood."

Bandoni began to speak again when one of his men rushed onto the patio, "Sir, come quickly!"

Bandoni jumped to his feet and asked, "What is the meaning of this?"

The Tye brothers followed their boss back to the front of the estate where they saw several men, huddled around the closed front gate, peering out.

Bandoni yelled, "Move! What is going on here?"

The crowd thinned out, exposing the heads of the messenger and his driver sitting on the back of small remote controlled toy dump trucks with the word, "LIAR," written across both of their heads in sharpie.

Bandoni rubbed his face and muttered, "Dannazione!" He turned to the brothers, "Once my new accountant arrives, he will be instructed to double your current rate. Now, I should not tell you this next part, but Liam's rate has decreased by 60%." He paused when he saw a smile touch Marcus' lips. "When it gets back to Liam," Bandoni continued, "it will be part of that egotistical bastard's punishment that I told you."

Darius looked at the men still standing at the gate. "You told everybody, Sir."

Bandoni smiled despite having the decapitated heads of two of his employees' yards away from him. "Yes. Yes, I did." He glanced toward the front gate. "Liam is the reason they are dead. He screwed up big time."

The brothers silently followed as Bandoni started to walk back to where they had parked. "I wish your visit could have been more pleasant, but I will contact you soon. Look for a black envelope with instructions."

***

"Now that we've been promoted, what do we do about the casino?" Darius asked his brother as they made dinner.

Marcus turned the news channel on and kept the volume low enough to carry on a conversation.

"I don't want to give it up, man," Marcus started, "But, maybe we can, like, put a hold on it for a while, or scale back how often we run it?" he said, rubbing his scar before continuing, "at least until we find our rhythm with this new gig."

"Yeah, I agree. We can figure out the logistics later and tell Marlon. I don't want to piss off Bandoni."

Marcus scoffed, "That fat fucker's all hot air."

Darius laughed. "Heads, Marc. We were having a conversation next to severed heads. They were just delivered to the man."

"I thought that was awesome!" Marcus yelled from the living room after he walked away to focus on the news stories.

"You would," Darius said to himself, shaking his head.

"Dude! They found the Italian Coochie guy!" Marcus yelled.

...grim discovery at an Italian restaurant downtown. Philip Elio, the owner of the very popular Cucina Italia, was found in the restaurant's freezer. It has not been made clear if this was an unfortunate accident or foul play. We will stay on top of this story as the investigation continues...

Marcus hit the mute button before a story on gas station fires started, and looked at his brother with a smile on his face.

"What?" Darius asked.

"I feel like we're finally gonna get what we deserve, brother."

Chapter Twenty-Eight

E.I. Bandoni was frustrated with all he had to do now that his accountant and good friend was dead. He also needed to make sure the families of the dead men that accumulated over the past couple of days were taken care of. He decided to take a break from the logistical work of his organization and clicked on his television.

...story as the investigation continues. Now, for some breaking news: Four gas stations along highways 42 and 60 have caught fire, causing delays on those busy roads. Crews from several counties, including some from across the river in Indiana, fights to bring them under control. Officials are convinced of arson and may even be the work of domestic terrorists. Luckily, two of the fired started in the restrooms and have not reached-

Bandoni muted the TV and called Liam Stacey. He rubbed his face and sighed while he waited for Liam to pick up.

"Liam, are you watching the news?" Bandoni asked when he answered.

Startled by the initial question, Liam answered, "No sir, I'm not."

"Are you near a television?"

"I am."

"Turn to the news. WAVE, specifically," Bandoni instructed. A moment later Bandoni could hear the broadcast over the phone, matching the lip sync of the field reporter in front of the first fire which was now contained, on his own television set.

"Are those ours?" He asked his employee.

"Sir, I'm supposed to collect from them tomorrow." Liam could hear the deep sigh over the phone, "What should I do?" Liam asked.

"Collect from the other stations today before they go up next. Tell the employees to close and arm themselves. I'll dispatch a few men to help each of them."

"I am heading out now, Sir."

"Be fast, Liam."

Bandoni hung up the phone and pressed the button on the intercom for Dante to call the gas stations.

"Tell them to close their bathrooms to the public and that Liam is coming with further instructions."

"Yes, Sir."

"And have eight of my men pair up and each go to the remaining stations." Bandoni continued, "I must assume these are distractions to thin the men protecting me. These investments are important, but not that important. Tell all of the men on the estate to go to code red for the time being."

"As you wish, Sir."

***

Thirty minutes later, Liam had already collected from two of the gas stations and provided them with instructions. As he pulled into the third station, he noticed a car with a Solomon's Knot sticker on its back window. It was parked off to the side and facing out towards the road at the other entrance. He recognized the symbol from Robbie's coin that held the O'Connell family crest.

He parked near the empty car and decided to take a quick look around the building before heading inside.

Liam didn't want to assume the arsonist was working alone. He saw the two employees together and relaxed at the counter but noticed no one else from where he stood. This particular gas station had outdoor bathrooms that required a key. Before going inside, Liam thought he should check for smoke first, because a lock could easily be picked if someone wanted to get in badly enough. Finding no indications of a fire, he quickly went back to the front.

Peeking around the corner of the wall, Liam's eyes narrowed as he spotted the arsonist placing the nozzle of one of the four pumps back into its cradle, but no cars were at any of the pumps. Without hesitation, Liam curled his body around the wall, taking aim and firing two shots toward the assailant. Shots were fired back, narrowly missing Liam's head as fragments of mortar from the bricked side flew. Liam's gaze shifted towards the large pool of gasoline that was running on the concrete toward the store where propane tanks were stacked, intensifying the gravity of the situation.

The O'Connell arsonist, undeterred by Liam, swiftly made his way towards his car, popping the trunk with his remote key as he ran. The two employees ran out the front to see what was happening and unintentionally blocked the view of the one person there to help them.

"Get the fuck back inside!" He yelled at them.

Once they scrambled back into the store, Liam's eyes widened as he observed the menacing road flare in the arsonist's hand. Realizing the imminent danger, Liam stumbled to his feet and sprinted towards his own vehicle, desperately trying to put some distance between himself and the impending explosion. With a swift motion, the arsonist tossed the flare towards the pool of gasoline, causing a sudden burst of flames that illuminated the darkening evening sky followed by billowing black smoke.

As Liam ran around the back of the store, he was delayed by the back door swinging into him as the employees ran out to save themselves. Liam managed to reach his car. He started the engine and quickly reversed away from the building just as a thunderous explosion rocked the area, engulfing the surroundings in a massive plume of smoke once the propane tanks caged against the store reached their boiling point.

Amidst the chaos the arsonist's car sped away. The fire suppression system that the arsonist failed to disable went off, deploying a sodium bicarbonate-based dry chemical agent from under the canopy. It smothered the flames around the pumps, but the store was engulfed in flames that the fire department would have to tackle.

Liam realized that the arsonist had vanished into thin air, leaving behind only a trail of destruction and unanswered questions. Undeterred by the setback, Liam continued down the road before the authorities arrived, his mind racing with thoughts of how to locate the elusive arsonist. After a few minutes, he slammed his fist against the steering wheel. With the look of defeat etched on his face, he reached for his phone and dialed Bandoni to report his findings.

"Mr. Stacey, what do you know?" Bandoni asked.

Liam cleared his throat, "Sir, it's definitely the O'Connell's. They are hitting our businesses."

Bandoni asked, "Do you understand this is all because of you? Do you see how much this is costing me?"

Liam closed his eyes tightly to the reminder of his foolishness. "Yes, Sir," he said through gritted teeth.

"We must strike back now," Bandoni declared.

"I'll get right on it!" Liam exclaimed.

"NO!" Bandoni shouted. "This is the Tye Brothers job now. You come back here once you're done collecting. You are done for the day."

***

Darius and Marcus received a black envelope before their dinner had time to digest. In it was a list of three men to hit immediately.

The first, Peter, was the easiest. Darius spotted him at a local coffee bar, sitting at a small table on the edge of the fenced off patio alongside the public sidewalk.

Marcus stopped the car a block away and Darius instructed his brother to circle back around the block and pick him up.

Darius walked down the street toward the shop and as he approached his mark at the table, he concealed the knife Mike gifted him along his side. As Peter began to sip his coffee, Darius grabbed a fistful of his mark's hair with his left hand and plunged the knife deep into the jugular vein in the right side of his neck.

Blood started to spurt out with every pulse and the mark eventually dropped the porcelain coffee cup onto the bricked patio.

Before vanishing like a ghost, Darius smiled when he heard the waitress scream for help.

Their second mark, Isaac, was more difficult to locate, but after a few hours, they spotted him driving away from town toward the O'Connell compound.

The Tye brothers followed behind and initially planned to run him off the road but failed. Isaac, now on high alert, was swift. He was able to navigate away from the Tye brothers' failed pit maneuver and sped away.

Darius was able to gain speed and quickly closed the gap again. Marcus leaned out of the passenger window and fired three rounds into the back window. The car swerved and regained control.

Darius pulled his gun with his left hand and steered with his right, firing a single shot, he was able to hit the side mirror. He fired another single shot, and it scraped along the driver's side of the car.

He yelled over at his brother, "I can't steer and get a good shot!"

"Just drive. Let me do the shooting," Marcus yelled back before climbing out of the passenger window to perch on the door, using the roof for stability.

Isaac spotted this in the rearview mirror and slammed on the brakes. Darius swerved and Marcus quickly slid back into the car to avoid being launched from it.

"FUCK!" he screamed. "I had a shot."

Darius gritted his teeth, "He's fucking tricky, that little shit."

As Darius regained control, Marcus attempted it again. Darius hung further back from the car and allowed Marcus to get set. Once he was perched with the target in his sights, he slapped the top of the car three times and Darius punched the accelerator. As they approached the car from behind, Marcus started firing.

After the fourth shot, he noticed Isaac's body reacting to a direct hit as he appeared to go limp, and the car started to coast along.

Marcus slid back into the car and said, "I got his ass!"

Darius pulled up along the side of the car going at a considerably slower pace than before, and Marcus looked over as they became face to face. Isaac was trying desperately to stay conscious, drive, and defend himself. There was blood splattered on the interior of the windshield from the shot he took in the neck. Struggling to breathe, the second member of the O'Connell organization with a neck injury that evening, looked over at the brothers and with his last bit of energy, pulled his gun up to shoot Marcus.

Marcus smiled and cracked his neck to the side before firing his gun, hitting Isaac in his face, splattering most of his brain into the passenger seat and along the window and door. The car continued to coast off to the side of the road, hitting a drainage ditch, and then traveled along the ditch until it hit a culvert and came to an immediate stop.

The Tye brothers sped away and headed toward their third mark, Bryan "Sully" Sullivan.

As Sully stepped into his garage, he glanced at his phone and noticed a missed call from Mannix, prompting him to check his voicemail and attend to any pressing matters that may require his attention.

"Hey brother, be careful and get here as soon as you can. Things have escalated."

He could tell something was amiss when he arrived at the O'Connell compound. The front drive was filled with the vehicles of most of the employees. Sully parked and spotted one of the security guards, "What's going on?" he asked.

The security guard, looking a bit unsettled, replied, "Bandoni retaliated."

"Shit," Sully said under his breath as he continued up the steps. Two guards nodded at Sully and opened the doors letting him inside. He entered the room Mannix used as an office.

The moment his boss saw him, he filled him in about Peter and Issac. "I have some intel that Bandoni brought in two ringers he had riding the bench. Well, until now. We don't know much about them, except that they're brothers."

"We're not going to stand here and let Bandoni send his thugs to pick us off one by one. We will be fighting back with full force, but," Mannix turned to fully face his right hand man, Sully, "I can't do this without you."

He waited for Sully to nod in understanding before continuing to address the rest of the men, "If you have a routine, alter it. I'll send you each the details of your assignments once we have a firm plan on how to proceed."

The room cleared out with the exception of Sully. Mannix looked over at his old friend and admitted, "I don't know if we'll survive this." He sighed as he sat down in his chair, "Bandoni really hurt us when he hit that warehouse two years ago. I didn't want to give him the satisfaction of knowing that."

Sully nodded, "What's the plan?"

"I need more information on those brothers. I want your focus on them. Also, I believe we have some time. Bandoni is looking for a new accountant, and having these new hitmen on his books tells me he's scrambling. Liam Stacey was the one who bothered me the most, but Bandoni clearly put him on ice."

Sully smiled and said, "Understood. Let me dig around about the brothers. I'll find out who they are. Do you want someone on Stacey?"

"Yes. Fine, you pick someone to keep an eye on Stacey. Don't engage unless absolutely necessary," Mannix said. "He may turn out to be an asset before we kill him. I have a feeling he'll talk after the way his boss has humiliated him. For now, we continue the attacks on the Bandoni properties and kill his men on site. You focus on the brothers."

Midday sank into evening and dusk set in. The hills glowed with the setting sun and the sky put on a show of pinks and amber.

Throughout the day, the Tye brothers heard reports of two other business attacks and one of Bandoni's men was killed. After some brief information gathering, they discovered Sully, a devout Catholic, attended evening Mass on a regular basis and asked Bandoni to put the church Sully frequented on surveillance for them.

Darius received a text from Dante that their man witnessed Sully entering his church. The brothers pulled up to it moments later.

"Let's wait for him to finish and then follow him home," Darius suggested.

Marcus, looking at the decor outside the church, took note of the head-carrying cephalophore statues of Saint Osyth of Essex and St Juthwara who were martyred at Halstock in Dorset, and St Justinian of Ramsey Island in Wales.

He smiled, looking at Darius, "I have an idea. Stay here and keep a lookout."

Darius nodded and watched his brother walk around the back of the SUV in search for something before crossing the street to the church. He noticed his brother strapped a machete to his back.

A half an hour went by, and Darius watched as the handful of church members began to leave. Eventually the Church was quiet. Darius had a brief moment of worry until he saw his brother on the side of the church.

He watched as he propped something up against the wall. The darkness shrouded what Marcus was working on, but Darius could tell it was taking a lot of effort.

He continued to watch until Marcus jogged towards him.

"What the fuck? Is any of that your blood?" Darius asked, reaching up to kill the interior light.

Marcus smiled, "Dude, he didn't even see it coming."

"What did you do?" Darius asked.

Marcus pointed at his project and said, "Drive up that way and take a look."

He pulled up toward the side of the building, angled the headlights, and saw Bryan Sullivan. His body was propped up with the legs crossed, holding his severed head in his own hands.

Darius quickly drove off with a smile growing on his face. "That should get heads rolling," he said before laughing. "That was fucking awesome, man."

Marcus looked over and said, "It got stuck on the first whack. I looked over and his face was all -" Marcus paused to mimic a frightened and surprised face. "I had to pull it out and do a second chop. It's so bloody inside."

Darius shook his head, "Jesus!"

Marcus smiled, "I got some on him, too."

Chapter Twenty-Nine

The demise of Sully came as a devastating blow to the O'Connell organization. His untimely death instilled fear and apprehension among the non-familial employees, prompting many of them to contemplate resigning. These individuals harbored concerns for the safety of their own families, believing that they too could become targets.

Outside the organization, the news of a beheaded man found on the grounds of a Catholic church reverberated throughout the public, causing widespread panic. The media extensively covered this peculiar death, which occurred amidst a series of fires, fatalities, and shootings in the vicinity. The cumulative effect of these events heightened the sense of unease and uncertainty among the general population, further fueling their anxiety, and creating a factitious need for security that Bandoni capitalized on.

Bandoni, who had previously made a substantial contribution to the mayor's re-election campaign earlier in the year in hopes to gain favorability in the town, seized this opportunity to extend a helping hand to the Chief of Police. He proposed providing complimentary public security services through his recently established security practice.

Mannix O'Connell clicked off the television and violently threw the remote control against his office wall, smashing it to pieces. He couldn't stand watching as Bandoni stood shoulder to shoulder with the Mayor and Chief of Police in the town square while they talked about a more secure community.

He knew then, that if he continued, he would not only have to deal with Bandoni's men, but the government authorities as well.

Mannix was increasingly becoming short on personnel. Majority of his hired help had left. Some even sought employment with Bandoni's organization which was growing by the day. The rift between the families continued, but the fighting slowed until weeks went by without a death.

One of the guards walked into his office and stated a letter was delivered to the front gate. As he stood there with the letter, the guard chose that moment to inform Mannix that it was his last day. He let out a sigh and waved him off after he placed the letter on his desk. He opened the letter to see it was an invitation from Bandoni to meet at the library again. He became furious, tossing the letter opener across the room and swiping the papers off of his desk.

Later in the week, Mannix showed back up at the library conference room early, before any of Bandoni's men arrived. He decided to come alone and walk around the library, up and down the aisles, looking at the books. He knew today was going to be the last day of his organization and he felt that this was a final goodbye to the place he loved. Eventually, after spotting some of Bandoni's men milling about, he slowly walked to the back conference room where he spotted a figure sitting inside as he pushed open the door.

"Eustachio."

"Mannix," Bandoni replied.

Mannix O'Connell continued into the room allowing the door to close behind him and pulled out a seat and plopped down.

"I know we have our differences, but I would like for you to join my family," Bandoni offered.

Mannix, too proud to accept defeat right away countered, "Why don't you join mine?"

Bandoni lets out a chuckle, "I do love your sense of humor, Mannix. I also still have respect for you and my offer is serious."

Mannix looked down at the floor before looking back up at his rival to speak. "I can't."

Bandoni inhaled deeply and allowed the air to escape through his lips before pulling a gun from his jacket. He laid the gun on the table directly in front of him.

Mannix, looking confused, started to speak, but was immediately interrupted.

"When you employ the security, you can dictate who can carry the weapons," Bandoni explained, predicting his old rival's question.

He smiled and continued, "I figured you would be too proud to join me, so I have another option for you."

He lifted a briefcase that was sitting on the floor, next to his chair, and set it on the table. He opened the case to reveal money.

"I will buy your operation for one million in cash. Your properties, your home, the rest of your staff. All of it."

Mannix scoffed, "My home alone is worth over 1.5 million. This is ludicrous!"

Bandoni smiled again, "The other option is I kill you right now, dispose of your corpse and seize your properties for free. Your choice."

Exasperated, Mannix set his head in his hands.

"Okay, but I just ask for one favor."

Bandoni sat back and folded his arms. "I'm listening."

Mannix leaned in and pleaded, "I will disband my organization and everything else you said but let me hold onto the one property my daughter lives in when she's home from school. She never wanted anything to do with the business. She's a good girl with a lot of potential and her friends are here."

"The condo downtown?" Bandoni asked.

"That's the one."

Bandoni was thoughtful for a moment, "I'll allow that."

Mannix leaned back in his chair and said, "Fine, then I accept."

Bandoni slid the briefcase across the table and stood up. He holstered his gun and a smirk danced across his face.

"I will give you until the end of the week to vacate your home and transfer all your acquisitions to me. I am glad we could come to an arrangement."

Mannix waved him off and sat, feeling empty inside as his empire came to a crashing halt for a measly one million dollars.

Mannix O'Connell had one more order of business to take care of before he tucked his tail between his legs and left Kentucky. He sent a text to Shane, one of the few men who chose to remain in the family, to meet at the compound one last time. While he waited, Mannix contacted his lawyer to prepare all properties, besides the condo for his daughter, Siobhan, to be transferred to Bandoni. He knew his daughter and she would not want to go anywhere else on her breaks from school. She loved her childhood friends, and this would give her a safe space to enjoy life with the people she loved.

Shane knocked softly on the opened door of the office Mannix sat in, looking for movers on the internet.

"Shane, are you still sure you want to join us in Boston?" he asked as he waved the young man in.

"Absolutely, Sir. Was there something you needed me to do?"

"Find Liam Stacey and put a bullet in his brain. When you're done, that bag," Mannix pointed to the very bag Bandoni handed to him earlier that day, "has a million dollars in it, and it's yours. You can collect it when you rejoin us in the northeast."

***

Liam sat alone in his living room with a glass of bourbon neat and 3 lines of cocaine left on the tray in front of him. He glared at a TV he was barely paying attention to. The Tye brothers were doing his job better than he ever did, and Bandoni loved them. What they did to Bryan Sullivan was a thing of beauty.

"Fuckers. I just need those fucking brothers to screw up," Liam said to himself before snorting one of the lines. He'd still be running the show if it weren't for those guns, he thought. He was humiliated over those stupid guns.

"You stupid fuck," he muttered just before downing the two fingers worth of bourbon. He snorted another line before getting up to refill his drink.

Liam walked back into his living room with his drink to find a man, in his mid to late twenties, standing to the side of the TV.

"Well, this is new," Liam said, raising his glass of bourbon to his lips.

Shane smiled, "This is for Robbie," as he took aim toward Liam's head.

Quickly, Liam flung the drinking glass from his lips toward Shane and leapt toward him. He tackled Shane as a shot went off just past his ear. They scrambled on the floor with Liam gaining enough control over the gun that the next time it went off the barrel was pressed deep under Shane's chin causing the bullet to tear through his tongue, exploding through a nasal cavity and lodging into his brain.

Standing up, Liam looked down at his would-be assassin, "Fucking rookie! You think you can take me down? I'm Liam fucking Stacey, you bitch-ass shit stain!"

He noticed the broken glass of his freshly poured drink all over the hardwood floor. He snorted the third line of coke and poured another drink before sitting down again. He picked up his phone to report what happened to Bandoni but put his phone down reconsidering his next move.

Liam sat still for a very long time with the body of O'Connell's pathetic hit man laying on his living room floor.

"Well, O'Connell's gonna pay for this." Suddenly energized, Liam started pacing.

He stopped in the middle of his floor and began laughing uncontrollably.

Chapter Thirty:

Late May brought beautiful weather to Kentucky and Bandoni was excited for his nephew to come home for his summer break.

Bandoni folded the paper and asked, "Has my nephew's room been prepared? He will be home this afternoon."

Dante nodded, "Yes sir, the staff just finished getting his room ready and his car left an hour ago. He should be here before lunch."

Bandoni smiled, "Very good. We will have lunch and catch up."

The morning gave way to the hot afternoon, causing the staff to raise umbrellas shielding the seating area of the garden. Sprinklers were set to mist the surrounding area to provide a pleasant dining experience for Eustachio Bandoni and his nephew Brenden, who he had not seen in ten months.

Lunch was just about prepared when Brenden's car pulled up to the Bandoni estate. Brenden stepped out of the car and two men approached the trunk to collect his luggage.

Dante stepped up and greeted Brenden.

"Your uncle is excited for your arrival. I hope you're hungry. He had lunch prepared for you."

Brenden smiled and pulled out his earbuds, "Yeah, I could eat."

He shoved his wireless Bluetooth headphones into his backpack and followed Dante up the stairs.

E.I. Bandoni approached the main foyer as his nephew stepped inside.

"Ah! You've arrived, how wonderful!" Bandoni joyously exclaimed.

Brenden smiled, "Hey, Uncle E."

"Please, place his bags in the guest room," E.I. Bandoni directed the help.

Brenden bit his lip and stammered, "Uh, about that Uncle E., I have a request."

"Please, let's talk in the garden, lunch awaits us."

Brenden nodded, "Yes sir."

As Brenden sat, his anticipation got the better of him and he blurted out, "I'm not going to be staying with you the entire time this visit."

Eustachio lowered his spoon quicker than he intended and it clinked off of a ceramic coaster. "What? Why not?"

"No offense, but I'm planning on staying closer to downtown with friends."

Eustachio scoffed, "Why would you sleep on couches? No, that is beneath you. This is much nicer."

Brenden shook his head, "I'm planning on spending a lot of time with a certain friend and-"

"A woman?" E.I. interrupted.

"Yes, Uncle E. A woman from school, but also, I plan on being with my friends too," Brenden explained.

"She can stay with you. No one will bother you."

Brenden laughed, "You mean it now, but we both know that's not true. I promise to come over every day and if you have anything planned for the two of us, I will mark it in my calendar."

"Aye, fine! Do what you want. You are growing up too damn fast," Bandoni said, before taking a quick sip of his tea.

"I heard you went to war with the O'Connell family." Brenden approached the topic of business.

Bandoni smiled. "Mannix set up shop in Boston with his cousin. Their organization is twice the size it was here. It's almost impressive," he smiled again before asking, "Have you given any thought to joining me? We run the whole place now. You could make a lot of money."

"Let me see where this Summer takes me first. I still have another year before I can graduate, anyway."

***

With the Bandoni mafia preoccupied with their growing power and new community dynamic, Marcus and Darius were making much more profit than they ever expected with their casino. They decided to buy a house outright and remodel the Dollhouse basement to maximize the space. Marlon was not thrilled, but it helped pay the bills. They temporarily moved operations downtown to the basement of a bakery called, 'Batter Up Bakery,' formerly owned by the O'Connell family.

Marcus looked over at his brother on the phone who was becoming increasingly furious.

"Fine. As soon as you can, get started," Darius said, just before ending the call.

"What?" Marcus asked.

"The fucking contractor can't start working until the plumber gets in there to reconstruct the pipes. This is a fucking nightmare!" Darius yelled, extremely frustrated.

Marcus laughed, "We're okay. We've got the set up in the bakery and we're making so much money that we're really not missing out on much. It's going to be fine."

Darius shook his head, "Yeah, I know. It's just annoying that the renovations at the Dollhouse are taking so long. They have to gut the entire basement!" Darius was more worried about Marcus having too much time on his hands, because the casino kept his brother happy and busy.

Darius groaned, "This was a mistake."

Marcus looked over, "Calm the fuck down. It's going to be okay," he said, sitting up. "Let's go blow off some steam."

They swung by the store and picked up a twelve pack of beer and headed out to a small little wooded riparian river cove on the Ohio. Marcus chugged a beer and walked down toward the water and placed the can on a rock. Darius did the same before they both walked back up the riverbank.

Marcus smiled, "Okay. The first to shoot their can, wins. Ready?"

Darius nodded.

"Go!"

The brothers fired their pistols and hit their cans at the same time.

Darius smirked and said, "We're getting too good at this."

They continued drinking and shooting until eventually, they begin tossing cans and shooting at them like clay pigeons.

About an hour goes by and they ran out of ammo and beer.

Marcus saw a huge smile on his brother's face and said, "Hey, let's get out of here and head to Batter Up. We need to set up for tonight's game."

Darius nodded and said, "Thanks for this. I needed it."

At the bakery, the brothers set up the chairs and table in the basement. Marcus walked up the steps to the main level and was spotted by a young woman.

"Excuse me, sir?" she said, trying to get Marcus's attention.

Marcus looked around to realize she was talking to him. He smiled as he walked over and asked, "What can I do for you?"

She was looking at the bread menu and asked, "I was wondering if you have any marbled rye today."

Marcus smiled, "I'm sorry. I don't work here, but I'll grab someone for you."

She smiled at Marcus and said, "Oh, I'm so sorry for assuming. Thank you so much."

Marcus became smitten by her smile. "Sure," he said, being brief.

He walked away and grabbed the baker from the kitchen. He watched as the beautiful woman paid and left the shop. Marcus walked out into the side alley and spied as she got into her car and drove off.

Darius spotted him and walked up. "What are you looking at?"

Marcus smiled and said, "An angel."

"A what?" Darius asked, perplexed.

"I just saw the most beautiful girl I've ever seen."

"Oh, Jesus fucking Christ! Not this again. You're not going back to old habits, are you?" Darius asked in a harsh whisper.

Marcus shook his head, "Not with her. She was so nice to me. I need to find her."

"For fuck's sake, Marc. Let's get out of here. We need to get ready," Darius said.

As they head toward home, they stop at a light across town. Walking out of a shop was Marcus' angel.

Marcus spotted her and yelled, "Oh shit! There she is. Look!"

Darius looked over to see a stunning red-haired woman, standing in the midday sunlight, loading goods into her car. The sun shimmered through her hair as the breeze picked up, sending her hair over her shoulders like a dancing flame.

"Wow, that's her?" Darius said with admiration.

"She's mine, brother. I saw her first."

Darius smiled, "Sure. She's yours. You gonna talk to her? Or are we just browsing?"

"Yeah, I'm going to talk to her," Marcus said, as he suddenly opened the car door.

"What? Wait!" Darius yelled.

Still waiting at the light, he watched his brother from the car. It turned green and the car behind him honked.

The woman looked toward the sound and spotted Marcus walking her way. She smiled as he started to speak, "Ma'am, excuse me, did you find the bread you were looking for?"

"Did you follow me here just to ask that?" she asked, amused.

Marcus smiled, "Well, yeah. You left the bakery before I could ask you."

"I thought you didn't work there?"

"I don't. I'm just a curious person who needed a good ending to this marbled rye mystery," Marcus replied.

"Ah! I see," she said, impressed with his wit.

"What are you doing tonight?"

Darius circled the block and parked near where his brother got out.

The beautiful woman smiled more, and her cheeks flushed with color.

"What? C'mon, I want to take you out," Marcus pleaded.

"Well, I have plans with my boyfriend," she said, breaking the news.

"Boyfriend? Aw, come on. You'll have more fun with me. I promise."

She looked over and spotted his brother in the car behind him, shaking his head.

Looking back at Marcus, she said, "I don't even know you. And besides, your ride is here."

Marcus looked behind him at his brother and back at her. "He can wait. I'm Marcus. There, now you know me."

"Hardly!" she said with a laugh.

Marcus winked and said, "Well, get to know me then."

"I'm so sorry. I can't go out tonight," she repeated.

Darius honked the horn and shouted, "Come on, Marc! We gotta go!"

"You better get going," the woman said with a smile.

Marcus stood firm and said, "Not until you tell me your name."

"It's nice to meet you Marcus, but I'm not telling you my name."

Marcus smiled and said, "I guess I'll just call you Angel, then."

"Oh, wow. That was good," she admitted.

"Good enough for a date?" Marcus asked.

She shook her head, "Seriously, you should go."

Marcus winked and said, "See you around."

He slowly backed away until she looked up and smiled one last time. Marcus waved as he got into the car and his brother sped off.

They arrived home to find a black envelope on their door. Marcus snagged it and continued towards the kitchen. He grabbed a slice of leftover pizza and tossed the envelope on the table.

Darius got a beer from the fridge and cracked it open. While chewing, Marcus said, "Gonna jump in the shower," walking past his brother.

Darius took a swig and nodded as he swallowed.

He looked over at the envelope and then decided to take a shower himself.

Darius walked back into the living room, running his hand through his wet hair, and saw Marcus on the couch.

"Did you open it yet?" Darius asked, nodding toward the coffee table.

"No, not yet. Be my guest, though," Marcus said as he tied his boot.

Darius swiped the envelope from the table and used his knife to open it.

"Fuck!" he exclaimed. "We gotta cancel the game tonight."

Chapter Thirty-One

That night, Brenden reserved a table at a new Italian restaurant. He requested the floor around their table be filled with pink and orange roses. A big green balloon was tied to her reserved chair. The limo he ordered dropped them off in front and he watched her face when she saw their table.

"Happy Birthday, Siobhan!" he said as they approached.

Siobhan felt the frisson of excitement. Goosebumps rose on her arms and legs as she smiled warmly to the other patrons in the restaurant who were applauding.

"Is my face the same color as my hair?" she asked Brenden as they were seated.

He laughed, "I didn't pay for the movie star treatment, but if they want to give it to you, go with it."

"Wine list?" The waiter asked, handing it to Brenden.

"I think we should let the birthday girl order now that she's legal," Brenden teased.

The couple enjoyed their dinner and especially the wine. They decided to take another bottle back to her condo, a more intimate setting.

***

"I'm still pissed that we had to move the game to tomorrow," Darius complained. They sat in the parking lot of the address they received a few hours earlier.

"Eh, I needed a distraction tonight so I'm happy for it," Marcus said, smiling.

"Still thinking about your red-headed angel, huh?"

"I just wish I had a name to go with that perfection," Marcus said, as they waited for the light to eventually go out in the condo where their mark lived.

"She looked a bit young, man," Darius teased.

"Any woman who looks at me is either disgusted by my scar or they're rude. She smiled at me. A real fucking smile."

"She did seem to flirt with you, but other women have flirted with you before."

"Strippers don't count. They want tips."

"Ah, and you hope your angel wants a different kind of tip."

Marcus gave his brother an incredulous look.

"Oh shit, you are a smitten kitten. I can't joke like that about her?" Darius asked, surprised.

"Nope. That kind of woman should be placed on a pedestal and worshipped."

"Do you want to change her name from Angel to Goddess?" Darius continued to tease.

"Maybe I do," Marcus said with a smile.

Darius pulled out a deck of cards and raised his eyebrows at his brother.

"Oh, fuck yeah," Marcus said with a smile. "Wanna play War?"

After a few minutes of playing, Darius approached a topic he had been afraid to talk about. "How do you pick?"

"Pick what?"

"The Tree Girls."

Marcus raised an eyebrow, "Oh, um, they just seem like their life isn't going to get better, and death would be kinder."

"So, you believe you're doing them a favor?"

"Kinda. Like mom."

Darius was taken aback, "What the fuck do you mean, 'Like mom,'?"

"Her life wasn't going to get better. She's happier in death. Free." Marcus said flatly as he laid a card down, "War!"

Marcus asked, "What do you think the note meant about playing with our food before we eat it?" changing the subject.

"I think the organization likes to assume we rape, pillage, and plunder when we do a job," Darius said in disgust.

"Oh, and since the mark is a female..."

"Exactly."

"Honestly, something feels off about this. Wait, do you think it's a trap?" Marcus asked.

"I don't know."

Marcus rubbed his scar. "Yeah. We don't even know if this chick's alone."

"Marc, you know we can handle anything that gets in our way."

The brothers played games and continued to talk about Marcus' infatuation, until Darius noticed the lights had gone out.

"We should go get this done," he said.

"Sweet."

***

Sweaty and panting, Brenden laid on his back as Siobhan curled up into his side, his arm wrapped around her naked body as she laid her head on his chest and closed her eyes.

"I don't know if I can top all of this for your birthday," she said with a yawn.

"Oh," Brenden started as he kissed her head, "You never have to do much. Besides, we can just repeat this last part and I'd be the happiest man alive."

She giggled, "Can you reach the light?"

Brenden stretched and turned the bedside lamp off. He began tracing her bare back with his finger, lulling her to sleep. Her left leg draped over the sheet and over Brenden's leg, exposing her buttocks as she continued to cool.

Her left arm laid across his abdomen while the fingers of her hand splayed over his chest, feeling his heartbeat.

She was jolted awake when Brenden sat up in the bed.

"What is it?" she asked.

"I heard something," he whispered. "Did you set the alarm?"

"Oh shit," she whispered back, "I don't remember doing it."

"Stay here," Brenden said, as he got up to investigate.

Siobhan sat up and pulled the sheet up over her breasts. Brenden pulled his dress pants up, leaving them unbuttoned, and the belt hanging loose.

"When I walk out of the room, I want you to hide in the closet," he said, and she nodded.

Before he made it all the way to her bedroom door, a figure of a man stood in the doorframe.

Brenden started, "Who the fuc-" as 3 bullets from a suppressed Heckler & Koch USP hit center mass.

Siobhan produced a short, surprised scream and stopped. She was too scared to move. Darius continued into the room, paying more attention to the man he put down to make sure he was dead. Focused on the scream, Marcus came in behind his brother, with his gun locked on their mark.

She was a vision. Even scared, Marcus thought she was the most beautiful woman to ever walk the Earth.

Darius put one more bullet in Brendan's head, startling his brother and Siobhan as they stared at each other.

"What the fuck are you doing?!" she screamed and launched her naked body at Marcus from the bed.

"Oh, shit!" Darius exclaimed, coming to the realization that his brother's infatuation was none other than their mark, Siobhan O'Connell.

Marcus easily side stepped her assault and caught her in his left arm. She struggled as he pulled her hair to bring her face to his. He trapped her against his body and for a brief second, he inhaled her scent and felt what it was like to have her up against him.

"So, I guess I have your name now, Siobhan," Marcus said before pivoting, causing Siobhan to fall to her knees.

Marcus put the gun to the side of her head.

He looked up at his brother, "Pity," he said, before pulling the trigger and walking away.

Chapter Thirty-Two

Later the next day, they were informed of an emergency meeting at the Bandoni estate.

As they approached, they noticed the bustling atmosphere as every employee and family member was rushing to the meeting.

They saw Liam as they got out of their car. Darius hurried toward him and asked, "What's going on?"

"Someone killed Brenden, the nephew, and his girl last night. Bandoni's on the phone with Mannix O'Connell breaking the news to him."

Darius asked, "Why is he calling Mannix?"

Liam answered, "His daughter, Siobhan, was Brenden's girl."

Marcus turned to his brother, his eyes wide. Darius felt sick.

In the briefing, the brothers paid little attention.

They knew the details and didn't need a refresher.

Darius kept his eye on Liam who acted nonchalant, yet eager, to want the culprit caught. He even found social media posts of the two young lovers to show Bandoni's men.

"Marcus and Darius Tye!" Liam shouted over the murmuring in the conference room. "The second we find out who did it, you will be dispatched to take care of them. Be on stand-by and ready to go at a moment's notice."

All the brothers could do was nod, as eyes turned in their direction before the murmuring continued.

Darius hopped in the car and started to pull away before Marcus could even close the door. His anger was festering more and more as time went on.

"What the absolute fuck, Marcus?" he asked.

"She said she had a boyfriend, but never, in a million years, did I think it would be Bandoni's nephew."

"That's not what's upsetting me. Who ordered the fucking hit?!" Darius yelled, slamming on his brakes when the light turned red.

"Do you want me to drive?" Marcus calmly asked.

"I want you to build a time machine, so we can ask Bandoni directly if he ordered that hit and avoid all of this."

"Hmm, that I cannot do."

"Fuck! You even said there was something off about this. Remember?"

"Yeah, and Bandoni's gonna use his resources in the police department and make this case a priority, too."

"Fuck!" Darius yelled.

***

A week and a half passed before the funeral. Bandoni met with Mannix, and they agreed on a cemetery, plot, and service. Mannix went back to Boston with a promise that Bandoni would keep him updated on their investigation.

The day before the service, Liam was called into Bandoni's office.

"Mr. Stacey, I need you to find me an investigator," Bandoni said.

"Why, Sir?"

"This was a hit by someone who has no love for either the Bandoni or the O'Connell family. Someone knew of their relationship and the police are useless. I need someone who will be motivated to find Brenden's killer."

"I understand, Sir. Who should I get to investigate?"

Bandoni wiped the moisture from his face, shrugged, and said, "Someone neutral. I still don't know who would have done this! Have you heard of any other organizations in town? CIA? FBI? I can't trust anyone working for the government at this point. Find me someone who can work outside the law."

Liam shook his head, "No, Sir. I'm just... I am so sorry, Sir. I'd give anything to make this easier. I'll find you the best investigator I can."

Bandoni scoffed, "I have never been less in the mood for your ass kissing, Liam. Just, do as I ask and get out of my sight."

The Tye brothers were in attendance at the funeral, mainly to avoid suspicion amongst the family. Darius noticed a younger brunette woman tossing a flower onto Siobhan's casket. She tried so hard to be stoic, but a sob caught her off guard and she covered her face.

Back at the Bandoni estate, the brothers separated and started talking to others about the tragedy.

Darius noticed the same woman from the funeral and excused himself from the conversation he was in.

She was sitting alone in the corner and sipping on a mixed drink.

"Hey, I'm Darius. I saw you earlier at the funeral. How did you know Siobhan?"

She looked up and smiled warmly at him, "Oh, she was my best friend and roommate at school," she said with a sniffle. She wiped her nose with a tissue, and Darius handed her a new one.

"Thank you. Darius, right?"

Smiling, he said, "Yeah. What's your name?"

"Kelly. Kelly Kinton," she said.

"Nice to meet you, Kelly."

She nodded and looked away.

Darius, trying to avoid being awkward, asked, "Can I get you anything? A drink?"

Kelly held up her glass, showing that she already had one.

Darius smiled and said, "I guess I'm not very observant."

She smiled back, knowing he was just trying to be kind.

"It's okay. It's not a great atmosphere to meet new people."

Darius nodded, "Yeah, the last one I went to was for my best friend."

"Oh God, I'm sorry to hear that!" Kelly said.

"It was rough," he replied. "So, I understand what you're feeling if you ever want to talk."

Kelly studied his face as she smiled, "Be careful, Darius. I just might take you up on that offer."

He took in a deep, shaky breath. Marcus caught his eye, gesturing toward the door.

"Man, I don't want to stop talking to you, but I promised we'd leave soon."

"We?" Kelly asked, trying not to sound disappointed.

"My brother and I. He's over there," Darius said, pointing with his drink.

"Oh," she said unashamedly, as her relief was obvious. "Well, I don't want to stop talking to you, either."

"What are you studying in school?" he asked to keep the conversation going.

"Physics," she said with a big smile.

Darius stumbled over his words, "Whoa, Physics. That's uh, um _"

"Boring. I know."

"Boring? Nah, come on, it's not boring. It's," Darius sighed, "Impressive."

"Are you saying you're impressed, Darius?" she asked.

"Yes, ma'am. I'm very impressed by you," he said, with a sheepish grin.

"So, what do you do?" she asked.

"We work for the Bandoni family. My brother and I. Well, sorta. We're like contractors."

"What kind of contractors?"

Darius tried to backtrack, "Odd jobs, this and that. Whatever they need done, really."

Kelly smiled at Darius and stayed quiet while they gazed at each other.

"What?" he finally asked.

"Siobhan was my best friend and Brenden was over a lot. So, I know what the Bandoni and O'Connell families are all about. You don't have to whitewash it for me. I'm into honest men. Whether they're bad or not isn't my concern."

"Are you staying in town?" Darius asked.

"I was going to leave tonight."

Darius paused for a moment, "Stay another night. Let me take you to dinner."

"Are you asking me out on a date at a funeral?"

Darius pursed his lips, "Well, since you like honest men, yes. I am definitely asking you out at a funeral."

"Hmm, I do like a bad boy," she teased as she handed him her drink and brushed past him to leave.

"Are you leaving so soon?" Darius asked, flustered that she was out-flirting him.

"I have a hot date to get ready for; and besides, weren't you just saying you guys were about to go?"

"Yeah, I did say that," he admitted.

***

Liam Stacey did a quick internet search, and his eyes were caught by a name, Clifford Dee. He knew Mr. Bandoni would not want him to leave a message so when he got Clifford's voicemail he hung up and decided to go directly to the address on the site. He was about to go in when a stocky built man with a slight limp came out and jumped in a dark green Mustang Bullitt.

Liam followed him to a pizza joint, where he got two boxes, then to a motel on the edge of town. He watched as Clifford went to the second floor with the pizza. Liam walked over to the only other car in the lot, a rusted white Toyota Celica. He spotted a shiny metal medallion that seemed way too valuable and out of place in that vehicle. He adjusted his fedora to shield him from the mid-afternoon sun and broke into the car to snag the medallion.

Hearing a commotion overhead, Liam turned to see Clifford Dee running down the steps followed by a scrawny guy with a gun.

Liam drew his own gun and Clifford, who turned to run under the stairs, lurched to a stop, raising his hands when he saw him. The thug behind Clifford was struggling with the sunlight as his eyes hadn't adjusted from the dark hotel room. He couldn't see Liam who fired one shot, hitting the thug directly in the temple.

His friend followed quickly behind and was also met by Liam's bullet.

"Clifford Dee?" Liam asked. "Yeah?" Clifford responded, squinting in the sunlight.

"My name is Liam Stacey," he said. "I have something for you. A gift."

Coming to the realization that he couldn't flee, and that Liam Stacey wanted to give him something, Clifford put his hands down.

"A gift?" Clifford asked.

"First, here!" he said, as he tossed the medallion in Clifford's direction.

"Where'd ya find this?" Clifford asked.

"In their car. It's what you're looking for, right?" Liam asked.

"Yeah thanks, but did you have to shoot those guys?"

"They were going to kill you, and my employer wants to hire you. He can't if you're dead."

"Who's your employer?"

"His name is Bandoni."

***

Back at Bandoni's estate, Liam and Clifford arrived as the last of the repast attendees were leaving.

Clifford stepped out of the passenger side of the car and was approached by a man in a black suit. He spotted the outline of a Beretta pistol inside his jacket as he walked up. He raised his hands for the second time in a span of an hour.

"He's with me, Fredrico!" Liam shouted over the hood of the car as he rounded the front.

"Mr. Stacey, who is your guest?" Fredrico asked.

"Mr. Bandoni needs a tracker, and Clifford Dee here's the best in the county."

Clifford gave Fredrico a tight-lipped smile.

Fredrico called into his radio, "Mr. Stacey's here with a Clifford Dee to see the boss. Can he see anyone right now?"

He held his earpiece to hear the communication.

"I will send them up," he said back.

Liam strolled into Bandoni's office and said, "Mr. B, please meet Mr. Dee."

Unpleased with the joke, Bandoni ignored him.

"Mr. Dee? Please sit."

Bandoni looked over at Liam and said, "Mr. Stacey, please leave."

Liam scoffed, "Sir?"

"Now, Liam!"

He nodded, closing the door behind him.

E.I. Bandoni gave Clifford Dee the rundown of what happened to his nephew, his old rival's daughter, and his reasoning for an outsider to figure it out.

"Liam will be made available to you for any questions you may have or access you may need."

Clifford tried to speak, but Bandoni held out his hand and continued, "You will be paid handsomely. The second you find out who, I want names, and then, I want them handed over to me alive and bound."

"With all due respect, that last part is a felony, Sir."

"You can either be paid a great deal of money and do the job I give you, or you can be buried in my garden, and I'll find someone who wants my money. Your choice."

"Handed over to you alive and bound. Got it!" Clifford said flatly.

Chapter Thirty-Three

Liam dropped Clifford off at the motel parking lot to get his Mustang and sped off. Clifford Dee gave himself a moment to process what had just happened. He took the recently acquired medallion to the person who hired him to find it and collected his fee. As he arrived home, he found a section of an outdated newspaper at his door. He examined it as he walked inside and saw three red circles drawn in sharpie. He put his keys down and spread the paper to get a full look. The circles surrounded three different letters. Y, T, and E. They were all circled in an article titled: The Bandoni-O'Connell: Romeo and Juliet Murders.

Clifford grabbed his cell and texted the newest number in his contacts.

Liam was waiting on the other side of the park, across from Clifford's place, when he got the text he was hoping for. Ten minutes later, Liam was being invited into Clifford's home office. He showed Liam the article with the circled letters.

"What does the YET mean to you?" he asked Liam.

Liam played dumb. He looked at the article for as long as he thought looked convincing. "T, Y, E. It's TYE. As in the Tye brothers!"

"And they are?" Clifford asked.

"Bandoni's latest enforcers. Frick and fucking Frack," Liam said.

"You don't sound too fond of them."

"I was flawless and now I've been relegated to an errand boy, and now a babysitter. No offense, by the way."

"None taken. So, why would they be a part of this? It sounds like they've got a good thing going."

"They're killers, Mr. Dee. We ran the O'Connell's out, and they're bored."

"I guess I better get eyes on them," Clifford said.

Liam smiled, "You're motivated. I like that. I'll drive."

Liam drove Clifford a street over from the brother's new house and parked. He pulled out his binoculars and another pair from the glove box for Dee.

"Marcus could be with Darius, but I'm certain that Darius is not in the house right now."

"Well, someone's there, look," Clifford said when he saw a large man come out on the porch to drink a beer.

"That's Marcus," Liam revealed, as they both watched him absentmindedly touch his scar.

"They're rarely separated."

Clifford thought Liam sounded nervous. "Why don't you go try and find Darius? You seem familiar with his habits and where he might go," he suggested.

"What will you do?" Liam asked.

"I'll keep an eye on the big guy here."

"Okay, but don't be deceived, Dee. He may look house-broken, but I assure you he's as feral as they come. Marcus will drop you without a second thought."

Clifford was well-armed, and with permission to borrow the binoculars, stepped out of Liam's car to be picked up in the same spot at a later time.

He watched Marcus leave the porch and walk into the woods. He wasn't too keen on following a killer into the woods at dusk, no matter how many guns he had on him.

He laughed to himself, "I think this is how horror movies start out."

Clifford kept a safe distance but was losing visibility. He eventually turned around as the woods became too thick to navigate. He lost him.

Clifford decided to walk on the sidewalk around the neighborhood to get familiarized with the landscape and vehicles that were parked around the Tye home. He planned to return alone, at first light, to see if Marcus did anything in the woods that would raise a red flag. He still thought of the suspicious circumstances surrounding the clue left on his front door and knew he couldn't take any of this at face value.

***

Darius was nearly giddy when he pulled up to Kelly's hotel. He hadn't felt this hopeful in a really long time. He never thought he would ever have a chance with a woman like her. He brought her purple tulips. As he stood at her door, he wondered what she was going to do with flowers in a hotel room. He thought about tossing them and then she opened the door, startling him.

"I'm nervous so I've been checking the peephole every 10 seconds," she blurted, with a laugh.

"Well, I was just in the middle of convincing myself that flowers were a bad idea," he admitted, taking a moment to fully look at her. He could barely hear her sweet laugh, as he took in the sight of her. She was picturesque in a lavender and white sundress with sandals. The light musky fragrance she wore intoxicated him. He took in the dainty pearl that hung from a thin gold chain she wore around her kissable neck. Matching pearls hung on the ears he wanted to whisper into.

"Flowers are never a bad idea. Thank you!" she said, as she invited him in. Kelly moved quickly as she grabbed the hotel ice bucket from the dresser and walked into the bathroom to fill it with water. Darius was unsure what to do so he strolled over to look out her window to see her view.

"Try not to be jealous. Not every view has a brightly lit parking lot and a bypass," she said from behind him.

He laughed at her quick wit and was turned on even more. "This view really does suck," he agreed.

"Well, I'm a college student, and my daddy isn't as connected as others, so I get what I can afford," she said with a shrug.

"I love how open and honest you are," Darius said, without thinking.

She noticed he surprised himself with his admission, and she suddenly felt warmth deep in her belly. "Well, how's this for open and honest?" Kelly began, as she grabbed her purse and walked towards the door. "You're gonna have to royally fuck up tonight to not get laid."

Darius could feel the smile on his face but not his legs. He quickly regained his composure and closed the space between them. "If I ever royally fuck up anything with you, I'm an idiot. Dinner?"

Kelly cocked her head to the side. "Lead the way."

"Do you like Chinese?" he asked her, walking to his car.

Kelly and Marcus talked and laughed all through dinner. He was fascinated listening to her talk about her classes.

"You have to be bored?" she asked him.

"Quite the opposite, actually. I could listen to you talk for hours. I don't have to understand what you're talking about to enjoy it."

When she realized she was doing all the talking, she engaged him with a question about his childhood.

"Marc and I were born not far from here, but we moved around a lot in foster care after our parents died."

"Oh my god! I'm so sorry. No wonder you and Marc are so close. It makes sense."

"Yeah, but Marc is... special," Darius started, "He was in an accident that caused a brain injury. It changed him, his personality and..." Darius struggled to find the words, "I don't think I could ever leave him. Does that make sense?"

"It does. I hope to get to know him."

Darius was more nervous about that than anything else.

"Let me pay for you to stay longer. Do you have anything going on for the rest of this Summer?" he asked, reaching for Kelly's hand.

She didn't know what to say and thought she'd tease him, "We haven't even had sex yet. It could be awful."

"Let's do it right here on the table and find out," he quipped back.

She laughed, "Lo mein, everywhere."

Darius watched her laugh, eat, and talk as though everything she did was a work of art. He gave his brother so much shit for the way he talked about Siobhan. The sudden thought of Siobhan made Darius wince. How was this going to work if she found out they were responsible for her best friend's murder.

"Dari? You okay?" Kelly asked, snapping him out of his thought spiral.

"I don't want this night to end, but I'm so ready to take you back to the hotel."

Kelly pouted, "Wanna get rid of me now?"

Darius shook his head slowly. "I wanna get rid of the rest of the world, and just keep you."

Kelly felt the warmth deep in her belly again like before. "We should probably leave now."

"Check!" Darius yelled out.

Darius took her hand to help her out of his car, feeling as though someone was watching them. He quickly glanced around, putting a protective arm around Kelly and escorted her into the hotel. He was on alert until the elevator doors closed. Kelly felt him relax and leaned into him, nuzzling his neck and inhaling his musk. She loved the feel of his arm wrapped around her, and she felt safe and warm. She had already started to unbutton his shirt when the elevator doors opened to her floor. Scrambling to retrieve her room's keycard from her purse, she could barely get the door open with Darius kissing her shoulder and playing with her hair. Darius walked in first and turned around, pushing Kelly into the closing door so he could make sure it was locked without breaking stride. She wrapped her legs around his waist while her back was firmly pressed against the door. She heard him lock the door and put the chain on, before carrying her over to the bed. Darius turned and sat on the edge of the bed with Kelly straddling his lap. She continued her work on his shirt buttons as he kissed and nibbled her neck. A soft growl escaped his throat close to her ear and she trembled. Finding the edge of her dress, he slid his hand up her thigh. After undoing the final button, she wrestled the shirt off his body and placed a hand on his belly as he laid back. Her touch caused him to inhale sharply. Darius noticed the curtains were still open and he silently cursed to himself. Kelly started to undo his belt when he gently grasped her wrists and sat up. He placed a tender kiss on her lips and picked her up again, letting her feet slide to the floor. He walked over to the curtains and slid them closed. When he turned back around, Kelly had slipped her dress off and stood wearing only the dainty pearl jewelry.

***

After driving around for an hour and a half, Liam finally located Darius' car heading to a hotel. He watched as Darius got out and walked around to the passenger side, helping a beautiful young brunette out of the car. They disappeared into the lobby of the hotel, and Liam waited to see if Darius would come back out. A movement in one of the windows eventually caught his eye. He watched as a shirtless Darius closed the curtains.

"Well, that explains Marcus being alone. Good for you, Darius. If anyone needs to get laid, it's you," he said to himself, as he sent Clifford a text, he was on his way back.

Liam dropped Clifford off in front of his condo after comparing uneventful notes. He needed to bide his time until he could pit the organization against the Tye brothers. Clifford Dee was becoming a different kind of problem for him.

Chapter Thirty-Four

At dawn, Clifford stood at the edge of the woods near the spot he witnessed Marcus enter the night before. He saw the same cars in the driveway and surrounding the house. The lights Marcus left on, the night before, were now off. Using that as proof that the known killer was no longer lurking in the woods, Clifford started his investigation with a flashlight in his hand and his gun on his hip.

It wasn't a particularly large area of woods, but it was thick. After about thirty minutes, Clifford came upon a small clearing as sunlight filtered through the leaves and hearty branches. He clicked his flashlight off as he walked closer to a macabre scene.

An hour and a half later, Clifford was in his home office, making a phone call.

"Hello sir, I'm looking for Margaret, is she available to speak?"

"Sir, I'm sorry to inform you, but my wife, Peg, died two years ago. Is there something I can help you with?" Harold asked.

"I'm very sorry to hear about your wife. I was calling to ask some questions about two boys who stayed with you many years ago."

Harold scoffed, "We got so many kids, I don't know if I'd be of any help at all. It's hard to keep track, ya know?"

"Their names are Darius and Marcus Tye."

There was silence on the phone for a few seconds. "What do you want to know about those boys?"

"So you do remember them?" Clifford asked.

"Yeah. I remember 'em."

"I can be up there in about two hours. I'd like to talk to you in person."

"Do you have my address?" Harold asked.

"Yes, sir, I do," Clifford responded.

***

Darius woke up with Kelly's naked body wrapped around him. She was nestled perfectly in the crook of his left arm with her head on his chest. He kissed the top of her head and covered the hand she rested on his chest with his own.

"I have to check out soon," she groaned as she stretched.

Darius brought his right arm around her body as he shifted to trap her on her back. Propping himself up on his left elbow, he gazed down at her, smoothing the hair from her face to give her a long soft kiss. His hand left her face and trailed down her body to rest on her left hip. When he felt her body react to his touch, he suddenly stopped.

"Do not move from this bed. I'll be right back."

She thought about arguing but was afraid to break the spell she was under. Kelly watched as Darius got up and tossed his pants and shirt on while grabbing the keycard before kissing her again, gesturing for her to stay put.

About twenty minutes later he came back with a plate of Danish and two cups of orange juice. He put everything down on the dresser next to the TV and playfully shed his clothing.

Kelly giggled as he climbed back into bed and scooped her up against him. "Your room is paid for, for another day, if you want it," he said, as he nuzzled the back of her ear and neck, his hand moving from her hip to her belly.

Kelly tried to keep her mind clear to what he was saying, "Are you serious?" she panted.

"I am. Stay at least one more day." Darius begged, "Please?"

She turned to face him. "Are you sure?" she asked.

"Honey, I feel like missing you would shatter my world and I'm not ready to feel that."

***

It was well after lunch when Clifford got back from Indianapolis. He pulled up to the little deli where he chose to meet Liam.

"Bandoni's riding my ass. Tell me you found something connecting at least one of the Tye brothers to Brenden's murder," Liam said, sliding into a chair and removing his sunglasses.

Clifford swallowed his bite before saying, "Man, you look rough. Did you get any sleep?"

Liam sniffed, "I'm good. What'd you find?" he asked impatiently. Clifford noticed Liam Stacey appeared agitated, his one leg bouncing restlessly.

"Well," Clifford started, as he grabbed his folder and opened it to reveal a couple of photos. "I went back out to the woods Marcus walked into last night. I found a bunch of crude traps. I also saw a variety of animals hanging in the trees."

"What the fuck are you telling me right now?"

"I saw a fox, an opossum, several squirrels... It was a bit unsettling, and I've seen some shit."

"Alright, how does this have anything to do with Bandoni's nephew?"

"I'm not sure just yet, but let me tell you about everything I did find."

Liam gestured for him to continue as he sniffed again.

"Well, I found the names of an aunt and uncle that they lived with. I called them last night and they wanted nothing to do with anything I had to say. I did manage to get a little information as to why they gave them up to the state."

"Wait," Liam interrupted, "What happened to their parents?"

"You're getting ahead of me," Clifford said with a smile. Liam gestured again for Clifford to continue.

"Marcus had a brain injury in a car accident and his personality changed. One day, their cousin's pet hamster was found hanging in its cage. Then, the boys go to their first group home. I spent some time this morning with one of the people that used to run it. He showed me these," Clifford said, as he spread out three photos."

"What the fuck am I looking at?" Liam asked in disgust.

"Rats. All hanging from under a bed. Marcus Tye's bed, in fact. They're hanging just like the hamster."

"Okay, budding serial killer, I see." Liam surmised.

Clifford nodded, "But wait," he paused for dramatic effect, "There's more. A few years later, Darius aged out of the system, and Marcus was left with his last foster parents. The foster mother was murdered."

"Marcus?" Liam asked.

"Well, we may never know. But you tell me, Rope was found around her neck, but she wasn't hung like the animals. Plus, and unfortunately, she was a crack whore. So, a lot of different DNA was found on, in, and around her with a plethora of suspects."

"Jesus Christ," Liam said, under his breath.

"I haven't gotten to the best part."

"How much more can there be?"

"Well, the accident that caused Marcus' brain damage was caused by his father. Just before he strung up their mother. The cops shot him as he hung her in the very tree the car hit. They witnessed it all."

"There's a lot of hangings in this story," Liam quipped.

"Right? I thought so, too. Harold, the guy I talked with, said that he and his wife were certain that Marcus was the Tree Girl Killer and even went to the police, but were dismissed."

Liam's eyes grew wide with that bit of information. He thought for a moment and then asked, "Didn't they find the last girl a few years ago?"

Clifford nodded, "Three or four years ago, yeah."

Liam thought for a moment. "Did you find anything about them in Tennessee?"

Clifford smiled, "What do you know about Tennessee?"

"I know Darius killed a cop there." Liam had no trouble giving dirt on one of the Tye Brothers.

"I didn't see anything on that, but they were in the state around the same time the Tree Girls in Tennessee were found."

Nodding, Liam said, "Sit on this for a bit, would you?"

"What are you thinking?"

Liam replied, "I just want to be completely sure before running to Bandoni with this information. If they are the Tree Girl Killers, that's one thing. But there's nothing to tie them to Brenden and Siobhan's murder. That's what we need."

Clifford stammered, "Those look like a legit hit. The Tye's work for Bandoni. I just don't think they'd have a motive to kill them."

Liam tried to hide his annoyance with the P.I. he hired. He thought Clifford Dee was a hack, but he was actually good at his job. He'd have to get rid of him soon.

"Siobhan was a beautiful young woman. Maybe one of them hit on her, and she rejected them. Their ego couldn't handle it so they went to kill her but didn't expect Brenden to be there." Liam looked up at Clifford, feeling proud of his possible scenario idea, expecting him to finish the thought.

Clifford sighed, "Yeah, that's possible. I mean anything's possible with a killer who can be set off by anything. You told me last night; he wouldn't think twice about putting me down."

"The stories Mike told me-"

Clifford interrupted, "Wait, who's Mike?"

"He was a good guy. Mike's the one that vouched for the brothers. He knew them when they were kids."

"We should talk to him. Harold mentioned a Mike."

"Mike's dead. Killed on a job," Liam abruptly stated.

"A hit gone wrong?" Clifford asked.

"The organization does more than hits, Mr. Dee. He was actually destroying one of the O'Connell's warehouses with-," Liam stopped for a moment and smiled at the coincidence, "with the Tye brothers."

"Do you think they did something?"

Liam shook his head, "No. Darius took Mike's death hard. I think one of the O'Connell's got him before the fire."

"Yeah. Harold said Mike ran away and the brothers weren't the same afterwards. They must have always been tight with one another," Clifford added to the argument against blaming the brothers for Mike's death.

Liam nodded, "Probably pissed he didn't take them with him. Well," Liam slapped the table, "let's keep digging. I don't think it's enough to loop Bandoni in yet. Lots of theory, not enough proof. We need more."

Clifford nodded, "You're right. I'll keep at it."

Chapter Thirty-Five

"Can I meet your brother before I leave?" Kelly asked Darius after her third extra day at the hotel.

"Wait, you're leaving?" he joked as he pretended to be stabbed in the heart.

"My parents will think I've been abducted if I don't give them better proof of life than texts. Plus," she looked around the coffee shop, "I'm running out of clothes."

"Tell you what, let's grab your clothes and we'll wash them at my place while we hang out with Marc. We can all get dinner and then you and I go back to the hotel to," he turns to dramatically look directly at her, raising his eyebrows up and down, "Not sleep."

"I need to hydrate," Kelly groaned, and Darius laughed into his coffee, splattering it everywhere.

"Do you mind adding my shirt to your load of laundry later?" Darius asked with a hopeful expression.

"Not even a week and you've already got me doing your laundry," she quipped.

"Are we about to have our first fight?" he playfully asked.

"Wanna skip to the make-up sex?"

"Yes. But I should probably hydrate too," he admitted.

They left to get her suitcase full of dirty clothes from the hotel. Darius received a text before they left the room.

"Shit. I forgot my brother and I have a game tonight," he said, as he responded to Marcus.

"What game?" Kelly asked.

"We're in charge of a weekly poker thing and I forgot it was scheduled for tonight."

"Okay. Why is there a problem?"

"It's a late-night thing."

"Ah, not a problem. I'll drive my car over to your house. I'll do laundry while we hang out until you have to leave for the game. When the laundry's done, I'll pack it up and meet you back here."

"I've never been so motivated to get through a game."

Kelly grabbed her keys, "Just stay hydrated. And maybe eat some protein at dinner."

Kelly parked her car in the street, and Darius carried her suitcase inside. Marcus came down the stairs fresh out of a shower, his wet hair slicked back. Setting the suitcase down, Darius made the introductions. He was worried how Marcus was going to react, given his history with women and with Mike. Darius knew this was a risk and he admitted to himself that Kelly's planned departure might be for the best. He would visit her, no matter where she was.

"So, you're the reason my brother's so happy all the damn time," Marcus playfully accused, as he shook her hand.

"I'd better be," she retorted with a smile. "And you must be the most important person in his life. It's an honor to meet you, Marc," she said, squeezing his hand a little before letting go.

Marcus blushed and asked if he could get drinks.

"Actually, Marc, give us a few minutes. I need to change and show her the laundry room," Darius said, running up the steps with the suitcase. He gestured at Kelly to follow him.

As they left the room, Marcus said, "I'll order pizza, if that's cool with everybody."

Kelly followed Darius to his bedroom after they agreed to pizza and he locked the door, stripping out of his coffee-stained shirt. Kelly sat on his bed looking around. He was a minimalist when it came to decorating. He cursed himself noticing he left some of his weapons sitting around. Darius watched her study his room and waited to see her reaction.

"It's cozy." she finally said. Her words dripped in sarcasm and her eyes twinkled. Darius slowly closed the space between them, not once breaking eye contact.

"You should probably wash what you've got on now, too," he whispered, as he slowly started to undress her.

By the time the pizza arrived, Kelly and Darius were walking back downstairs. She was wearing a pair of old sweatpants and a hoodie. He loved seeing his clothing on her body.

A few hours later, it was time for the brothers to leave for the game. They both promised it would be as quick as they could make it. Darius kissed Kelly at the door.

"It should only take two hours, tops. I hope to get to you before you fall asleep," he said as he kissed her nose.

"If not, promise to wake me?" she teased.

"Oh, I promise. Lock the door and don't answer it for anyone," Darius said, before kissing her again.

Marcus impatiently cleared his throat behind him.

Darius looked back to glare at his brother. Marcus couldn't hide his smile and walked away, whistling.

***

Bandoni was breathing down Liam's neck to motivate the P.I. to find whoever was behind the hit. The police believed it was motivated by jealousy or even a suicide pact, which infuriated him. Liam blamed Brenden for his own death. No one knew he was with the O'Connell girl. Marcus and Darius did exactly what they were told, and they did exactly what they always do. Pivot and leave no witnesses. If Bandoni ever found out Liam was the one behind it by using his favorite henchmen, all three of them would be dead, but he'd be tortured first. Liam had spent the past few days randomly finding and following one of the Tye brothers. He noticed they were separate more often than together and soon realized that Darius was consistently seen with the same beautiful brunette. He was angry they had his job, making his money, and now, Darius was walking around with arm candy.

Liam hadn't slept in two days. Opening the center console of his car, he found his small baggie of cocaine. He had to tie Marcus and Darius to the hit without implicating himself. If he could prove, without a shadow of a doubt, that one or both of them were the Tree Girl Killer, Bandoni would have them taken out immediately. He'd be back where he belonged. He had to find the proof before Clifford figured anything else out. Then he would expose Clifford to the brothers. While they're busy with him, he'd convince Bandoni they were hitmen gone rogue and serial killers.

He did another bump from his baggie before getting out of his car, near the Tye house. Liam already went through their old condo the organization owned and came up with nothing. Now he needed to get into their house to look around. The lights were on inside, but their SUV was gone. Liam went around to the back and picked the lock of the door on the side of the house. He watched as the brunette walked downstairs with a suitcase and set it by the front door with her keys. She made her way into the kitchen and Liam became nervous that she would find him. Assuming she was done upstairs, he snuck around her and quietly ran up the stairs to search the bedrooms, hoping she'd leave the house soon.

After she set her suitcase and keys by the front door, Kelly went to the kitchen to grab one more slice of pizza before heading back to her hotel. She had changed back into her own clothes and laid the sweatpants on his bed. His hoodie, however, was packed in her suitcase. She wanted to take it home because it smelled like him. She smiled to herself thinking about wrapping herself in his hoodie and texting him from her own bedroom. She sprayed a mist of her perfume on his bed to give him the same feeling. Kelly sighed as she started to feel melancholy. She reached her hand up to play with her necklace and realized she left it in Darius' bedroom and made her way back upstairs to retrieve it.

As Kelly rounded the corner to Darius' room, she saw a man she didn't recognize kneeling on the floor, looking under the bed. Liam jumped to his feet when he heard her startled gasp. Kelly turned to run, and Liam knew he couldn't risk her telling the Tye brothers that he was there. He saw the boot knife Mike gifted Darius on the dresser and grabbed it as he chased her down the stairs. Kelly flew down the steps and snagged her keys, leaving her suitcase as she ran out of the door. She never made it past the front lawn. Liam was faster and she wasn't the first person he had to chase down. He tackled her, knocking the wind out of her. He struggled with her to get her onto her back. Kelly screamed, punched and clawed with everything she had. After a brief struggle, he straddled her and plunged Darius' knife into her chest. He stayed still until her arms fell to her side and her last long breath escaped her lungs.

Panting, Liam sat back and looked around. Luckily, the house was set back from the rest of the neighborhood. He left the knife in Kelly's chest and took her keys to open the trunk of her car. Liam placed her body in the trunk and went back for her suitcase. When he came back to her car, he opened the suitcase and pulled out an old large hoodie. Liam grasped the handle of the knife and pulled it from her chest, covering the hole it made with the hoodie. He used the sleeve of the hoodie to clean the knife and shoved it into his waistband. He made sure to lock the front door and closed it. Leaving the house the same way he found it, he had to concede that getting rid of the brunette's body was top priority and if he couldn't use the time to search their house, he'd frame them for her murder.

Liam drove Kelly's car and transferred her body to the back of his SUV after he laid down one of the plastic sheets he saved for such an occasion. He drove to one of the 24-hour hardware stores the city had, and bought rope with cash before driving to some random woods off highway 31. He worked as fast as he could and raced to get back to her car, put it somewhere, get home and shower.

***

"I can drop you off at the hotel instead," Marcus offered his brother, after they left the game in the bakery.

Darius shook his head, "Nah. I don't like her driving me around. I'm old fashioned, I guess."

"Never pegged you as a sexist," Marcus quipped.

Darius laughed, "I have to touch her, and if she were driving, we'd end up crashing."

"Couple Killed in Crash. Cause: Foreplay," Marcus teased.

The brothers laughed and joked as they pulled up to their house. Darius carried his keys with him and got in his car as Marcus continued inside, waving to his brother.

Darius went well above the speed limit to get to the hotel. He didn't see her car but didn't think anything of it as he ran through the lobby. He chose the stairs, believing the elevator would take too long. Keycard in hand, he walked into her room and saw the bed was empty. He turned the light on in the bathroom and even looked behind the shower curtain. Darius tried calling her cell and it went straight to voicemail. He got back in his car and retraced the route between the hotel and his house, looking for her car. He tried calling again and this time, he left a message.

"Hey, I can't find you and I'm getting really worried here, babe. Please call me when you get this. Don't text. You call me. I need to hear your voice and know you're okay. Did you decide to go back home? Seriously, whatever it is, I just want to know you're okay."

He sent a text to Marcus and when he got back to their house, his brother was waiting outside for him.

"I checked the house, she isn't anywhere in there," Marcus stated with his keys in his hand.

"You got to help me find her, Marc."

Chapter Thirty-Six:

Diego Muñoz was lounging in his backyard on a sunny Monday morning when he received a phone call.

"Detective Diego Muñoz?" The voice on the other side said.

Muñoz, swallowing his coffee, cleared his throat, "Yeah, this is me."

"Hey, this is Detective Martin DiPietro of the Broward Valley police department here in Kentucky. I heard you were the lead detective investigating the Tree Girl killings."

"Once upon a time, I was, yeah, but I'm retired now. Has there been another one?"

Martin answered, "We think so. Are you up for a drive? I could really use your expertise on this."

"Text me the address, I'll leave now."

A few hours later, Muñoz found the police station and flashed his old badge at the desk and asked for Martin DiPietro. The officer pointed toward his desk.

"Detective DiPietro?"

DiPietro looked up, "Yeah."

"Detective Diego Muñoz," he said, introducing himself, holding a large folder.

Martin smiled and stood to greet the man, "You made record time."

Muñoz smiled and asked, "So you think you got yourself a Tree Girl?"

Martin slid a photo across his desk as Diego sat down. "She was stabbed in the chest and then hung. The knife was not found at the scene, but there was blood on the rope, so it suggests that they used the knife to cut the rope after they stabbed her."

Muñoz rubbed his chin, "Interesting."

"What's interesting?" Martin asked.

"None of the other victims were stabbed. They were all strangled and hung up."

DiPietro countered, "Maybe something went wrong and the killer had to stab her? Maybe they were afraid she was going to get someone's attention?"

Muñoz looked at the picture again and asked, "Was the rope Manila, cotton-twisted? One inch?"

Martin said, "No, it was nylon."

"I have my doubts this is the work of the original killer," Muñoz said, opening his folder.

"Why do you say that?" Martin asked.

"The rope is wrong. We never released it to the public, but the killer used twisted manila rope, not nylon. Also, the killer always kept their victims hanging just an inch or two off the ground. It gave the appearance they were standing near whatever tree they were hung from. This poor girl was hoisted pretty high."

Martin compared the photos from previous victims.

Diego Muñoz reminded, "Also, none of the victims had any type of punctures or cuts and this one had a stab wound to the heart. I assume that was the initial cause of death?"

Martin nodded, "It was."

"One more thing, the strangulation is what will give him away because our Tree Girl Killer has had some type of injury to one of his hands and he leaves a very specific bruise on the victim's neck."

Martin asked, "So you think we are looking for a copycat?"

Diego Muñoz nodded, "It has to be. The killer or killers haven't killed in a few years and then this? Either they changed their M.O., or it's someone new." He looked at the picture of the victim and asked, "Have you identified her?"

"They're in the process," Martin started. "We believe it's a college student named Kelly Kinton. She went missing a few days ago. Her parents are on their way to the morgue to ID her as we speak."

"Who was the last to see Kelly alive?"

Martin smiled and said, "I was told she was in town for the Siobhan O'Connell and Brendon Bandoni funerals and was seen hanging with one of the Bandoni employees. One of his enforcer goons by the name of Darius Tye."

Martin's desk phone rang. He leaned over and picked up the receiver. "DiPietro," he said into the phone.

He listened intently for a moment and said, "Thank you," before turning back to Muñoz. "It's Kelly Kinton. Her parents just confirmed."

"Her identity is also a red flag."

Martin looked up, "Why's that?"

"The other victims were women who might not be reported missing for a really long time, if ever."

Martin thought about it for a moment, "The others were transients, sex workers or drug addicts."

"Exactly, "Diego stated. "And this victim was a healthy young college student who had family and friends"

"Care to join me as I take a run at Darius Tye?"

"Buy me a cup of coffee on the way?" Diego Muñoz asked, as he slowly raised up from his chair, favoring his bad knee.

Darius heard a loud knock on the door and sat up in his bed. He glanced in Marcus' room on the way downstairs and noticed he wasn't in it. He looked out the window facing the driveway on his way to the door and recognized an unmarked police cruiser. He moved quietly to look through the peephole to get a look at their faces.

Martin knocked again and loudly said, "Mr. Tye. Detectives Martin DiPietro and Diego Muñoz here. We need to ask you some questions about Kelly Kinton."

Darius didn't want to answer the door but thought that they might know what happened to Kelly.

He let out a huge sigh.

"What about Kel? Did you find her?" Darius asked.

"We're trying to piece together a timeline. When was the last time you saw her?" Martin asked.

Darius shook his head, "Thursday night. She had to do her laundry, so I let her come here. I had to go somewhere with my brother for a couple hours and we planned to meet back at her hotel after, but she wasn't there."

Martin nodded, "Is your brother here?"

"No. I haven't seen him today."

"Was he with you the whole time that night?"

"Yeah, Marcus was with me. We don't know what happened to her. When I couldn't find her at her hotel, Marcus and I split up to look, but..." Darius rubbed his eyes when they started to sting, "Sorry, I was in the middle of a nap."

Martin smiled and noticed the red rimmed eyes of someone hurting, "No worries. What was your relationship with Ms. Kinton?"

Darius sighed again, "Well, I thought things were going well. We'd barely left each other's side since last weekend."

Diego Muñoz nodded and asked, "Did your brother like her?"

Darius narrowed his eyes, "Yeah, he thought she was great. Where's this going? Wait, do you know what happened to her?"

"Her body was found yesterday in the woods off highway 31." Martin flatly stated.

Diego examined the changes of Darius' facial expressions.

"What?" Darius questioned, feeling sick.

"We're starting to believe she was a victim of the Tree Girl killer," Diego said, rolling the dice on a gamble.

Martin looked over, not expecting Diego to release that nugget of information so soon. He watched as Diego kept examining Darius' face as it changed.

"Tree girls? No. It can't be." Darius said, slightly shaking his head.

Diego was quick to jump on the denial with another question, "Why do you doubt that?"

"Well, I doubt it because I thought those killings stopped. What's it been, like, five years?"

"Not quite."

"I haven't heard about them on the news in a long while. I just assumed..." Darius trailed off as he started to spiral. He knew he needed to stop talking. "Sorry I can't talk about this anymore. I... I need to process."

Martin nodded, holding his card. "Understood. Thank you for your time and answering questions. If you, or your brother, think of anything that can help. Please call."

"Yeah," Darius said, as he took the card and shut the door.

As Martin climbed in the driver's seat he looked over with a stern look and said, "You gave him a lot of information."

Diego replied with a smile, "Did you see his face change when I said it was a tree girl killing?"

Martin nodded.

"He knows something about it," Diego continued.

"Maybe. But did you also notice he was genuinely surprised she was dead? You really think he knows something more?"

"I know so. He started getting really nervous about the tree girl talk."

Martin nodded as he started the car, "I think you're right that he knows something about the serial killings in general, but that doesn't explain Kelly."

"Maybe Darius is the serial killer who fell in love and the brother got rid of her," Diego Muñoz suggested.

"Why, though?"

"Kelly was a smart and beautiful coed. Maybe Marcus wanted her, he made a move, she rejected him and boom! Or maybe he was jealous that she was taking his brother's attention... I don't know why people do what they do to others."

Martin and Diego headed into the station with their coffee and walked up to Martin's office. Sitting in a chair out front was Clifford Dee.

"Martin DiPietro?" Clifford asked, as the two detectives approached.

Martin nodded, "That's me. This is Diego Muñoz. He's consulting on a case."

"Clifford Dee."

Martin shook his hand, "Nice to meet you, Clifford."

Clifford smiled and said, "You can just call me Dee. It's an Army thing."

Diego smiled as he shook Clifford's hand, "Army, huh? Thank you for your service, Dee."

"What can I do for you?" Martin asked.

"I'm a private investigator working on a sensitive case. I'm not at liberty to discuss it or my employer, but I came across something in my investigation that you might want to see," and he handed them an envelope full of pictures.

***

"Where've you been? The cops were just here asking questions," Darius rushed outside when his brother pulled up.

"Oh shit, about Brenden?"

"Brenden? No, Kelly."

Marcus turned to look at his brother, "She okay? Did they find her?"

Darius looked away for a moment as he swallowed a new lump forming.

"Dari," Marcus was at a loss for words, "What did they say?" he asked as he followed his brother back into the house.

"Someone hung her from a fucking tree," Darius said loudly, as he turned to face his brother.

"Oh, fuck!"

"I know you would never, but I need to hear you say it."

"I didn't touch her. I haven't..." Marcus stopped talking when he realized he didn't need to.

Darius lowered his voice, "Someone must know about you."

"Who?"

"Fuck if I know. But we were set up for that hit and now some-one did to Kel what you've done and," Darius started pacing, feeling Kelly's loss again, but this time it was tangled in anger, "I couldn't keep her safe, Marc. I couldn't keep Kel safe, just like I couldn't keep mom safe, I..." Darius continued pacing and his brother grabbed him mid-stride in an awkward bear hug.

"We need to leave. We can't work for Bandoni anymore. We have our go-bags, and we'll just take everything we can fit in the SUV, grab all the cash, and just fucking drive. We'll set up a casino some-where out west." He let go of his brother and stepped back to see if Darius liked his plan.

Darius took a deep breath, "We still have those old IDs, right?" he asked, and waited for Marcus to answer before continuing. "Let's go rent a storage unit. Then, we can come back and pack. I don't want to lose the casino shit. We should get a room at a motel, too. We'll just go back to what we knew before all of this."

Marcus smiled, "You and me Dari?"

Darius took a shaky breath, "You and me, Marc."

***

Martin flipped through the photos of dead rats hung by twine and shoelaces. He slapped them down on his desk and asked, "What is this?"

"I reached out to the old proprietor of a group home up in Indiana. The address is on the back of the photos. Those were found under the bed where Marcus slept. This is the same M.O. as the killers who are responsible for The Tree Girls."

Martin looked over at Diego and let out a huge sigh. Diego took a photo off of the desk and examined it. He looked over at Martin and said, "He's right. It's very similar. When were they there?"

"Mid-nineties," Clifford began, "After an accident that left Marcus with brain damage, and a bum hand. They left to go into foster care and bounced around. They get harder to track after that, but the last foster mother was found with rope tied similarly to these. She was found in her bed and not a tree. She may have been the first and our serial killer may have started taking human victims before he reached adulthood."

Martin put his head in his hands, "We talked to the wrong goddamn brother."

"Was it the right pinky finger?" Diego asked, "The bum hand. Was there an injury to the right pinky finger?"

"Yes, Sir, it was," Clifford confirmed.

Diego looked over at Martin, "I bet Darius already warned him. He did know something."

"You talked to Darius Tye?" Clifford asked.

Martin nodded, "Yeah, about an hour ago. The copycat's victim is his girlfriend."

"Holy Shit. They're probably going to leave town. Someone's setting them up for that one," Clifford declared.

"Not only that, but we have a copycat who's just as ruthless. Kelly may not be the only victim," Martin cautiously suggested.

Diego cleared his throat and said, "Gentlemen. I think I need to head back home. I solved my case. I didn't get the guy, but I solved it. I'm retired with my beautiful wife, Jen, who likes having me around. I think you guys got it from here."

Martin smiled, "But what about Kelly's killer?"

"Ah," Diego scoffed, "That asshole's your white whale."

"Thank you for your help, Detective Muñoz," Martin said as he shook Diego's hand.

"This isn't your case, either, but if you come across anything that could assist us, I'd greatly appreciate the help."

Clifford nodded, "Actually, I might. After I was hired for my case, I got a message on my door leading me to the Tye Brothers. Someone wanted me on their trail, and I think it's your copycat."

"Bring it by as soon as you can."

"Will do, but could I ask you for a favor?"

Martin was wary, "What?"

"Could you see if you can get your hands on the security footage from the Bluegrass Estate Condominiums on the night Siobhan O'Connell and Brenden Bandoni were murdered?"

"Give me an hour."

Clifford smiled, "Thanks. I really appreciate that."

"I hope you find what you're looking for."

Chapter Thirty-Seven

In the dead of night, Liam drove away from the local nature preserve, exhausted from his latest hobby, framing the Tye brothers as serial killers. It became his obsession and he thought of little else. He knew he made the mistake staging Kelly after he had stabbed her, so he made sure not to use a knife again.

He went home and straight into a shower to wash the woods and stench of death off him. He needed a nap before his scheduled meeting at 7 am with Clifford Dee at the Bandoni Estate.

He tossed the towel aside and laid on top of his bed naked, feeling the cool air of the ceiling fan on his wet skin. He looked at his phone to check the time.

"A four-hour nap should work," he said to himself, as he laid his head back and enjoyed the cool air for a few more minutes before setting an alarm.

Liam opened his eyes, feeling confused.

"FUCK!" Liam shouted as he realized the time was 6:52 am.

He snorted a line set up the night before, letting out a huge groan as his eyes teared up from the jolting stimulant. He wiped the excess from his face and shook his head before scrambling to get dressed.

***

Clifford was escorted into Bandoni's office. He carried a flash drive and still photos from video of the condominium's security cameras during the time around his nephew's murder.

Bandoni looked at Clifford, "Where is Liam Stacey?"

Clifford replied, "I'm not sure, Sir. He texted he would be here. Should we wait?"

Bandoni motioned for Clifford to sit. "No, I have no time for tardiness. Please show me what you have found."

"The night of the murders, two men were seen entering the building. The flash drive has videos and photos of them coming in from the parking lot. We enhanced the photos to show you one of them has a facial scar. I believe the two men are your employees, Marcus and Darius Tye."

"Yes, yes. I've seen these and that's a coincidence. I own that building and they could have been visiting anyone in there." Bandoni was dismissive and Clifford surmised that if he owned the building, he would already have seen this.

"You don't find the timing the least bit suspicious?"

"I would have but, look at the expression on Marcus' face." Bandoni picked up an image of the younger brother and pointed to his smile. "Marcus is never in a good mood. Always all business when he is on the clock. Do you know, I have never seen this man smile before?"

"Then, I must congratulate you on employing the two most meticulous and ruthless killers I've ever come across. The only problem is, one of them is the Tree Girl Killer, and I did uncover proof of that."

"What? Let me see!"

"Here is a copy of the evidence. I had to turn it over to the police."

Bandoni let out a long breathy sigh as he looked over the contents of Clifford's envelope. Eventually he opened a desk drawer and tossed two fat envelopes over to Clifford. "This is payment for your services and an advance on your next assignment."

"What is my next assignment?"

After a long dramatic pause, Bandoni said, "I want The Tye Brothers DEAD! I don't care how, but you get them this week and you get more money."

"I'm not a hitman!" Clifford yelled in astonishment.

"I've investigated you, Investigator," Bandoni started in a more controlled tone, "I know what you've done for your country. More to the point, I know what you're capable of."

Clifford could tell the mob boss was upset. "Even if I wanted to take this job you need to understand they'll be under surveillance. The news will break soon."

Bandoni had no time for excuses. "And whose fault is that? I didn't pay you to give the police anything. You have a week. I suggest you get to them before the police do and I want proof of their death"

Clifford stammered, "I don't know if I can do it in a week."

Bandoni shouted, "Fine! As long as you kill them and bring me proof. You have until next Friday. That's ten days! Or I send someone after you. Hai capito?"

Clifford nodded, "Consider it done."

"Go!" Bandoni demanded.

Clifford walked to his car as Liam pulled up. "Where were you? Bandoni's pissed."

"Oh, didn't find anything on the brothers, huh?"

"No, he wants me to kill them," Clifford said in a whisper.

"What?" Liam said, as he pushed past him.

Liam ran into Bandoni's office to find him looking out his office window.

"Mr. Stacey, you are late."

"Sorry Sir, I ran into a snag."

Bandoni turned around and walked up to Liam, grabbing his jacket with both hands.

"Tardiness is disrespectful. You are disrespecting me and my time!"

"I'm sorry, Sir."

Bandoni let go of Liam and he noticed some cocaine residue on his sleeve.

"You missed a little," Bandoni said as he turned away.

Liam took a deep breath, "Since the Tye brothers are out, I was wondering if I could resume my old job?"

The question instantly infuriated Bandoni. He turned and backhanded Liam across his face.

"You disrespect me and then ask a favor? You are lucky I still have a use for you."

Liam looked at his feet. "Sorry, Sir. What would you like me to do?"

"Get out of my face! That's what I want you to do! I will call you if I need you."

Bandoni sat at his desk and swiveled away, facing the window.

"If I turn around and you are still here, I will put a bullet between your eyes," Bandoni said through his teeth.

After a moment, Bandoni grabbed his remote and tuned into the local morning news.

The story about the Tree Girl Killers identified as Marcus and Darius Tye was breaking.

Chapter Thirty-Eight

The Tye Brothers worked through the night to move all the casino equipment and tables from the bakery to the storage unit. They knew their next order of business would be getting the weapons and money from their house and then the stash at the Dollhouse. They also wanted to collect the money Marlon owed them, plus interest.

"Let's go through the guns and ammo first. We can decide what we should store and what we need to keep with us right now," Darius suggested.

"Good idea. Let's get breakfast after."

"Okay. We should probably secure a room at a motel somewhere away from the city soon, too."

They drove past their house and spotted an unmarked cop car on the street.

Marcus hit the side of the door with his fist, "Fuck!"

"You knew they'd be watching the place. I'm thinking we sneak in the back."

"Well, we have to."

Darius parked around the corner, "If we go through the woods and hop the fence in the back, we can probably sneak in my bedroom window. I keep it unlocked with no screen for a quick escape."

Marcus looked over and said, "Let me go."

"Alone?" Darius asked.

"Yeah, alone. No sense in both of us getting caught if they're inside."

Darius sighed, "Do you mind getting Kelly's necklace for me?"

"Where is it?"

"It should be hanging from the corner of the mirror on the dresser."

Marcus easily made his way through the woods. He passed his crude traps and sprinted as fast as he could until he saw his own backyard. He ducked down, continuing his journey, crouched low until he was completely concealed behind the house. Using the railing of the deck, he pulled himself up to Darius' bedroom window, opened it and hoisted himself in. Marcus pulled his gun and cleared the house first before gathering anything. He pulled out his phone and sent his brother a text, *"House is clear. Keep ur head down."* He dragged a footlocker out from under his bed and put a good portion of its contents in one of the duffel bags he planned to use. He went to the safe and emptied all the money from it into two other duffels. He ran to the bathroom and grabbed a few items under the sink before returning to Darius' room and grabbing his stuff. Marcus reached for Kelly's necklace and tucked it into his pocket. He tossed the duffel bags out of the window and retraced his steps through the woods.

Darius relaxed a little when he received Marcus' text. He was still staring at his words when his phone rang in his hand.

"Bad news, guys. Bandoni's put a hit out on ya." Liam Stacey's voice sounded cheerful to Darius.

"Let me guess, he wants you to track us down?"

"Nope. That's why I'm calling. He hired someone outside the family."

"What's his name?" Darius asked through clenched teeth.

"Clifford Dee. He's actually someone I've underestimated before. He believes you guys are the Tree Girl Killers and I'd love for you two to take his ass down."

Darius sighed, "Shit."

"Look, lay low and keep an eye out. Dee drives around in a dark green Mustang Bullitt. We should meet in a few days. I ain't too happy with Bandoni right now so I want to help you get out of Kentucky."

"Yeah, okay," Darius said as he rubbed his eyes and looked around again, "We'll figure it out and then we can meet up where we used to by the silo."

"You might want to change your look," Liam suggested before Darius hung up.

Darius sat feeling agitated, alone in the car. His head was on a swivel. He hoped it was all a dream and when he'd wake up, Kelly would be there. He hadn't had time to really mourn her. Every time his mind drifted to her; he'd feel like his heart was being ripped out all over again. Feeling the familiar stinging in his eyes, he blinked and refocused his attention to the woods.

Each second felt like a minute, "Come on, come on!" Darius said to himself. A moment later Marcus emerged wearing two duffel bags on his back and carrying two others. Darius let out a huge sigh of relief and popped the trunk.

Once Marcus was in, Darius caught his brother up on his call with Liam. "Bandoni's using an outsider to kill us."

"Oh, really?"

"Stacey seemed impressed by this guy."

Marcus sneered, "So we know he hates him. Egotistical fuck. Hey, don't be mad but I turned on the gas and cranked the heat before I left."

"Shit like that only works in movies, Marc!"

They sat in a small diner off one of the backroads eating breakfast when the television began plastering their information on the screen. Marcus was in mid bite of his eggs when he saw a blurry picture of himself from security camera footage. Then a blurry picture of Darius popped up next to it.

"This just in, local authorities have confirmed the identity of the Tree Girl Killer as Marcus Tye. He is believed to be traveling with his brother, Darius Tye. The police are looking for any information regarding the whereabouts of the Tye brothers. Marcus is described as six foot two and approximately 235 lbs. with a facial scar on his right side and brown hair and hazel eyes. Darius is six foot with a muscular build, and is approximately 205 lbs., with brown hair and brown eyes. If you see either of these men, call the authorities immediately. Do not approach or try to apprehend them on your own. They are considered to be armed and extremely dangerous."

"Well, shit's starting to hit the fan now," Darius said quietly to Marcus, while gesturing for the check.

"If those are their only pictures, we may have a little more time than we thought," Marcus said, wiping his face with his napkin, and getting his wallet out.

"They'd have better photos if Bandoni were helping them. He does want us dead; he won't help speed up the cop's progress."

"I guess it's a good thing I got a haircut after that night, huh?" Darius asked after they got back in the car and continued on the back roads.

"Yeah, but my scar's going to get us spotted."

"Yeah, keep your hand up on that side and just stay in the car, I guess, until we're in a room somewhere."

Marcus thought for a moment, "We're gonna need to boost a car soon."

"I know, but the closest airport is the opposite direction, And, when we figure out where we can get one, we need to stick to older models. It's been awhile since we've had to steal a car. I don't trust anything new."

They continued past the county line on the backroads to get a room at a motel called Old Grimes Lodge. The motel was only a few miles from the Dollhouse and about a half an hour from the silo next to their childhood farm where they planned on meeting Liam.

They paid cash for the room, and once everything they needed was moved in, Marcus flopped on one of the beds.

"We should take a two-hour nap, Dari. We've been up for, like, thirty hours."

Darius had to agree with his brother that sleep was needed, "And maybe afterwards, we can grab some brisket sandwiches at that Kentucky River BBQ on our way to get some stuff. I say we get a week's worth of groceries, so we don't have to go out much."

Marcus sat up and looked at the small refrigerator across the room. "How much food can we fit in there?"

"We should probably avoid perishables."

"Will it hold milk? Will the freezer hold ice cream?"

Darius laughed, "Dude, seriously? Yeah, probably."

"Sweet!" Marcus said cheerfully, as he laid back down on his bed and passed out within seconds.

Darius set an alarm on his phone and laid down. His body was exhausted, but his mind would not let him rest. Thoughts of what they needed to do turned to listing those who wanted them dead. He also wondered who they could trust, who the copycat was, and finally, his thoughts turned to Kelly. He picked up the phone and added another two hours to the alarm and eventually drifted off.

Darius loved that his brother got excited over little things. It wasn't often he caught a glimpse of his baby brother, but every once in a while, the man before him transformed into the little brat he used to tease. After his nap, Marcus had the worst case of bedhead, and it amused Darius even more.

"Okay baby bro, let's get you that barbeque and some ice cream, but if you get dairy farts in the middle of the night, I am sticking a cork in your ass."

Marcus laughed, "Then, I'll aim and yell, 'Fire in the hole!' You'll be wearing an eyepatch for a month."

Darius ran into the Kentucky River BBQ place and grabbed the sandwiches he promised while Marcus stayed in the car. Luckily for them, there was a small out of the way grocery store that wasn't busy. Marcus relaxed a little while Darius went in and stocked up on a bunch of food and a small tub of rocky road, a chocolate puffed cereal, and a half gallon of milk for Marcus.

Darius put the groceries behind the driver's seat, jumped in the front, and pulled out of the parking lot. He noticed a green mustang sitting on the corner. He thought nothing of it, until he turned, and the Mustang followed. He made another turn, and the Mustang made the same one.

"Hey, Marc, you think that Mustang's following us?"

Marcus glanced in the side mirror, "I saw that car at the grocery store."

"Really?"

"Yeah, I remember thinking I liked the color."

"Fuck, that's the PI Bandoni sent to take us out."

"He caught on to us pretty damn quick!" Marcus said, sitting up straighter, focused.

Darius racked his brain for a solution. "I saw an apartment building up the street earlier. I have an idea, but I'll need your help."

"You got it."

"We're not going to kill him. I have some questions."

"Copy."

A few turns later, Darius pulled up near the apartment building just before a sectioned off spot on the sidewalk for a small construction job. The brothers made sure they were seen as they walked into the building's lobby. Darius watched as the Mustang turned into a lot across the street and parked. He felt his phone vibrate in his pocket.

"Found side exit"

And then nearly two minutes later:

"Getting out of car"

That was Darius' cue in his plan.

Clifford Dee stepped out of the Mustang and walked up to their car when he noticed Darius exit the building. He peered in the vehicle to see it was empty and then started to follow Darius.

Marcus spotted a metal pipe on the ground and picked it up, "Clifford Dee? Stacey says, 'Hello'."

Darius ran to help Marcus put Clifford in the back of their car, and then jumped into the driver's seat. "The old church?"

"Dude, that's perfect!"

They made a U-turn and headed back to the church hitting a pothole. "Well, if he wasn't out before, he is now," Darius said, dryly.

Marcus snickered, "You gonna ask if that cunt Stacey put him on us?"

"Ooh, I wouldn't call him a cunt, brother," Darius scoffed, "he doesn't have the depth or the warmth."

Darius and Marcus spent the next half an hour on the road, heading to the church. Clifford woke up once briefly, but Marcus made sure he wouldn't do that again for a while. The brothers dragged him into the church, stripped him, and tied him to an old table they found.

"When he wakes up, we'll get some answers out of him."

Marcus looked over at Darius, "Um, can we go and come back? We have frozens."

Darius snapped, "They'll be fine!"

"Dari, my ice cream!" Marcus pleaded.

Darius rolled his eyes and laughed. "Tell ya what, let's secure this jackass real good and give him another little whack on the noggin'. No one knows he's missing."

"Come back in a few hours and get your answers?" Marcus asked with a smile.

"Let's go eat some ice cream."

By the time they got back to their room, the ice cream had softened quite a bit, so they put it in the mini freezer and played a card game while they waited. Marcus wanted to turn on the news, but Darius was afraid he'd hear their names connected to Kelly's murder.

"When we get back, I should shave my head," Darius said, as he laid a card down.

"Yeah, I'm trying to figure out what I can do to make my scar less noticeable."

"Have you thought of adopting a weird homeless hipster vibe? Like, long cargo shorts with a long sleeve tee and one of those trapper hats with the flaps?" Darius said, jokingly.

"I'd never be able to pull that off."

Darius began to laugh, "You'd look like an undercover cop trying to pass as a sixteen-year-old in a high school."

Marcus got up and grabbed two plastic spoons and the rocky road. "So, what are we going to do if this guy confirms that Stacey's behind this? We're wanted. It's not like we can stick around much longer."

Darius looked up from shuffling the cards. "I really have a feeling he is. If so, I'll put a bullet in his skull myself."

He glanced over seeing his brother checking updates on his phone. "Are there better pictures of us out there?"

"Not yet. I refreshed all the local news sites a few minutes ago."

Marcus quickly shoved his phone into his back pocket. He didn't want to tell his brother he was reading headlines about more Tree Girl Killer copycat victims.

Darius continued shuffling the deck, deep in thought when a bag of chips hit him. Marcus sat with the ice cream and handed him a spoon. "I know you like to eat something salty when you have chocolatey ice cream."

Darius smiled at the thoughtful gesture. "Marc, let's just go back and kill that Dee-bag, and fucking kill Stacey too. He's worthless. Then, we'll get the money from Marlon, and get the Hell outta here."

"I would like to give Cinnamon a proper good-bye," Marcus smiled, and pressed his tongue against his cheek.

Darius shook his head in disgust and laughed at his brother.

***

They turned down the beaten gravel path toward the church. As their headlights illuminated the front of the building, they noticed the door was wide open.

Darius slammed on the breaks and shifted the gear into park. "Fuck!"

They jumped out of the car and ran inside to find the table broken, and no sign of Clifford Dee.

Darius kicked a wooden plank, punting it across the church. "Shit!" he shouted in frustration.

Marcus remained quiet. He turned around and walked out of the church to the car.

"Where are you going?" Darius asked as he followed his brother, gun drawn.

Marcus opened the back passenger door, "We tossed his clothes in the back seat. His wallet should be in his pants."

"Marc, you're a goddamn genius!"

Marcus spotted Dee's pants and felt the wallet, immediately. He pulled out the brown leather billfold and opened it to see the face of Clifford Dee on his ID along with all of his other important information.

"Aww, he's an organ donor," Marcus said as he handed it to his brother and pocketed all the cash inside.

"Let's pay him a visit tomorrow," Darius said as he started to get back in the driver's seat.

"Should we look around? He couldn't have gotten very far with no transportation or clothes."

Darius shrugged, checking the time on his phone. "Early morning hours and barely a soul out. He's having a rough time right now. He's just softening himself up for us."

Marcus wasn't so convinced, "He could go straight to the cops."

"Not if Bandoni sent him."

Chapter Thirty-Nine

Darius woke up to the late morning sun and startled himself when he walked into the bathroom. He had forgotten he shaved his head and when he turned the light on, for a moment, he thought a strange man was standing in front of him. He couldn't help but laugh at himself.

"What the fuck's so funny?" Marcus yelled from his own bed.

"The mirror's lucky I don't have a gun on me."

"You're not that ugly, Dari, you just look like something I'd clean my ears out with."

Darius laughed at the comparison. "Asshole. Maybe I should've bleached it."

Marcus scoffed, "Bleach what, your head or your asshole?"

Darius smiled, "My asshole."

"Ew! Hey, fetch me a bowl of cereal, would ya?"

"Fetch? I'm not a dog."

"My apologies, your royal highness. Please, if you would be so kind, put cereal and milk into a bowl and bringeth it to me so that I may enjoy some nourishment?"

"If I were the royal highness, why would I be getting anything for you?" Darius asked as he shut the bathroom door instead.

Dismissed by his brother, Marcus sat up in bed. "That's fair," he said to himself.

The early afternoon sun was in and out of the clouds as the brothers swung by the condo listed on Clifford's license.

"Swankier part of town, I see," Marcus observed, as he looked around seeing if anything felt off. They were taking a huge gamble being in such a public area in broad daylight. Marcus saw a wheel-chair bound black man under the shade of a tree, in the park across from the building. He wondered if it was an undercover cop. He smiled as he reminded himself that Clifford Dee worked for Bandoni not the cops and, admittedly, maybe he had been watching too many action movies.

They found Dee's condo and picked the lock to his front door. They did a quick look around to determine no one was there before heading into his office.

On the desk were a bunch of case files. As they started looking through them, an alarm went off.

"WARNING, YOU HAVE JUST ACTIVATED THE ALARM SYSTEM. THE POLICE ARE ON THEIR WAY."

Darius tapped Marcus and said, "Let's go!"

They both started to leave when Marcus turned back. He pulled the shredded paper out of the shredder and dumped it onto the desk with the files. He lit a match and tossed it onto the shredded paper mess. As he started to walk away, he tossed the match book at the fire, but it skidded across the desk beyond the flames.

Darius shouted over to his brother, "Come on, man, that wasn't necessary!"

"Fuck that guy. I hope it burns to the ground," Marcus retorted, as they picked up the pace to get back in their car.

"Only in movies, Marc. We didn't use an accelerant," Darius said flatly. He was exasperated; they still didn't have the answers he needed.

It was several hours before they made it back to their motel room. They ran a few errands, picking up suits from the dry cleaner, and paying for brand new fake IDs with passports. They knew they were taking another risk using Bandoni's ID guy, but he was only loyal to himself. If paid well enough, he'd forget you ever existed. They knew they needed to leave soon, but not until they collected the rest of their money from the Dollhouse.

Marcus grabbed the duffel bags from the trunk and brought them into the room. "We should get cases or luggage to carry this money in. The duffel bags are too cumbersome and a bit suspicious looking."

Darius nodded, "We'll head out first thing in the morning. We should probably wait until we get to Virginia to do the luggage shopping."

Marcus looked confused, "Virginia?"

Darius smiled, "They think we'll go southwest towards Mexico or through Ohio or Indiana to Canada. So, we'll go southeast first, maybe find a beach town and see where we go from there."

"I'm up for anything. This could be fun."

The next day, they ate a quick breakfast and rushed out the door to meet with Liam. Darius waited for Marcus to toss a duffel bag in the back before he jumped in the car. They were nearly halfway down the road before Marcus exclaimed, "Wait!"

Darius hit the brakes, looking around, "Wait, what?"

"Did you grab the other bag?" Marcus asked.

"What? I thought you got both?"

"NO!" Marcus said in exasperation. "I grabbed one and you were supposed to grab the other."

"I said, 'Grab the bags.' BAGS! Plural!" Darius shouted as he waited to make a U-turn.

They bickered the entire ride back. Marcus went in to retrieve the other money bag before finally heading off to meet Liam.

They pulled up the driveway to the old barn and silo and saw Liam sitting on the hood of his car.

"There's that smug asshole," Marcus said.

"Yep," Darius said, taking a breath, "You packin'?"

"Double. You?"

Darius smiled, "Yep. I can't wait to watch him die."

"Well, that's a Texas-sized ten-four!"

Liam watched as the Tye brother's car slowed to a stop and they got out. He wanted to kill them before they got close enough to make escape more difficult. He reached for the gun behind his back when an odd electronic sound caught the attention of all three men, and he froze.

He looked in the direction of the sound and recognized Nick, one of Bandoni's men.

"Aw shit!" he said, realizing he had been followed. He dove into his car.

Darius pulled two guns and started firing in Nick's direction while Marcus put distance between him and his brother to flank the shooter, who they assumed was Clifford.

Liam's cars kicked up dirt and dust as he drove down the driveway as fast as he could, nearly fishtailing out of control turning onto the road.

Nick tried his best to get back to the road where his car was, but Marcus caught up to him and put a bullet between his eyes.

"Well, it wasn't Dee. It was Nick," Marcus said, as he walked back to Darius.

"From the organization? That Nick?"

"My guess is he followed Stacey," Marcus surmised.

"That weasel high-tailed it outta here, too. Why does it feel like nothing's going right for us these last few weeks?"

***

That evening, they headed out to the Dollhouse to collect the last remaining cash they had stashed there and see what they could squeeze out of Marlon for the $50,000 they loaned him years ago. Marcus liked Marlon and he convinced Darius not to kill him if he didn't have it all. They didn't have the time to make good on any threats.

They paid for some drinks and watched the entertainment for a bit when a familiar face walked over to them.

"We need to get the stash from the basement," Darius told the bouncer, Josh, after he asked him to tell Marlon they were there for the money he owed them.

Josh smiled, "That's why I came over when I saw you. He's been expecting you guys to come for it. Just follow me. We'll get what you left from the basement first and then I'll take you to his office."

"This guy makes collecting so easy," Marcus said as he started to follow Josh.

"Oh, I should let you know, there's a small game finishing up and we had painters in there the other day, so mind the plastic," Josh warned them.

As they made their way down to the basement of the Dollhouse, Darius started to get a bad feeling.

It was dark in the room. "Where's the game?" Darius asked.

Marcus sniffed the air. "Where's the paint?"

Josh asked, "What paint?"

Marcus reached for his gun. "You said they were painting in here. There's no paint."

Out of the darkness, a shot was fired.

Darius grabbed Josh and yelled, "I will fucking shoot him! Shit! Marcus! Shit!"

A second shot rang out.

Several hours later, Marlon and Clifford were arguing in front of the same old church where a concussed Clifford Dee woke up a few days before.

Josh shook his head at the bickering and sighed.

He walked towards the edge of the parking lot and discovered a fallen branch lying across the opening of an old well.

"You fall in that well and no one will ever find you!"

-Colby Tye

Book 1:
Clifford's War: The Bluegrass Battleground